Torture
the
Artist

A NOVEL BY JOEY GOEBEL

Torture
the
Artist

A NOVEL BY JOEY GOEBEL

MacAdam/Cage

MacAdam/Cage Publishing
155 Sansome Street, Suite 550
San Francisco, CA 94104
www.macadamcage.com

Library of Congress Cataloging-in-Publication Data

Goebel, Joey, 1980—
    Torture the Artist / by Joey Goebel.
      p. cm.
    ISBN: 1-931561-77-X (Hardcover : alk. paper)
    1. Authors—Fiction. 2. Suffering—Fiction. 3. Literary agents—Fiction.
4. Authorship—Psychological aspects—Fiction. 5. Human experimentation in
psychology—Fiction. Title.
PS3607.O33T67 2004
813'.6—dc22

                                                              2004015297
Manufactured in the United States of America.

10 9 8 7 6 5 4 3 2 1

Book and jacket design by Dorothy Carico Smith.
Cover painting by Hieronymus Bosch.

For Nancy Bingemer Goebel, my mother, the best

Contents

Art is a good means to declare one's love to people,
without inconveniencing them.

∽20th-century artist Ernst Ludwig Kirchner

I'm proud of my body, on the dance floor. Show me what you got.
It's a thong.

∽21st-century artist Chad

PART ONE

I. RACHEL

1.

I am so sorry to be the one to tell you this, but you will never be happy.

I don't mean to hurt you by saying that. I say it because I think it is only fair that I be honest with you before we begin. I hope you appreciate this because no one will be fair or honest with you from here on out. So again, I'm telling you right now: You will never be happy. I've put it in writing for you, and you're very welcome.

I want you to go outside on the sunniest, sweatiest day of the year and quietly say it aloud. "I will never be happy." Even in the heat, you should be able to see your own cold, smoky breath acknowledge the statement. The only way to avoid seeing your breath is to say it proudly like a wise man. "I will never be happy!" Try it sometime.

When I think of you, I think of a cartoon cloud hovering over your head, a private torrential downpour. I see you soaking wet, your entire being drooping, and you're always sick because you can't stay dry. Depressed by the bad weather, you cry yourself a little river, but the tears evaporate and form into another cloud that rains on you even more. You can't win.

It will be sad. You will never get the girl. You will not save the world. You will never find true love. You will not find a trustworthy friend. You will never be satisfied. You will never have enough. The grass could always be greener. The grass will always need mowing. Your days will be long and contain no fun. Your nights will be lonely and not much else. You will always be waiting for better days that will never arrive. And you will most definitely never have peace of mind.

There will be days when you will collapse to your knees and screamingly plead your case to whatever might be listening. But The Thing Called

God can't help you, and It won't. I think of heaven as being a radiant crystalline metropolis, and in the tallest sparkling skyscraper, The Mayor stays busy making deals behind a door with no knob. He's forever inaccessible, not taking calls at this time. And then I envision all the perfect blond angels, devoid of genitalia and feet, congregating and pointing and laughing at all of us down here, saying "Those poor little things!" in between giggles. They will get a kick out of you.

We are more likely to answer or not answer your prayers than they. We will control your destiny and watch over you. Not gods or angels. Not the dead. Us. Men and women. Adults with tangled webs and hidden agendas. Former children.

We will allow you your needs but deny you your wants. We will see to it that any requirements for long-term happiness are kept just out of reach. If by some mistake you experience a sensation that resembles happiness, then by all means, embrace it for all it is worth. Make the most of it because we will not let it last.

Again, I'm sorry. It's true what they say. Life's not fair, especially for you. The only consolation I can offer is that the things you will be making amid all the loneliness and suffering will by far outlast your despair and our cruelty. Our torture is temporary, your work is forever. With this in mind, we all win in the long run.

So on behalf of everyone that you will ever meet, I apologize in advance for every heartache we will cause. You're in for a rough time, kid. Consider yourself warned.

Nevertheless,

Harlan

— A letter I wrote to Vincent when he was seven

2.

I had to be awfully drunk to write a letter that sobering. It was some sorry time like 2:30 a.m., and writing it was the last thing I did before going to sleep. It was something I had to get out while I was feeling it, so I sat down and violently purged it all onto hotel stationery.

This letter foreshadowed for Vincent the fifteen years he and I would work together. In those fifteen years, Vincent suffered from unrequited love, illness, and depression, among other afflictions, most of which I was directly or indirectly responsible for. An innovative entertainment company called New Renaissance hired me to cause this suffering so that Vincent would always have inspiration to create quality works of art.

The day after I wrote that letter, I made Vincent read it aloud to me. It was just him and me and the puppy I would later kill sitting in the living room of the home I would later burn down. Despite being only seven, he was able to read the letter perfectly, pronouncing every word correctly, including "genitalia." He was slowed only by the illegibility of my drunken penmanship.

I was not supposed to write a letter like that. If Mr. Lipowitz had known, I would have been fired, or probably worse. But because of that letter, I can always say that I let Vincent know the score from the beginning. Most children don't receive such honesty from adults. I wish someone had written me a letter like that when I was a kid.

But I don't think the cautions in my letter really had a chance to sink into Vincent's adorable brain. As soon as he was done reading, he tossed it aside on the thrift-store couch and began goofily dancing around me. He was trying his hardest to make me laugh, because he could see that I was on the verge of tears after hearing a child read the grim words of a bitter old man. A bitter old man who at the time was twenty-eight.

3.

I suppose I wasn't as callous as I had hoped to be if the little bastard almost had me in tears after knowing me just one day. But back then, one of my favorite things to dwell on was this: Which is sadder? The elderly, because of all the things they've seen, had, and lost? Or children, who are pitifully unaware of the things they'll see, have, and lose? This was sadder than both: a child who had the depressing wisdom of an older person. That's what got to me when Vincent read my letter. But I didn't cry.

The last time I ever cried was when I was eighteen. Rachel Hanks did it to me. She was the first girl I thought I loved.

Her favorite band was the Cure, her favorite TV show was *Twin Peaks*, and her favorite movie was *Deliverance*.

We had been together for about six months when I bore witness to the devastating revelation that she had been siphoning other boys' penises. I confronted her about her clandestine fellating, which prompted her to declare the end of our relationship. I was prepared for this, however, as my first band, the Botchilisms, had just broken up, leaving her little reason to stand by my side.

But I was not ready to surrender to my old loneliness yet. I still wanted her. She was a liar and a cheater and wanted no part of me; she was more desirable than ever. So we sat in her darkened living room and engaged in exhausting conversation, my weak rebuttals chasing her calculated refusals around in oblong circles, until she finally said, "Fine, Harlan. If you really love me so much, then cry for me."

"What's that?"

"Cry for me. Show me how much I mean to you. Squeeze out just one tear for me, and I'll be yours forever."

She was serious. At that point I hadn't cried since I was a knee-scraped child. I hadn't even cried when my father died a few years before, and here she was demanding a drop of grief just for her as she twisted her hair around her index finger.

I looked across the couch at this cruel mammiferous creature and the creases of her crossed legs, and I found myself attempting to cry. I thought of life without her, but it didn't make me sad enough. Our breakup had not yet occurred. I needed experience, images, memories, the past I'd preferred to avoid.

So I thought of Christmas Day at a nursing home and babies born brain-dead. I thought of flags flying at half-mast and cheaply made roadside monuments. I thought of JFK Jr. saluting his father's casket. I thought of the last night of a childhood summer vacation. I thought of *Terms of Endearment*. I thought of an old man alone eating a meal of French fries at Dairy Queen. I thought of my father, young, vibrant, and telling jokes, then bedridden and slowly dying, then young again. I thought about a beer bottle three-fourths empty. I thought about my childhood, especially the good times. And with this parade of depressing images passing through my mind, sure enough, a tear fell out.

It rolled down my cheek, and that girl, my supposed first love, licked it.

"I love the way tears taste salty like that," Rachel said, knowing she would dump me the following day.

4.

But I ended up not crying that day with Vincent. He wouldn't allow it. He had me laughing instead, yodeling like that little mountain climber from *The Price Is Right*, rubbing against my legs in imitation of a cat, anything he could do to make me happy. And he succeeded. I adjusted my countenance, stiffened my posture, and resumed my role.

My role was being Vincent's manager. He was supposed to perceive me as competent and professional, as an important adult always to be obeyed and trusted. I dressed the part, wearing my dad's old sports coats, the kind with patches on the elbows, a white dress shirt unbuttoned at the top, a plain, dark-colored tie that I always loosened around the collar, gray slacks, and seldom-polished black wingtips. I was supposed to exude an air of intelligence, sophistication, and professionalism despite the fact that this entire business was ludicrous.

Even at twenty-eight, I would have preferred to wear ripped blue jeans and a T-shirt. But for this job, I attempted to be suave, borderline debonair with a streetwise elegance. My rapidly maturing hairline was accentuated by my perfectly slicked-back brown hair with its widow's peak, the most essential part of my costume. My angular, Germanic face with its pronounced features was always clean-shaven. With my ears sticking out and my ridged nose, I was on the south side of George Clooney as far as looks go. Handsomely ugly at best, I compensated with something that some might call style.

It didn't matter what I looked like, though, because Vincent didn't care. He didn't care about the way he dressed, either. The poorly groomed, disheveled seven-year-old would never change.

"Vincent, do you understand what I'm saying in that letter?"

"Yes," he answered as he settled back down on the couch and picked up his puppy, a tiny brown terrier that looked just like Toto from *The Wizard of Oz*.

"What am I saying?"

"You're saying that everyone will be mean, and I'll be sad."

"Yeah. Now, I can help you become a great writer and get your stuff out to everybody, okay? But I'm telling you right now that it's going to be hard on you. I can guarantee you that it won't be easy."

Vincent stared at me and nodded, rubbing his puppy's belly all the while. One day he would write a song about this dog that would become a hit single everyone would assume was about a woman.

"So listen," I continued. "If you want me to leave you alone, just say so. Just tell me to go away right now, and I will, and you can have a nice, simple life without me."

He kept rubbing the terrier's belly.

"So do you want me to leave you alone?" I asked after a long pause.

"No."

"Why not?"

"You're nice to me."

"No, I'm not. You just read that letter. That was not a nice letter, was it?"

"But nobody ever gave me a letter before."

"Well, nobody ever gives me letters, either. I'm the only person I know that actually still writes them."

"Why?" Vincent asked.

"Because of e-mails and because no one cares enough."

"I never got one of those e-mails either."

"You're not missing much. I hate e-mails. I refuse to use e-mail anymore."

"Why?"

"Lots of reasons. What really got me fed up was when I'd have fifty unread messages and forty-nine of them were junk mail from companies, and most of those had really dirty things in them. But anyway, are you sure you don't want me to leave you alone?"

Two pairs of puppy eyes stared at me. This was Vincent's normal expression, sad and worried. For the rest of his life, people would be asking him, "Are you okay, Vincent?" just for him to answer, "Why do you ask?"

"Do you not like me?" he replied.

"Hell yeah, I like you. You're my fucking—I mean you're my frigging idol."

Vincent laughed and covered his puppy's ears. I didn't realize how profane I could be until I was in the presence of a child, just like I didn't realize how often I talked about death until I had been at a funeral home.

"The thing is, Vincent, is that you're brilliant. And I want to make sure that you use every bit of your brilliance so you can help as many people as possible by entertaining them without making them dumber. That's what New Renaissance is all about. But to do that, to use your brilliance as much as we can, we're not going to have much fun. Especially you."

"But you do like me?"

"Yeah. I do like you. That's why I'm telling you all this and giving you a choice even though I shouldn't. So just tell me to leave you alone and I will."

"That's okay. I might end up happy."

"But you won't."

"Yes I will."

"I know for a fact that you won't."

"Yes I will."

"No you won't."

"I will!"

"Won't."

"Will."

This went on for a while before I gave up.

"All right, Vincent. You win."

I thought about saying, "You brought this on yourself," but decided against it. Instead I said, "Why don't you turn on that big ol' TV for us so we can watch how bad it is?"

As he turned and reached for the remote control, I snatched the letter I had given him and tucked it into my coat pocket.

My favorite band is the Dead Milkmen, my favorite TV show is *Saturday Night Live*, and my favorite movie is *Punch-Drunk Love*.

Vincent turned on the TV, and I reached out my hand for him to give me the remote control.

"And, hey, who knows?" I said. "Maybe you're right. Maybe you can prove me wrong and end up as happy as anyone."

That was the first time I lied to Vincent, and with that lie began my awkward career as a young creator's shady angel, the kindly cruel interloper between his present and future. With this lie, I inoculated him with something that could prove to be as harmful as the poison I would later sneak into his drink. I allowed this fatherless, doomed person to maintain an illusion of hope, and I even made eye contact when I did it.

II. VERONICA

5.

At any particular moment of any night of the week, her image dwelt within the minds of at least a dozen lovesick men. The memory of her gorgeousness haunted them, reducing them to lustful weaklings staring at telephones. I know because I was one of them.

How such an unremarkable place could produce such an exquisite specimen, I will never know. But she somehow emerged elegantly from a murky small-town gene pool, and she had been breaking hearts ever since.

Even her name seemed too lovely for such an ugly town, and it sounded far too full of grace and glamour to be in constant circulation among the swinish male population of Kramden, a small town in southern Illinois. "Veronica. Veronica, Veronica." The name floated dreamily in their minds and made them momentarily forget the pain of their work-weary bodies. I imagine they whispered it aloud to themselves just to hear it. "*Veronica.*" "*Vuh-rawn-i-cuh.*"

Her features were all that you wanted them to be, nothing too big, nothing crooked, no pairs of anything asymmetrical. No imperfections on her sensual lips. Likely no cavities within her bewitching smile. Not a trace of acne on her creamy flesh. And her perfectly applied makeup was not at all needed.

It was painful to observe her petite body. It was a privilege to watch her move. Her captivating form constantly inspired "*damns*" and audible groans from awestruck male bystanders. She stood just over five feet, but the entirety of her length was voluptuously curved in the proper places and enveloped in taut flesh that seemed to glisten.

Her beauty was too much. It was downright powerful, more than capable of forcing even the most stubborn of members to defy gravity. Everyone had to have her. Everyone secretly wanted her, even the girls in certain ways. Some wanted her at any cost. Their lustful stares gave her beauty its authority, those greedy eyeballs sending out rays of frustrated energy that penetrated her fair skin and seared into the organs it protected.

She was twenty-two and three months pregnant with her fifth child. She was in the middle of an alcohol-fueled ecstasy binge in hopes of killing her unborn baby. She didn't feel like being pregnant. She didn't want to go through labor again because childbirth was getting so it wasn't worth the pain. It had hurt more each time ever since her third labor, which was fraught with complications. The doctors had a hard time getting Vincent to come out of her.

6.

IUI/Globe-Terner became the world's biggest revenue-producing media company when the International United Internet company and the Globe-Terner entertainment corporation merged in the 1990s. IUI was itself the product of a merger between two powerful computer companies, and Globe-Terner was the result of a merger between two media corporations. Since smaller companies weren't as viable in the new globalization, IUI/Globe-Terner surfaced as a unified corporate Pangaea that we consumers couldn't help but inhabit. It became a media empire we supported often without knowing it, as ubiquitously yet inconspicuously present in our atmosphere as carbon dioxide.

At one point, IUI/Globe-Terner generated revenue that topped its closest competitor by more than 50 percent. Within its all-encompassing realm existed one of the world's largest book publishers, the world's biggest music company, a majority of cable TV channels (including most of the news channels), TV shows on every network, more than 1,200 radio stations, more than one hundred concert venues, and a popular video game system. The company's presence was even felt in the national government, what with both Democrats and Republicans in Congress representing its corporate interests.

And although IUI/Globe-Terner is a titanic money machine kept running by thousands upon thousands of employers and employees, a mere individual was largely responsible for making it the commercial empire that it is. In the beginning, that ingenious robber baron named Foster Lipowitz dreamed of building a global satellite empire, and by the end of the century, he had.

By the time Vincent was born, Mr. Lipowitz's ownership stake in IUI/Globe-Terner was so large that he could not be fired. And thanks to the global oligopoly that had developed, he was as powerful as one being could be. He was able to do whatever he wanted, which usually involved sitting and plotting in his sprawling office with plasma TV screens on the wall, untouchable except through appointments made months in advance.

By Mr. Lipowitz's seventieth birthday, cancer had begun to chew his innards away, changing the way he looked at thousand-dollar bills and high-priced hookers, at dodging federal investigations of his accounting practices and shareholder lawsuits, at his decades of deceit and the brutal slaying of his competition. He began taking inventory of that big business of his, and he didn't at all like what he saw. He became concerned for his legacy, and from this concern, guilt, and disgust came the ideas that would become New Renaissance (an IUI/Globe-Terner company).

7.

When I met him, Vincent had only three siblings, and they all lived under the same soot-covered roof where they played with dog chew-toys and ate peanut butter their mom thoughtfully kept on the bottom shelf so they could reach it.

Vincent's oldest sibling was named Dylan. His father was probably a drug dealer who was twenty years of age to Veronica's thirteen.

Sperm Donor #2 was either a local high school football star or one of his best friends. An unhealthy son named Vincent died in less than two weeks.

The identity of Sperm Donor #3 remains a mystery, though Veronica hypothesizes that the child was the result of "some sympathy fuck" she had given when she was fifteen. Another unhealthy infant, this one lived, and Veronica once again tried the name Vincent.

Sperm Donor #4 was most likely a well-to-do surgeon, husband, and father of two. This altruistic donor was kind enough to provide eighteen-year-old Veronica and his newborn daughter, Sarah, with a small home, the one Vincent would grow up in and that I would later burn to the ground. The home was located as far out in the country as possible.

Sperm Donor #5 may or may not have been a smooth-talking thirty-five-year-old transient immigrant who married Veronica before abruptly leaving town. He not only provided Veronica with a third son, Ben, but also gave her his name: Djapushkonbutm.

Veronica Djapushkonbutm.

8.

Decades of insatiable greed and sinful business practices were only a minor part of Mr. Lipowitz's shame. What truly made the older, wiser, sicker man disgusted with himself were those abominations that he had made possible with this greed, those undeserving works that would forever be available to the public just because they were likely to make a bunch o' money.

For instance, one year more than 65 percent of IUI/Globe-Terner's motion picture revenues came from just three movies released in June and July. All three movies were special-effects extravaganzas with occasional dialogue. There was *Death 2*, based on a long-running comic book; *Smokey and the Bandit 2069*, a futuristic version of the 1970s film with Ashton Kutcher taking over the Burt Reynolds role; and *Extremers 3*, about sexy vampire spies who are into extreme sports.

In the years before the geniuses of New Renaissance infiltrated the market, Mr. Lipowitz had nothing to be proud of on television either. Reality shows dominated the screen. These shows were cheaply made since they required no writers or actors. They were often immoral, unintelligent, and perverse, but I actually enjoyed watching them. Reality shows gave me a chance to witness how young people behave and interact without actually having to be around them. But other than the fact that I could make fun of these people without their talking back, the shows had little value.

One of these shows produced by Empire Television (an IUI/Globe-Terner company) followed a disgustingly rich celebrity whose fame came from her humongous breasts and whose wealth came from marrying a one-hundred-year-old billionaire (now deceased). Another of these shows forced twelve supposedly attractive lesbians to live in a one-bedroom apartment. As for programs that required actual writing, few are worth mentioning. Most didn't survive through half a season. Networks tossed shows at television screens, and if they didn't stick within three or four weeks, they were yanked regardless of their quality.

Nothing, however, was as despicable as radio, which IUI/Globe-Terner had controlled for years. Rock music was at an all-time low, so homogeneous that it seemed only one band was now in existence, the one with an overproduced sound, a misspelled name, brooding vocals, dull melodies, and occasional rapping. Rap, also as homogenized as milk, had become intensely popular among young males. It turned out there was quite a market for a genre that largely relied on acting macho, dehumanizing women, and glorifying drugs and violent death.

Pop radio was an abortion. If the aforementioned bland, unintelligible rock or rap groups weren't being played, the alternative was horrifyingly lame boy bands or scantily clad Jezebels, neither of whom could play instruments or write their own songs. These acts had been manufactured by Terner-owned record labels, and provocative dance steps were all that compensated for their lack of musical talent. As for R&B, it could no longer be distinguished from pop. Neither could country.

It appeared as if the general public readily accepted any piece of excrement sent their way via mass production and airwaves. And although there *were* genuinely good artists out there from decades past and just below the surface of the current mainstream, Lipowitz knew that this easily pleased general public of his might never find them. He would have to bring the art to them. He would have to replace the inane entertainment that the masses were currently accepting with works of substance.

His favorite musician was Hector Berlioz, his favorite TV show was *All in the Family*, and his favorite movie was *La Dolce Vita*.

Lipowitz's hope was to see the values scale of mainstream entertainment tip toward art rather than commerce before he died. His cancer was growing slowly, and his goal could develop equally slowly. He wanted nothing less than to grow art, through years of educating and conditioning his young recruits. Lipowitz was rich enough to afford the latest experimental treatments to stunt the growth of his disease, which was helpful since he needed plenty of time. Vincent had not yet even had his heart broken by a woman.

9.

When Vincent was six years old, he was one of 457 children chosen to attend the New Renaissance Academy in Kokomo, Indiana. All of these children had been given a full scholarship that covered their room and board. Thousands of parents had called New Renaissance's toll-free number after seeing an advertisement that read:

ATTENTION PARENTS:

DOES YOUR SON OR DAUGHTER (AGES 5–12) DISPLAY
EXTRAORDINARY TALENT IN THE ARTS?

DOES HE OR SHE HAVE AN EXCEPTIONAL GIFT IN WRITING,
MUSIC, OR OTHER FORMS OF CREATIVITY?

IF SO, YOUR CHILD MIGHT BE ABLE TO HELP US IN OUR
EFFORT TO IMPROVE THE ENTERTAINMENT WORLD.

CALL NOW—1-800-555-4297

This full-page ad appeared for six months in all 1,535 magazines published by IUI/Globe-Terner. Veronica called after seeing the ad in the *National Intruder* tabloid. A receptionist explained to her that New Renaissance was establishing a special academy for artistically gifted children and that the staff would consist of the nation's top arts and entertainment authorities.

After confirming that Vincent met the age requirement and exhibited talent in both writing and music, the receptionist asked to speak to him. The children were always asked one simple question, to fill in this blank: I write because_____.

The receptionist wrote down Vincent's response: "I write because... you wrong."

The receptionist then sent an application to Veronica's home, one that required a writing sample from Vincent.

10.

The Ruler of the Earth
by Vincent

Once upon a time there was a little boy who secretly controlled the Earth. He was sick and couldn't do anything else. He must have got sick from licking dust, eating dirt, or taking baths in toilets. He also let fungus bugs crawl on him. He just stayed inside and ruled the planet. He controlled the earth from his bed and he did it with his pen and paper.

His mom didn't even know about it. His mom mainly liked smoking. She smoked so many cigarettes that you could build a Statue of Liberty from the ashes.

The little boy's name was Malgo-Dalgo. One day Malgo-Dalgo's mom found out about him controlling the planet because she was hiding behind the drapes and saw him doing it. She called people about it and told Malgo-Dalgo to make hers and his dreams come true.

The next morning Malgo-Dalgo woke up in a house bigger than all the continents put together. Then three men came to him. They said, "Sir, you're the ruler of the Earth. Solve our problems." The first problem was that Malgo-Dalgo's house was so heavy the Earth couldn't turn. So his house was knocked down to its regular size. The second problem was that his toys were stacked so high they blocked the sun. So then he only had eleven toys. The same toys he had before. The third problem was that some people couldn't move because of his money. So his money was taken away and he only had ten dollars. The same ten dollars he had before.

This was awful! Malgo-Dalgo wasn't the ruler of Earth any more. He was just a regular guy. Wait. This was great! Luckily, no more men came to give him their problems. Unluckily, some other men came and put his head in a guillotine and killed him. Luckily, nobody cared because he was just a regular guy now. Unluckily, he couldn't think, write, or lick. Luckily, he had no more headaches.

THE
N
D

—The writing sample Veronica sent to New Renaissance

11.

Foster Lipowitz wanted the New Renaissance Academy to be built in Kokomo because as a small college town in northern central Indiana, it was far away from the influence of Hollywood and New York. He figured New Renaissance would be less detectable to the media in a Midwestern state and therefore less likely to degenerate into some sort of happening or trend.

The New Renaissance Academy was a long, brown-bricked building that stood two stories high. Behind it, across a field, were two large student apartment buildings, one for boys and one for girls. In front of it were no signs or anything ornate, not even a flagpole. Anyone could drive past it on the highway without having the desire to actually look at it. It could have been just another office building with nothing going on inside but paperwork and small talk.

Inside, the foyer's walls and floors were made of white marble, and the ceiling was painted gold. The spacious classrooms had shiny wooden floors and on the walls hung paintings ranging from ancient to contemporary. On the front walls of the classrooms were large computer screens. Besides being a new-fangled chalkboard, these screens were also used to show movies, TV shows, and slides. Each classroom was well-equipped with the latest technology to ensure complete access to the past.

The school had no gymnasium or auditorium. The younger kids could go outside for recess, but they weren't forced to. All but one of the classes were electives. The only required class was "Basics," which taught addition, subtraction, multiplication, division, parts of speech, and other rudiments of academia. There were no math courses. Remarkably, Foster Lipowitz managed to get the academy properly accredited. I heard it was expensive.

Grades were called "years" at the academy. Students could choose to stop attending after completing any year. Eventually the teachers would deem them prepared to graduate, at which time they would be ready to embark on a career in their chosen entertainment field. Other than the fact that classes were divided by age groups, there was nothing arbitrary about this school. Students were there simply to perfect their craft and learn all they could about the creators who came before them.

Vincent would later make this school the setting for a movie he wrote, titled *Heartbreak Academy*. The movie was based on the social difficulties he experienced at the school during his teenage years, and eventually it became as beloved as such teen classics as John Hughes's *Sixteen Candles* and *The Breakfast Club*.

Vincent's class schedule was more complicated than the average New Renaissance student's because his interests were broader. His schedule couldn't emphasize just music or just film or just television because he was capable of doing it all, another reason we chose him. Here was his Year One schedule:

10:00-10:50—History of Rock 'n' Roll
11:00-11:50—Classic American Novels
12:00-12:50—Lunch/Recess
1:00-1:50—Basics
2:00-2:50—Writing I
3:00-3:50—Sitcoms
4:00-4:50—Deficient Cinema

Besides being the only required class, Basics held another distinction that could not be found in any syllabus or handbook. Each Basics instructor had been told to draft a behavioral case study on each student at the year's end. The students weren't aware their behavior was being documented, and the teachers didn't know why they were documenting.

12.

Student exhibits uncanny intelligence for his age. A definite prodigy. Writes at a remarkably advanced level. Frighteningly imaginative and creative. Wise beyond years. Fast, eager learner. By far most industrious in his class, often at the expense of personal growth.

Student is a complete social failure. Poorly dressed, badly groomed, unhealthy looking. Unpopular with peers because of his obvious intellectual superiority and tendency to isolate himself. Low self-esteem possibly linked to poverty. Rejects outdoors in favor of reading books inside. Withdrawn-rejected. Shy. Anxious demeanor and small, skinny physique makes student vulnerable to bullying. Often subjected to having books knocked away and name mockingly chanted. Turns his back when provoked, sometimes hides and cries alone. Seems to create fantasy world for himself by writing.

Student's occasional insubordination in class overlooked because of quality of his output and his strong work ethic. Thoughtful and polite, but often questions assignments and teachers' judgment. If reprimanded, student withdraws even more. Student's work is impeccable and constantly improving. Most common flaw is forgetting to write name on assignments.

Student could best be described as morbidly sensitive. Shows in his writing, to his credit, though sometimes could be perceived as disturbing considering the age of the source.

Overall, student shows extraordinary promise as a creator but is problematic as a functioning member of society. Potentially disastrous. A very sad case.

> —*New Renaissance Academy case study of Vincent,*
> *written after one year of attendance*

13.

When the academy was closed for summer break after its first year of classes, photocopies of the 457 case studies were FedExed to the movie star Steven Sylvain. Sylvain managed to read each file. He narrowed the hundreds down to forty, and these forty were FedExed to Foster Lipowitz.

In his sprawling office on the thirty-first floor of the IUI/Globe-Terner building in Los Angeles, Mr. Lipowitz sat behind his colossal desk and analyzed each of the forty case studies. He eventually dwindled the forty down to seven. These seven case studies were FedExed to me, along with a list of e-mails and phone numbers, leading me to interview seven different parents in hopes of finding the one student who best fit our agenda. One of these parents was Veronica.

Hello?
Hi. May I speak to Veronica Djapushkonbutm?
You are.
My name is Harlan Eiffler. I'm from New Renaissance.
Oh. What's up?
We're assigning managers to our more promising students, and Vincent is definitely one of them.
Like, what do you mean, managers?
Well, we want to provide our geniuses with someone to manage their careers so that they can focus on being creative.
So, like, someone to get them deals and stuff?
Yes. Well, with the help of one of our agents, that is. I'm really interested in managing Vincent myself. He sounds like he's got quite a future ahead of him.
Who have you managed before?
Well, I haven't managed anyone before. But New Renaissance is such a ground-breaking project that it doesn't really—
But if Vinny's supposed to be so great, maybe he could get some big manager.
Yeah. Well, I've been working with Steven Sylvain if that's worth anything to you.
Huh.
Anyway, I have some questions for you so we can learn more about Vincent.
Whatever.
Could you give me a brief history of Vincent's life?
Shit. He just turned seven. There ain't much to tell.
Just give me the highlights.
Well, let's see…I liked to have never give him birth. He's my second—well, third kid if you count the first Vincent.
The first Vincent?
Yeah. The one I had before this Vincent. He only lived, like, two weeks.
Does Vincent know that he has a dead brother with the same name?
Oh, yeah. He's been asking about that for as long as I can remember.
Excellent. Why did you use the name Vincent twice?

I just really liked it. I got it from that song that Tha Dawg Pak did. It was called "Vincent."

That's perfect. That song's about van Gogh.

Where?

Van Gogh. The artist.

Oh. I never really listened to the words. I just liked the beat.

Actually, Tha Dawg Pak was sampling from a NOFX song, but the NOFX song was a cover of the Don MacLean song, which was the original.

You sure do know a lot about music.

Thanks. I was a record reviewer before I did this. What's Vincent's middle name? I don't have it here.

He don't have one. I didn't start giving middle names until Sarah Michelle.

So you had a hard time giving birth to Vincent?

Right. Nearly twenty-four hours of labor, but they finally got him out. They thought he was gonna die, too. He's been sick his whole life.

How has he been sick?

Oh, you know what? He hasn't been that sick at all, come to think of it. Just forget I said that.

Ms. Djapushkonbutm, we wouldn't abandon Vincent over his health. Please answer these questions honestly. It would be to your benefit.

Oh, well, he's a weak, sick, little dude then. [Laughs]

How has he been sick?

He can't breathe good. He must have bad allergies. He's so little, too.

How's his vision?

I don't know.

Any other health problems?

No. One time he broke out all over in hives. Doctor said he was allergic to codeine from the medicine he was taking.

Allergic to codeine. Okay. So continue with his history.

Well, uh, I don't know. That's pretty much it. He taught himself to read a while back, I think with the help of one of my old boyfriends. And when he'd be too sick to play or whatever, I'd give him a pencil and paper, and he'd just lay there and write for hours on end. Then I seen that ad, and he got in y'all's school, and that's the biggest thing that's happened to him so far. Maybe y'all can help add to his history.

Are there any other important events in his life?

Nah. Not that I know of.

What about Vincent's father?

I don't know what to tell you about that.

Did Vincent ever know his father?

Hell no. I'm not sure I knew him myself.

Does Vincent have a stepfather?

Yeah, but he don't remember him. Mushtaque left me in no time.

Could you describe your relationship with Vincent?

What do you mean?

Are you close?

Yeah, we're close. I mean, I got four kids and another on the way. I'm as close to him as the others.

Do you argue a lot?

Not really.

Would you consider your parenting style to be dominant or lenient?

I dominate. He does what I tell him or else.

Or else what?

Or else…or else.

What is your occupation?

Stay-at-home mom.

Does mental illness run in your family?

I don't know. I think my mom must be bipolar, but I don't have nothing to do with her.

Does suicide run in your family?

Yeah. My dad killed himself when I was little. I think his dad killed himself when he was little.

Does homosexuality run in your family?

Don't think so.

Does Vincent ever try on your clothes or makeup?

My son is not a fag!

Okay! That's fine!

If you don't believe me, look in my magazines. All the girls' lips have turned blue from where he slobbered all over them kissing them. He already loves girls. I can tell you that much.

Good. That takes care of my next question.

What?

Does Vincent seem to have a strong interest in females?

Lord yes. I think that's all he really likes besides his writing and his music.

That's great. So have you noticed anything about Vincent's social skills?

Oh, he don't have any.

Have you noticed that he likes to be alone?

Oh, yeah. He'd just as soon watch his brothers and sister than be around them. He mostly just hangs out with his little dog.

Excellent. That's all the questions I have for you right now, so thank you for your time.

Are you gonna manage him or what?

He sounds perfect for us, but I'll have to meet you and him first. I'd like to visit his home and get some samples of his work. I'll also need some blood and stool samples.

That's weird.

Yeah. Listen. I'm not going to be your typical manager, but I think it'll work out because I don't think your son is a typical person, and Ms. Djapushkonbutm, what you and I have to do is make sure he stays that way so we can take him as far as possible.

Call me Veronica. So when you wanna come over?

14.

Vincent's childhood home in Kramden, Illinois, lay deep within an inconsequential realm of the Midwest known as "The Boonies." I later joked that he lived so far outside of town that I had to travel back through time to get there, and there is some truth to this. The farther I drove down that ridiculously narrow country road, the farther I went into the past. Ten miles in, nature began to regain its dominance, as man-made structures gave way to cornfields, cows, and trees. Twenty miles in, civilization ceased to be and the surroundings that my black Lincoln Town Car cut through may as well have been prehistoric. And when I picture that road ending adjacent to Vincent's home, I imagine the nasty little inflatable swimming pool in his front yard as the sacred spot where an ambitious, idiotic creature once crawled out to commence the monkey business of history.

The first time I pulled into his gravel driveway was the summer after Vincent's first year at the New Renaissance Academy, the day before I was kind enough to show him that depressing letter I wrote. I saw three little kids playing in that swimming pool. One was brownish, one was white, and one was something similar to beige. When I got out of my car, which was loaned to me by IUI/Globe-Terner, the children stopped whatever they were doing and stared at me blankly.

"Hey. What's going on?" I said, already looking for my genius.

"Nothing," said the girl before she splashed me with water. The two boys quickly followed suit, and I laughed.

"I bet none of you are Vincent, are you?"

"No way!" yelled the brownish boy. "He's a pussy. What do you want with him?"

"I'm not telling," I answered obnoxiously. "But you had better be nice to Vincent."

"What for?" said the girl.

"Because his life might be more important than all of your lives combined."

Then the brownish boy jumped out of the pool and grabbed the hose. He said, "Hasta la vista, baby," and sprayed me to his siblings' delight. I stood there and took it.

"You dumbass," I said. As I walked over to the white shack of a home and rang the doorbell, the boy concentrated the water blast on my backside.

Veronica opened the door, and I think the kid may have stopped spraying me. I'm not certain because at that point, I had already begun fantasizing about possessing every centimeter of his mother's body.

I met her when her ravishing looks were climaxing, and it only took one mighty glance from her to make me sick. I was prepared to resign myself to a life of biting my lip and picturing her naked, and that would be okay. I would look but never touch. I would store her away for when I got lonely. She was an impossible dream, better kept at an alluring distance than reaching for her and failing as I surely would, being the pathetic mortal I was.

I especially loved her eyebrows. They were thin and slightly arched and looked like they had been painted. I can't remember the color of her eyes.

She changed her hair's style and color so frequently that it would be pointless to focus on any one arrangement, although any coif I ever saw was praiseworthy. I could only guess her natural hair color, but I know that I liked it best the way it was that day, black and disarrayed.

"Dylan, you asshole!" she screamed. "Apologize to him *now*, or you're spending the night in the shopping cart."

"Sorry."

"That's okay," I replied.

I entered the foul-smelling house as I stared at Veronica's sinfully perfect ass. She wore short denim shorts and a wife-beater tank top.

"Look at you. You're all wet."

In more ways than one, I thought.

"I don't mind. It felt kind of nice, actually. It's so hot out there."

It was almost as hot in the house. I smelled the summer sweat of children.

"Vinny! He's here!"

Vincent bashfully scuffled in with a towel over his head, looking like a sad little shepherd boy. He wore blue jeans and a white undershirt, and he was indeed small for his age.

"Hi, Vincent. It's an honor to finally meet you. I'm Harlan Eiffler."

"Hello. They got you, too, didn't they?" He took off the towel to reveal his dampened black hair. He then offered the towel to me.

"Oh, that's okay. Thanks anyway."

"Go get him a clean towel and some of Jeff's clothes layin on my floor," ordered Veronica.

"You don't have to do that," I said.

"Yes he does. I don't want you gettin my furniture all wet."

Vincent obeyed.

"Vincent normally don't go outside, but he waited for you all day out there," said Veronica. "He finally come in to put on some dry clothes."

"Sorry I was late. I had one other student to visit between here and St. Louis."

She didn't reply, causing an awkward silence in which I pretended to be interested in the carpet.

Vincent returned with a clean towel and some clothes.

"Sorry they did that to you," he said.

"Oh. That's all right. We'll have to get back at 'em later, though."

"Go take him to the bathroom to change," said Veronica.

A few minutes later, I returned to the living room wearing an oversized basketball jersey and extremely baggy pants. It seemed pointless to put on my wingtips, but I did anyway.

Veronica and Vincent sat on the couch, Veronica with her legs crossed, Vincent wanting to laugh at me. He waited until I laughed first.

"What? What's so funny?" asked Veronica.

"Harlan looks funny in that outfit," said Vincent.

"He does not!" snapped Veronica. "And you call him Mr. Eiffler."

She was even sexier when she was angry.

"But Mom, I bet he doesn't want to be called Mr. Eiffler because he's not old and doesn't want to be made to feel that way."

"Oh, really? Well, which do you prefer to be called, Mr. Eiffler?"

"Harlan is fine. I always hated my last name."

"Whatever, then. You can sit down if you want, Harlan," she said.

I sat on the recliner and noticed that Veronica was shaking, as evident in the quivering of her ample cleavage.

"So now what?" she asked, her eyes darting around the dinky living room.

"Um, well, you and I already talked on the phone, so actually now I'd like to talk to Vincent alone, if that would be okay."

Veronica immediately jumped off the couch.

"I'll be in my bedroom if you need me."

She looked me in the eyes when she said this, and I realized that her purpose in life was summed up in that one sentence. Vincent watched me as I gawked at his mother running to her bedroom, her breasts bouncing.

He grinned at me, and I think even back then he understood. He already had the general idea of what made the world operate. I don't see why he couldn't have; animals have it figured out well before they turn seven.

15.

Now that Veronica was gone, I was capable of taking in my surroundings. I saw the walls were decorated with magazine cut-outs of Brad Pitt, Tom Cruise, et cetera. Where there weren't magazine clippings, there were old tape marks. The wall behind the thrift-store couch was shrouded by tabloid covers with eye-grabbing red and yellow headlines proclaiming things like "ANNA NICOLE SMITH'S BOOBS EXPLODE." On the brown plush carpet lay beer cans and ashes. A big-screen TV took up nearly half of the room.

"What does she have me wearing?" I asked.

Vincent laughed. "Those are her stupid boyfriend's clothes."

"So your mom has a boyfriend?"

"Many boyfriends."

"Do you like any of them?"

"No, but none of them like me either."

"Why don't they like you?"

"I don't know. They're here for Mom, not me. They don't talk to me."

"They sound like a bunch of losers to me."

Vincent giggled. He would later base a sitcom on his childhood living situation. The premise of the show, titled *My Mother's Men,* was that each week a new boyfriend came to live with a dysfunctional family. With a different male lead each week, the show remained fresh and popular for several seasons.

The dog that looked like Toto scampered in and jumped on the couch to sit on Vincent's lap.

"That's a cute doggy. What's its name?"

"Wynona."

"Hey, Wynona. Hey, furry friendly," I said in a high-pitched voice. She answered me with a wide-eyed gaze before laying her head on Vincent's lap.

"So has your mom told you why I'm here?"

"She said you want to be my manager and help me make money later on from the things I write and make us rich."

"You're right, except the money isn't that important to me, believe it or not. Just so we get your stuff out to the public someday, just so it sees the light of day, I'll be happy. The goal of New Renaissance—and I'm sure you've heard your teachers talk about this—our goal is to replace some of the stupid crap that's out there with good stuff that you guys will provide us. So the main thing I would be doing as your so-called manager would be to make sure that you keep on writing and that you keep on writing good stuff."

"Why?"

"Why what?"

"Why do you want to make me keep on writing?"

"Don't you like writing?"

"Most of the time. But why me?"

"Because we at New Renaissance think that you have a lot of potential. We see some great things coming from you, and we want to guide you early on in your career—before your career even begins—because we want your work to be as good as possible. Does that sound all right with you?"

"Yes. But what will it be like?"

"What do you mean?"

"How will you do all that?"

"Well, if I become your manager, you'll still go back to the academy in the fall. It would be like last year only I'd be visiting you every once in a while and looking at your work. And I'll call you to see how you're doing and see what you might need help with, and in the next couple of years you'll be learning how to write screenplays and music and technical things, and then eventually you'll be writing things that we can shop around. But I'll be there for you every step of the way. So would you mind me bugging you like that for the rest of your career?"

"No. I'd probably like it."

"So it sounds like something you'd want to do?"

"Yes."

"Do you have any questions about anything?"

"What are your hobbies?"

I laughed. "I don't know if I have any...I love listening to music. I like playing the guitar. And I like reading. That's pretty much it. Why?"

"I just get curious."

"That's good. Any more questions?"

"Not right now."

"Well, if you're willing to let me be your manager, then I guess we can make it a done deal."

"Okay."

"Will you go get your mom, please?"

Vincent put Wynona on the couch and ran over to the closed door of his mother's bedroom. He knocked.

"Mom?"

"What?!"

"Harlan wants to talk to you."

"Tell him to come here!"

I walked over to her bedroom door, which was adorned with a Kid Rock poster.

"Ms. Djapushkonbutm, I have some papers I need you to sign."

"Come in!"

I nudged open the door to see Veronica sitting on her bed hugging her smooth, pale legs, rocking herself back and forth while smoking a cigarette. She was sweating, and her room was filthy.

"What do you need?" she asked, her voice trembling.

"I need you to sign some papers. I want to be Vincent's manager, if you'll agree to it."

"Yeah. Okay. Give 'em here."

"Actually, I have them out in the car. I need to talk to you about some things first before we go through with this."

"I can't deal with this right now," she said, smoke coming from her mouth.

"That's fine. I've already made reservations at the Economy Inn over in Vincennes, so I'll be around tonight and tomorrow."

"I can't deal with this right now," she said.

"That's perfectly all right. Are you okay?"

"Yeah. I'm fine. Why would you say that? I just can't, you know, like, don't worry about it."

"That's fine. How about I call you tonight, and perhaps we could meet somewhere to talk. Would that be okay?"

"Yeah. Just call me later."

"All right. I'll call you later tonight. Thanks for having me over."

"You're welcome. Could you shut the door?"

She still rocked back and forth. I shut the door behind me. Vincent was in the hall looking up at me.

"Is your mom okay?"

"Yes," he replied. "She gets that way when she's pregnant."

16.

I used to think there was not a more poetic location than a hotel room. For some it is a home for a night, an oasis just off the interstate to rest road-weary bones, a place intended for continual abandonment. For others it is an adult playground, a shelter for sin, a boudoir with no memory. It can be full of life by way of debauchery or family togetherness, or it can make you feel desperately lonely and restless. The atmosphere of an evening in a hotel room is determined by the number of its occupants. When you're alone there, you feel it.

After I bought a fifth of Maker's Mark at one of Kramden's three liquor stores, I checked into the nearest hotel, which was in Vincennes, Indiana. I called the six other candidates' parents to tell them I had chosen another student to manage. I called movie star Steven Sylvain to tell him that I had found the ideal kid, but he wasn't home. I got ice for my ice bucket and drank whiskey and water from a clear plastic cup with the Economy Inn logo on it. I didn't bother eating. I watched television until the sun set, thinking of Veronica all the while. I eventually decided that I had given her enough time to clean up.

"Is this Veronica?"

"Yeah."

"This is Harlan."

"Oh. Hey, Harlan."

"Hey. Are you about ready to meet with me?"

"Oh. Yeah. Can I call you back later, baby?"

"Oh, uh, yeah. Thanks. But the things I need to talk to you about, they're really important."

"Okay. Let me call you back. I've got company right now."

"Do you want my number?"

"I got it on the caller ID. I gotta go. I'll call you back."

That's when the loneliness and restlessness crept in, watching the digital clock and the phone, hearing those bass-heavy door slams coming from the hall, trying to think about my job and Vincent, all thoughts leading back to Veronica.

At around midnight I again called *People Magazine*'s former "Sexiest Man Alive," Steven Sylvain, but he still wasn't home. By then, I was drinking the whiskey straight, and the red numbers on the digital clock were continually scrolling downward due to my unreliable vision.

At around one, I heard a knock on the door.

She was now wearing tight blue jeans and an equally tight red T-shirt. I sat on the bed. I made sure she sat in the chair.

"I hope you don't mind me popping in. My company wouldn't leave, so I finally just said fuck it and left him back there."

"That's quite all right, Ms. Djapushkonbutm."

"Oh, please. Call me Veronica. I hate my last name. I'm seriously thinking about changing it."

"You should. I changed mine."

"Really? What did yours used to be?"

"Eifflerdorf. I dropped the *dorf*."

She laughed, and I wanted to marry her.

"Before I got married, mine was Spinetti. I don't like that one either, though. I wish it was Thunderheart or something like that." Her lips were in my hotel room. Her body was no longer just in my brain.

"So what'd you think of Vincent?" she asked.

"Vincent? Oh—I loved him. He's so precocious. I was just amazed."

"He really liked you, too. He kept bugging me about you after you left. He usually don't get so happy like that."

"Yeah. I noticed he kind of has a sadness about him."

"Oh, man. I mean you just don't understand. That kid gets so sad I don't know what to do with him sometimes. It'll just happen out of the blue. Like, one time, Andre brought in some mint chocolate chip ice cream, and we fixed the kids a bowl, and Vincent couldn't eat. We were like, why ain't you eating, and he started to cry and left the room."

"Why was he crying?"

"He said he had got to thinking about that serial killer—remember that one bad serial killer from around here that got the chair a while back, the one that only killed prostitutes?"

"Yeah."

"Vincent said that mint chocolate chip was that guy's last meal before they electrocuted him. And I was like, so what? And he said that the killer probably loved eating mint chocolate chip ice cream when he was little and he probably always wanted to eat just ice cream for supper but his mom wouldn't let him and so then he was eating it for his very last dinner because he knew it didn't matter 'cause he would die soon."

"He's so sensitive."

"Yeah. He just cracks up over nothing. He's fucked up like that."

Veronica looked all around the room.

"Hey. I think I've been in this room before—ooh! Can I have some of that whiskey?"

I thought about asking if it would be safe for her unborn baby but quickly decided I couldn't say anything. I fixed her a drink.

"Listen, I definitely want to be Vincent's manager. There's no doubt about that. But there's something else I need to talk to you about."

She swallowed the whiskey with ease.

"We—New Renaissance—we have this idea that I'd like to run by you."

"Give it to me."

"Now, it's going to sound crazy, but we're deadly serious about it."

"Come on and give it to me."

"All right. The situation is, well, are you familiar with the idea of art coming from suffering?"

"No."

"Okay. Ever since there has been art, ever since people have been creating things, there's been the idea that to make art, especially great art, it has to come from some sort of suffering that the artist endures. Maybe it's a loss of some kind or a broken heart or bad health. The point is that the suffering serves as inspiration. The artist feeds off of it."

"Like Kurt Cobain?"

"Sure. So you understand what New Renaissance is all about, right?"

"Pretty much," she said from behind her cup.

"We're kind of like old-time patrons for the artists. And the founder of New Renaissance, who is a very powerful man that can really pull some strings, he has this other idea. It's a highly secretive idea, and to make a long story short, if that's possible at this point, well...to be perfectly honest—"

"Could I have another drink?"

"Certainly."

I got up to fix her another drink. I fixed myself a double.

17.

"We want to secretly manipulate your son's life and cause him to suffer so that he will always have inspiration to create great art."

"Huh."

"Yeah."

"And so he would never know about it?"

"Not unless you told him. You and I and just a few other people on the planet would know about this. It has to be that way in order for it to work."

She took a big swallow of whiskey and ran her fingers through her shoulder-length hair, pushing it off her face.

"So what do you think?" I asked.

"I think it's stupid. What are you gonna do to him?"

"I'm not sure yet. Whatever it takes to keep him inspired. For instance, when he gets older, we'll see to it that he has no girlfriends. One of our top priorities would be to keep him lonely. I think loneliness is essential for Vincent's work because it not only causes pain, but it also allows the time and environment necessary for the creative process. You follow me?"

"He don't need a girlfriend anyway. You'd be doing him a favor."

"You're probably right. But to answer your question, I don't really know the specifics of what we would be doing to him. There's really not a blueprint for something like this. I mean, we aren't going to hurt him physically or do anything dangerous to him. It will mostly be psychological. And I can guarantee he'll be in good hands because I would personally be doing the dirty work while at the same time managing his career. But I would need your complete cooperation to pull this off."

"What would I have to do?"

"To put it bluntly, you would help me lie to Vincent. I know this sounds like an awful thing to do, but we think the end will justify the means. We think that Vincent is going to give the world a lot of great things and make a lot of people happy, and you and I will be pushing him the whole time. Plus, if you agree to this, you'll receive payment in addition to a percentage of the money from the deals we'll make someday."

"How much payment?"

"About $2,500 a month."

Veronica finished her second drink and crunched on an ice cube.

"Yeah. Why not? Let's do it," she said.

"You don't have to give me a decision right now. You can have as long as you need to think about it."

"The way I see it, bad shit will happen to Vincent anyway. Shit happens to everybody, you know? It don't matter that it's you that'll be causing the shit to happen. If it wasn't you it'd be somebody else, maybe somebody worse than you. Shit happens no matter what, so you might as well get paid for it, right?"

"I had been thinking the exact same thing. I've found that's the best rationale to justify what I'm doing. But you know, Veronica, I don't feel right about this whole thing at all."

"And it seems like there'd be way more good coming from this than bad," said Veronica.

"Well, I should hope so. Are you sure about this, though? You can have more time."

"I don't need more time. Let's do it. But if things get too bad, can we stop screwing with him?"

"Absolutely. You can pull the plug on us if it gets to be too hard on him. We might pull the plug ourselves if we feel like it's gone too far."

"So am I supposed to sign something?"

18.

Vincent's fate was sealed at an Economy Inn at around 2 a.m. I went over all the contracts with Veronica, the one that allowed me to become his manager, the one that offered her consent for our project, and the one in which upon signing she vowed secrecy regarding said project.

She signed everything and said, "You know, it won't hurt for that boy to go through some stuff. He's had it easy so far. When I was his age, my dad had already killed himself, and my mom wasn't around much, and when she was she was whoopin me."

"That's so sad," I said, and she proceeded to tell me her life story, up through every baby, including the one she was currently incubating in her body full of chemicals. She was eventually done talking, and I had stared at her as much as possible.

"Well, Veronica, thanks so much for coming over. And also thanks so much for allowing us to do this," I said, pointing to the contracts.

"Shouldn't we shake on it to make it official?" she asked.

"I guess so."

She stood up and extended her hand toward me. It was hot. When I was done shaking it, she rubbed two of her fingers against my palm. She put one knee on the bed.

"You know, for something this big, to make it official, we should probably do more than just shake hands."

"Oh."

She pushed me against the headboard and straddled my lap. I stroked the top of her thighs slowly. She took off her shirt and arched her back so that her black bra and the ripe bosom it cradled were in my face. She played with her hair, messing it up. I was already swollen with desire.

"Do you want me?" she whispered.

"Obviously," I said. She kissed me gently as she began rhythmically rubbing her groin against mine. She smelled like Vapo-Rub and tasted like whiskey.

She arched her back again as she reached her well-toned arms around to undo her bra. Her entire image was scrolling downward because of my whiskey vision, but for just a second I managed to focus on her sexy, blood-shot eyes, which appeared to be rolling back into her skull.

"Get off me," I said.

She abruptly stopped rubbing against me. She let her arms fall to her side.

"What?"

"Get off of me and go home to your kids."

"They're in bed. It don't matter."

She tightened the grasp of her thighs around my torso. I pushed her away.

"Get off me, Veronica!"

She laughed in disbelief.

"Whatever."

She dismounted and put her shirt on. I stood up.

"Are you a faggot or something?"

"No, I'm not a faggot."

"Don't you want me?" she asked, genuine anguish on her face. Her eyebrows slanted pitifully.

"Yeah. I want you."

She suddenly wrapped her arms around me and curled one leg around my thigh. She kissed me as hard as she could.

I freed my tongue from hers, pushed her away, and screamed, "Please, get the hell out!"

"Whatever," she said and left.

I finished off what little remained of the whiskey. Then I tried calling out-of-work actor Steven Sylvain to ask him if they could find someone else to do this, but he still wasn't home. I sat down and wrote Vincent the aforementioned letter with the drunken penmanship, still fully aroused.

III. WYNONA

19.

When fifteen-year-old Veronica was struggling to squeeze out Baby #3, a.k.a. Vincent, I was struggling to finish my last semester of college. I had always hated school because I didn't like being around people. I hated the classroom environment, sitting so close together in those rows of desks, all those warm bodies, all those heads pointed in the same direction, thinking similar thoughts. Despite my aversion to my classmates, I did well in school without trying, and it's a shame I persevered through sixteen years of education just to be expelled the spring semester of my senior year.

I turned twenty-one that semester, making it much easier to acquire alcohol. I fell into the habit of attending class drunk, a habit that deeply enhanced my time within the beige walls of school. For the past four years I had sat quietly, always next to one of those walls, writing crude things about my classmates in my notebook instead of taking notes. I cringed at the utterance of the words "group work," and rather than dealing with choosing a partner or joining a group for some childish and pedantic exercise, I casually left the room and came back toward the end of class. But with a few coats of liquor on my brain, class became more tolerable. I remained quiet but allowed myself to be careless. I finally felt at ease.

The drink made dormitory life more tolerable, too. I found myself leaving my room more often and even drinking with others. Normally, the music I heard emanating from their rooms was enough to discourage me from leaving my own. But with enough whiskey in me, I could surprisingly tolerate their kind of music for short periods of time.

That last semester I was often hung over and could barely function in my morning classes. Those bright classroom lights were always hurting

my hangover eyes. I've noticed that the most awful places seem to have
the brightest lights, those long, tubed fluorescent ones. Classrooms, hospitals, doctors' offices, workplaces, public places—all the locations I
dread—all have lights like these. These lights are never flattering and
bring out your every blemish. These lights shriek, "Look! Here it is! This
is your reality! Look at it! It's so ugly!" Shadows can't form in light like
this. Everything is perfectly lit and unavoidable. I eventually started
wearing sunglasses to class.

I was expelled from school when a teacher finally discovered I had
come to class drunk. He was in the middle of a lecture exalting Rasputin,
explaining how hard he was to kill, when I had an unrelated thought that
seemed reasonably profound at the time. I had to share it.

"You know what I just realized!?" I shouted, forcing everyone to turn
around and look at me in my back corner, next to the wall. It was probably the third sentence I had said in that class all semester. The only time
I volunteered to speak in class was to make a joke, and opportunities for
humor were rare.

"What?" the teacher replied.

"Something absolutely horrible has happened to everyone in this
room."

I loved having all those eyes on me. Everyone looked scared. No one
knew what to say, so I continued.

"No. Seriously. Everybody in here is carrying around these unspeakable...*things* in their heads. And these are the things that made you who
you are, but you never even talk about them. It's kind of similar to—well,
have you ever thought about before you take a shit, you're walking around
carrying it in you for a while? It's like that. Yet, we all just...*sit there* like
we don't have this stuff in our body, like nothing has ever happened to us.
We sit in here in these desks like everything has been okay and normal.
Does anybody understand me?"

A few students were cracking up laughing, including me.

"What is the point of all this?" asked the plain, middle-aged professor.

"I know. That's just it. What is the point of all this?" I slurred. "The
only thing I can think of is if you take the horrible thing—the shit—and
make it have a point. You gotta use it. 'Cause otherwise, then it is pointless. I mean, when you're on the crapper—"

"I'm going to have to ask you to leave my classroom."

"Okay. Sorry."

I staggered out the door and was never allowed back. I later chose to believe that at that precise moment, Vincent emerged from his mother's bloody uterus, crying and screaming.

20.

Steven Sylvain was born unto the public eye in the romantic comedy *Love from the Heart*, a sleeper hit. Shirtless in every scene, Sylvain quickly captured the attention of the female demographic with his lean, well-built body, ruggedly handsome face, and cool, brooding manner. He secured this role after catching the eye of a casting director who saw him squat-thrusting at a Los Angeles gym. The twenty-nine-year-old Sylvain worked at the gym and then went by the name Steve Jablonski.

His small but sexy role in *Love from the Heart* led to a string of increasingly larger acting jobs. He played one of many heroes in the ensemble disaster piece *Catastrophica*. Touted as the ultimate disaster film, *Catastrophica* featured such cataclysmic forces as earthquakes, hurricanes, tornadoes, tsunamis, floods, and fires, all of which occur simultaneously in New York City after a meteor shower bombards the Atlantic Ocean. One of many Christ figures in the film, Sylvain's character, Johnny, sacrifices his body to save New York from a fire tornado. The film pulverized box office records.

With his fame rising, Sylvain's next big break was his first co-starring role in the psychosexual cop thriller *Circumstantial Heat*. A thirty-three-year-old playing a twenty-something rookie cop, Sylvain was paired with established actor Kurt Russell. Russell played the callous but wise veteran cop who mentors his young partner in the ways of the law, love, and life. An embarrassing box office failure, *Circumstantial Heat* at least served as a catalyst for Sylvain to meet Bob Kuntzweiller, the head of Dead Line Pictures (an IUI/Globe-Terner company).

Following the orders of Foster Lipowitz, Kuntzweiller chose Sylvain for the lead in *Blood Lust*, his first starring role. With *Blood Lust*, Sylvain became a bona fide action hero, idolized by men and women alike. As Johnny Lane, a vigilante cop with nothing to lose, Sylvain used *Blood*

Lust as a showcase for his athleticism, martial arts skills, and ability to play a tough but likable everyman. Massive audiences cheered on Johnny in every scene as they waited for those oft-quoted one-liners that preceded a punch, kick, gunshot, or bomb detonation.

"You were just a rough draft. Consider yourself proofread." (BANG!)

21.

I am one of those fortunate souls who had a mother who genuinely cared for him. When I was ejected from school, she was incensed not by me but by the college for being so strict with its zero-tolerance policy. When I returned to my safe suburban home in St. Louis, she welcomed me back with unconditional love. But when I decided that my next move would be to temporarily relocate to California with my band, she told me I wouldn't have a home when I came back.

Until then, my mother had always supported my music career. Prior to my move to Los Angeles, she saw my playing guitar and singing as a healthy form of escapism, which I needed. When I fronted the Botchilisms from age thirteen to age eighteen, she allowed me to practice two nights a week and play shows on the weekends, lots of them out-of-town shows at seedy clubs, park shelter houses, and VFW headquarters. She also encouraged me to start up my second band, Dumbstruck Juggernaut, because she knew I hated college, and music seemed to be the only thing that made me happy.

But now my education had come to a halt, and my backup career as a history teacher was out of the picture. Me being in a band was not cute anymore. My mother felt I was throwing my life away on music, and she was right. I shouldn't have been pursuing rainbows in L.A. when I had a loving home with a wonderful mother and caring older brother back in St. Louis. My mother had been better to me than any other human ever had, but I told myself that I would get that lucrative record deal once Dumbstruck Juggernaut received some big-city exposure, and I would make her proud by becoming rich and famous, and then I would buy her everything she ever wanted, and that would make up for everything bad or wrong I had ever done, and all the troubles I had ever seen would not have been in vain, and everything would be fine from then on.

22.

By the time the first *Blood Lust* hit theaters, Sylvain's real-life reputation as a Hollywood bad boy was already well established. Notorious for reckless partying, paparazzi brawls, and countless affairs with fellow celebrities, Sylvain was a one-man marketing department constantly generating hype for himself. Furthermore, his new riches allowed him to turn his old cocaine habit into a lifestyle, and he was in and out of rehab as much as he was in and out of his female costars.

"Hey, hey, hey. Bombs away." (KABOOM!)

After three more *Blood Lust*s and *Love from the Heart 2: Lost in London*, Sylvain played the lead in the World War II picture *Sea to Shining Sea* and for the first time enjoyed critical praise for his portrayal of morphine-addicted Sergeant Jack Slate. Then after a lengthy stay in rehab, Sylvain reluctantly signed on for the fifth and final installment of *Blood Lust*. The filming of this movie, *Blood Lust 5: Last Rights*, was discontinued after an on-set freak accident left Sylvain partially mutilated.

"There *are* no options." (RAT-A-TAT-TAT-TAT!)

The accident occurred in a scene that involved Johnny and his female lead having sex on a moving moped zipping through an exploding dynamite factory. It was a *Blood Lust* trademark to have Johnny fornicate with the female lead in the midst of a chaotic action sequence. Always a proud man, Sylvain insisted on doing his own stunts, especially when these stunts were during sex scenes.

"I get off on this shit!" (KAPOW!)

The moped accident and the multiple explosions that followed left the right side of Sylvain's body charred and shredded. The tabloid rumors of him losing his penis were false, though the less-told rumor of him losing his right leg was true. After the accident, Sylvain lost the starring role for a movie based on *Miami Vice*, a role he had been promised. And though Sylvain's prosthetic leg looked normal in a pair of pants and his scars weren't visible under a shirt, the scripts abruptly stopped coming to his agent. And then his agent abruptly stopped calling. At forty-one, Steven Sylvain's career was over.

This fact was made achingly clear when Sylvain was not invited to be in *Catastrophica 2: Genesis*. This would make sense because his character

died in the first *Catastrophica*. However, *Catastrophica 2* was a prequel.
"Toodle-oo, motherfuckers." (KRRBANG!)

23.

I now realize how foolish I was for making that pilgrimage to L.A. with
my band. But it seemed like the right thing to do. I was no longer comfortable at my home. I felt guilty when I was around my mother after
being freshly expelled from the finest private college in the state. She had
been so proud of me for earning a full scholarship to go there. Now I was
an embarrassment. She once bragged to her friends that I had done so
well on my ASVAB testing in high school that the FBI called our home.
Now when conversing, she avoided bringing up my name.

She knew that I had once been a smart and careful person. I was once
the type of guy who felt naked without a seatbelt. No sneezes went
unblessed in my presence. At my first few band practices I sipped on apple
juice while the other boys were getting drunk. I was nerdy and thoughtful. I was harmless and studious. I had sense.

Music made me stupid. This was gradual but unavoidable: getting so
excited the night before a show that I couldn't sleep, taking a huge dose
of Nyquil to help me sleep, loving the Nyquil buzz so much that I didn't
go to sleep, taking some of Mom's diet pills the next day since I didn't
sleep. Getting so nervous before shows that I couldn't keep my food
down, being offered a drink to calm my nerves down, feeling the liquor
twice as much because I hadn't kept the food down. Altogether skipping
dinner in favor of drinking, getting more and more stupid, feeling my
stage presence getting better and better, getting to the point where I
wanted a stage permanently attached to my feet, even if I had to adhere
it to the soles of my Chuck Taylors with the glue I had been sniffing.
Getting paid in applause and attention, not bothering to finish the books
I had started reading. This is how music made me stupid.

My stupidity reached its depths in California. Those two years in L.A.
are nothing but a big, dumb blur to me. Needless to say, no record labels
would have my band despite our hard work. We even departed on a two-
month tour but became a part of the catch-22 that victimizes most bands
at our level. To have a successful tour, you have to be a popular band, and

to be a popular band, you need to have a successful tour.

Sick of the constant rejection and squalid living conditions, we returned to Missouri. I moved in with my drummer and secured a job writing record reviews for *Volume*, a music magazine based in St. Louis. Begrudgingly accepting that I would never become a successful musician, I immersed myself in this trifling writing job that would result in me becoming one of the more important unknown entertainment figures of the new century. But still unknown.

24.

RECORD REVIEWS

D-PRAYVD
Always and Never
(Continental Recordings)

It pains me to waste this very ink on critically appraising a band like D-Prayvd. After all, this is valuable space that could be used to squeeze a little more cleavage into this publication. However, it would be a sin to excuse this abomination of an aural experience from the severe chastising that it so fully deserves.

I am once again amazed that enough people had enough faith in an album like this to actually get it recorded, let alone mass-produced and unleashed upon the public. Of course, that D-Prayvd has been given a future makes perfect sense considering the country that spawned it celebrates mediocrity and shuns anything resembling originality. Thus, D-Prayvd's bland, average sound should find success in America, considering that audiences here will simply settle for *anything* in ways of entertainment. It's on TV; it must be good, right?

Wrong, fool. That such pure staleness and banality could be encapsulated and processed into compact disc form and released with hundreds of thousands of dollars behind it has nothing to do with quality. Bands like D-Prayvd (and there are *a lot* of them), or more specifically, the businessmen who allow bands like these to flourish, are entirely *quantity*-driven. Their job is to minimize risks by going for the easy sell, and their creed is "be safe and profit." And these days, judging by their uninspired output, independent labels are just as guilty.

I can almost hear the conclusion of the meeting that made the release of *Always and Never* possible:

RECORD EXEC: So you're asking me to release something that is basically just a collection of predictable noises and lifeless, forgettable melodies sung in a voice that cannot be distinguished from eight other lead vocalists of bands you are blatantly copying?

MORON FROM D-PRAYVD: Yes.

RECORD EXEC: Sure! Why not?! You got yourself a record deal!

I realize I haven't yet described the actual content of this record, nor will I because there is none. This style of so-called modern rock is a dead horse that has been beaten, skinned, sliced, refrigerated, served, eaten, digested, regurgitated, and eaten again. Without hearing a second of this record, you have heard this band and you have seen their video. Yet you will still, in all likelihood, buy this godforsaken product.

The whole situation saddens me.

— *A typical music review I wrote for* Volume Magazine

25.

My editor at *Volume Magazine* had warned me to stop giving such vindictive reviews, especially to the releases on Continental Recordings. Continental was a subsidiary of IUI/Globe-Terner, which also owned Globe Inc., which published *Volume Magazine*. I told my editor that once he gave me one CD to review that was unique, creative, and of above-average quality, I would tone down my candor. That one CD never came, so I was eventually fired.

Because I had been so good about saving money, I was able to bask in unemployment for several months after losing my job at *Volume*. My accumulated money wasn't the result of miserliness; I just never bought much. By that point I had every record I wanted, and the only things I found worth buying were books.

But I wasn't leading much of an existence. The highlight of my week was grabbing my roommate's girlfriend's posterior. The idiots would suddenly begin making out as we were drunkenly watching Conan O'Brien. With her face occupied with his, she assumed it was he groping her, not me from across the sofa.

Outside of such grab-ass, I hated being around that happy, horny couple, and I could sense they wanted me out. But with no income and no other friends to turn to, I couldn't leave. I was stuck in the lovers' afterglow with my books and my music. I was frustrated and futureless, and slowly running out of cash. When the call came, I was willing to answer.

26.

Talk.

Hello. May I speak to Harlan Eiffler?

This is he.

Hi. My name is Richard Resnick. I'm calling on behalf of New Renaissance. We—"

I'm broke. Please take me off your list, and go to hell.

Wait! Don't hang up, Mr. Eiffler. I promise we're not after your money and we're not selling anything. I'm calling because we want you to come work for us.

Why me?

We love your writing.

You mean my record reviews?

Yes.

What place are you calling from again?

It's called New Renaissance. It's a new organization that promotes the rebirth of quality in the entertainment industry.

How do you plan on doing that?

For starters, we're building a school, a special school for exceptionally creative kids, and we're going to groom them to be the creators of tomorrow.

The creators of tomorrow?

Yes. I noticed in your writing that you are not satisfied with the creators of today.

You just said something there.

Would you be interested in meeting with us?

I don't know. What would my job be?

We're not quite sure yet. I know that you'd be working with the kids in some capacity.

I like kids.

Good. We've been looking for someone like you. Judging by your writing, you share the same attitude as New Renaissance, and we'd love to put your attitude to good use.

Can you send me some literature or something on this?

No. I can't because we don't plan on making any brochures or anything like that. What we were thinking is that we could send one of our guys to meet with you in St. Louis. How does that sound?

Sounds okay, I guess.

When would be a good date for us to send someone out to you?

Whenever. I don't have much else going on.

Great. Then I'll be talking to the agent you'll be working with and see when he can fly out there. And by the way, you may be interested to know that the agent is Steven Sylvain.

The action star?

Yes.

(laugh)

> — *My first telephone conversation with a New Renaissance employee,*
> *a year before meeting Vincent*

27.

I didn't recognize Steven Sylvain at first as he awkwardly strutted down the Lambert–St. Louis International Airport terminal. Only thinning wisps of his formerly abundant black hair sprouted from the top of his skull. His face appeared slightly bloated, and he was on the verge of having a beard. His washboard abs had distended into a prominent gut that his blue Hawaiian shirt casually draped. With this shirt he wore a nice black suit, aviator sunglasses, and new Nike tennis shoes with no socks.

I stood in Sylvain's path, my hair shagging in my eyes and my blue jeans ripped. He was likely expecting something smarter-looking and almost walked around me.

"Mr. Sylvain?" I asked.

"Guilty."

"I'm Harlan Eiffler."

"Oh, yeah. Hey, how are ya?"

We shook hands.

"I'm decent. How are you?"

"I need a drink. Let's get a drink."

Before I could ask him how his flight was, a young woman ran up to him screaming.

"Steven, I was one of your biggest fans!"

"You look pretty petite to me," he said in his famously cool, raspy voice.

"Ooh! Will you say it? Will you say, 'I get off on this shit,' for me? Please?"

"Sure."

Sylvain ducked his head down and paused as if he was summoning the muse of theatrical arts. He raised his head and suddenly bore an intense countenance.

"I get off on this crud!" he yelled at the girl.

"But it's 'shit.' 'I get off on this *shit*,'" she said, obviously disappointed.

"Now it's 'crud,'" said Sylvain confidently. "Laters."

A moment later another young woman came up screaming.

"I'm your biggest fan. Can I just hug you?"

"Yeah. Come here and hug my fat rear."

As the girl hugged Sylvain, I noticed he smelled her hair.

"Thank you," said the girl.

"No. Thank you. Be good now."

It took us thirty minutes to make it to a bar because as we walked across the bustling airport, people constantly stopped to ask for an autograph, photograph, hug, or one of his catchphrases. He accommodated everyone.

"You sure are patient with them," I said.

"Well, I haven't always been like that."

His favorite band was the Rolling Stones, his favorite TV show was

E! True Hollywood Story, and his favorite movie was *Braveheart*.

We finally made it to the Cheers bar, where Sylvain picked a booth in the corner and sat with his back to his audience.

"So. You're Harlan Eiffler."

"That's I."

"I've read your crud."

"Yeah?"

"Yeah. They gave me a bunch of it so I'd know what I was dealing with. I'm guessing you probably don't like my movies, do you?"

"They're entertaining."

"I'll be honest with you, Eiffler. I don't like 'em," he said as he smoothly lit a cigarette. "I don't like 'em one bit."

"What? My reviews?"

"No. My movies."

The waitress approached.

"Hi. What can I get you two?"

"Maker's and water," I said.

"Dewar's on the rocks."

"Hey! Aren't you Steven Sylvain?"

"Guilty."

"What happened to you?"

Sylvain took a deep drag from his cigarette, squinting his eyes the way single men so often do as they smoke in bars.

"I caught a bad case of AIDS, darlin'. What are you doing after your shift's over? Maybe I could get with your butt in the back of my El Camino."

"Oh. I—I'll be right back with your drinks."

"Works every time," he said.

"That was great," I said, genuinely impressed.

"Let's not dwell on it. You probably have a lot of questions for me about this job, right?"

"Yeah."

"That's what I'm here for. Ask me anything."

"I was kind of wondering how *you* got involved with this New Renaissance deal."

"Yeah. Right. How did Mr. Pretty Boy Action Hero get involved with something of worth?"

"I didn't mean that."

"Forget it. It's kosher."

Sylvain plopped his right foot on my side of the booth.

"You want a footrub?" I asked.

"Yeah. I want a footrub, you jack-rear. Just touch my leg."

"I don't want to touch your leg, Mr. Sylvain."

"Just gently caress it. And call me Steve."

When I shook my head, he pulled up his pant leg to reveal a tan prosthetic leg. The waitress brought us our drinks without saying anything.

"*Blood Lust 5*. Sex scene. Moped."

He returned the foot to his side of the booth.

"What happened?" I asked.

"They had me bonin Heather Graham as she was driving the 'ped, right? But an explosion goes off at the wrong time and shakes the 'ped, and I fall backwards over the front of it. Then Heather drives over my leg, and I can't move, and two more explosions get me. Long story short, it went gangrene, and they finally had to amputate."

"That's awful. I bet Heather Graham felt bad."

"Yeah. But it wasn't her fault. I didn't even want to do that movie. The studio pressured me into it. So anyhow, Foster Lipowitz got to feeling guilty about everything, you know? He felt guilty about laying the pressure on me to do that crap film, and about me getting maimed in a stupid stunt, and about not hiring me after I was crippled. So a while back, Lipowitz invited me over to his house, which I hear is rare for him. He told me he was sorry for everything, and he wanted to give me this important agent job. So now he takes good care of me, and he says I'll have this job for as long as I want as long as I don't get back on the drugs. So that's how I got a job working for New Renaissance."

"Who's Foster Lipowitz?"

"I'm impressed," said Sylvain. "That's usually where I would've been asked if it was true about losing my cock."

28.

"I still have all my genitals," said Sylvain.

"I'm happy for you," I replied.

"In fact—funny story—my publicist started that rumor."

"Why?"

"To overshadow the rumor that I lost my leg. So anyhow, about Foster Lipowitz. It's funny how no one knows who he is. He practically controls everything you see and hear. You've heard of IUI/Globe-Terner, right?"

"Of course."

"Lipowitz is its CEO. So that puts him in charge of the IUI Internet company, Terner Bros. Movies, Terner Bros. Music, and all their subsidiaries, and the subsidiaries of the subsidiaries. What am I leaving out? Oh, yeah, Globe Books and all of its imprints. But now he runs New Renaissance, and let me tell you, it's his pride and joy."

"But hold on. That magazine I was writing for was published by Globe."

"That's how we knew about you."

"Well, if you people think I'm so special, why was I fired?"

"Lipowitz probably didn't even know you were fired. He's so far up that he doesn't know what's going on further down the hierarchy, you know?"

Upon Sylvain's signal, the waitress brought us two more drinks.

"Anyhow, forget record reviews. Now you are personally going to play an active role in getting quality crud out to the public. We think you're perfect for this job. Just what Lipowitz is looking for."

"What's he looking for?"

"Someone who is furious about the way things are and smart enough to be able to do something about it. You seem furious about the state of music, am I right?"

"Yeah. I mean, it pisses me off when I see the talentless idiots out there that are making it big."

"Do you feel the same way about movies and TV?"

"They're worse in some ways."

"And we know how smart you are from your writing and from the fact that the FBI was wanting you when you were sixteen. That's great."

"How did you know about that?"

"We know it all, Eifflerdorf. Your habit of truancy in grade school. The time you sold the dog that belonged to your neighbor. Lipowitz has a lot of important friends. More like business associates. He can get any information he needs whenever he needs it."

"You're wrong. I actually sold lots of other peoples' pets. That was the only time I got caught."

"That's interesting. Can you tell me anything else you didn't get caught at?"

"Why?"

"This is like a job interview. I need to know."

"Well, in college I stole other students' textbooks and sold them at the bookstore. They'd come in class and be like, I couldn't do my homework because I lost my book. Ha ha."

"Sounds like you got a mean streak."

"Yeah. I have a nice streak, too, though. I did that stuff so I wouldn't have to get money from my mom. Things were hard enough on her as it was."

"You could've got a job, you jack-rear."

"I don't like being around people."

"Are you good at lying to people?"

"Why? Does this job require lying?"

"If it did, would you not be interested?"

I let out a frustrated sigh. "I don't know. You'd have to tell me exactly what we're talking about here."

"Yeah. Right. Okay. Let's get my rear to the hotel, and I'll put in a call to the home office."

Sylvain finished off his drink and threw a one-hundred-dollar bill on the table as he slid out of the booth.

"All that for the waitress?"

"I feel bad about the AIDS comment. It's company money anyhow. That's something you should know about this New Renaissance gig. For a company that's not out for money, they sure do have big pocketbooks. You'll be set for life if you take this job. You'll do better than you ever would've as a rock star. By the way, I heard your CDs. Your bands were pretty great. You should be rich by now."

"But I wasn't into music for the money," I said.

"Of course not. But what were you in it for?"

"I loved entertaining people. That's really the only way I feel comfortable around people, when I'm putting on a show for them."

"Then you really are perfect for this job."

29.

Sylvain told me to wait in the lobby of the Omni Majestic while he made a phone call in his room. I sat and watched the people come and go for twenty minutes before he came back down.

"Let's go back to my room," he said. "We need some privacy for this."

"For what?"

"I just got permission to declassify your job info, you jack-rear. That's what."

We walked into an elevator.

"What is that word you keep calling me?" I asked.

"Jack-rear."

"Like jackass?"

"That's the one."

"Why jack-rear?"

"Since I got this job, I've been trying to turn things around, you know? And Lipowitz got me thinking. He said New Renaissance isn't going to rely on sex, drugs, violence, and profanity to sell things. He said it's about true creativity. He said that New Renaissance is really about the talent of the writers, because that's where everything begins. Everything begins with the word. So with that in mind, I'm cursing less and talking smarter. That means no more 'ass.' Just 'rear.'"

Sylvain sat my rear down in his suite and slowly explained the ludicrous idea of secretly manipulating an artist for the sake of art. He explained how he would be a go-between for Lipowitz and me and how, as an agent, he would help me get this tortured artist's works out to the public. I replied to his ideas with disbelief and laughter, mostly laughter. I laughed until I almost cried.

"You know," said Sylvain, "This plan isn't as crazy as it sounds. Did you know that the United States government subjected Fidel Castro to some weird, secret torment? They gave him exploding cigars and tried to poison him so that his beard would fall out."

"What's that got to do with anything?"

"I'm just saying, some crazy things like what we're doing have been done before with the greater good in mind. Did you know a movie studio gave Shirley Temple hormone injections to stunt her growth? Then they hired taller actors and bigger furniture to make her look smaller."

"So?"

"So it's not unheard of for the entertainment industry to be control-ling a kid and that kid's environment. That goes way back. Like most classical music composers were child prodigies. Their parents and patrons exploited them, all right, but they gave the world beautiful music for all of eternity. So do you want to deny the world beautiful music for all of eternity?"

"Maybe I do."

30.

Dear Mr. Eiffler:

Salutations. I am attempting to orchestrate an intellectual revival for America through an innovative patronage system which you know as New Renaissance. I have been told that as of Mr. Sylvain's departure from St. Louis, you were undecided in regards to our proposal. This is com-pletely understandable. I acknowledge the fact that this idea is unortho-dox, bizarre, and in some ways, dare I say, immoral. However, it is crucial to our cause and an essential step in changing the direction of our culture. Forgive the cliché, but the end justifies the means.

Before I proceed, allow me to commend you on your fine service to the music industry. Your writing is entertainingly venomous, and more important, it is accurate. I was given copies of your more acrimonious reviews and agreed wholeheartedly with all of them, even though I was responsible for many of the records. In these reviews, you articulated thoughts that I was unable to. I have tremendous respect for writers and the written word, which is another reason why you are such an attractive prospect to me. Thank you for teaching me, Mr. Eiffler, as I am eager to learn despite my antiquity. I am now seventy and have several decades of intellectual stagnation to make up for.

As should our country! I am sure you have noticed that the entertain-ment industry is in a state of decay. As a man who regretfully admits play-ing a key role in this decay, I feel it is my responsibility to rebuild enter-tainment into something that I can be proud of.

For decades my businesses have operated on a reprehensible but widespread entertainment theory: In order for profits to go up, the products must be dumbed down. In place of well-written, thought-provoking material, we have often chosen to give the public meaningless works of stupidity, sex, and violence. I believe it was J. Krishnamurti who said something like, "In lieu of creativity, artists emphasize sex," a statement made obvious in today's music videos, hit movies, and television shows.

I do not know whether dumbed-down entertainment has gradually diminished the collective intellect of the nation or if their cerebral laziness came first and we merely catered to it. Whatever the case, I will do my part in bringing about quality, meaningful works to the people. How it will affect them, we shall see.

These aforementioned people *will* see and hear these quality, meaningful works because my system *will* work. The rebirth of entertainment will begin with a revamped version of another decaying institution: education. At the New Renaissance Academy, which will open this fall, a select staff of talented instructors will groom and train our elite class of prodigies. After their raw talent has been thoroughly refined and perfected, they will work on new creations for film, television, and music, the three main areas of our concern since they affect modern mainstream culture much more than, say, literature, plays, or paintings.

New Renaissance artists' creations *will* reach the public because I will make sure of it. I think you are now aware of the influence I possess as CEO of IUI/Globe-Terner. I consider New Renaissance my duty because I am one of the few men who has the clout, connections, and power to ensure it succeeds, and with my news channels and magazines, I can manipulate world media.

You might be asking: What makes you think that today's audiences will even *bother* with quality films, TV shows, and music? After all, it seems they prefer sex and violence to material that requires actual thought. My solution is simple: We will use the established celebrities they are so crazy about as bait. While the typical American patron may not be interested in original, creative material that pushes artistic boundaries, he or she *is* interested in Mel Gibson. The words that originate in the minds of New Renaissance geniuses will be filtered through the bodies of Hollywood stars and attractive musicians. I can guarantee these stars' cooperation because many of them owe favors to the man who helped set them in their current constellations. Meanwhile, the New Renaissance geniuses must remain relatively obscure.

As with most modern institutions, entertainment relies upon business and technology. Hence, the 20th century saw such innovations as agents, managers, publicists, and other sycophants, not to mention mass production, new advertising techniques, and the Internet. I have mastered the business and technological elements that entertainment depends upon, but art has suffered for it.

Might I suggest that entertainment has killed art? The perpetrators of entertainment are more likely to be sex symbols than true artists. This is our fundamental problem. Instead of art, we have entertainment, and instead of artists, we have pretty faces seeking fame, fortune, and pleasure. Suffering is kept to a minimum while profits are kept to a maximum.

Henceforth, I want to bring back art at all costs, or at least strengthen the art side of entertainment. This means summoning the artistic spirit that seems so lost upon contemporary souls. This means finding a true artist and keeping him that way. That is where you come in.

I firmly believe that we can produce the ultimate artist by carefully conditioning his life for the sake of his art. If our project proves to be a success, I plan to make this innovative approach commonplace in building artistic careers. Art is but an imitation of life. We would simply be providing material.

The idea of a tortured artist seems foreign to contemporary times, doesn't it? Once today's artists attain success, they enjoy the fame, riches, and love that soften their creative edge. Many of them don't have a creative edge to begin with, and if they do experience some sort of torment, it is often self-induced. The average entertainment figure may endure alcoholism, drug abuse, adulterous marriages, excessive sexual appetites, and depression. Besides depression, their problems arise from their hedonistic lifestyles. There is no true suffering present. Again, everything is pleasure-oriented for these well-paid party animals.

We will attempt to seek out and develop the polar opposite of the hedonistic millionaires who have been entertaining us and shaping our asinine culture. We will encourage our artist not through rewards such as money, fame, and sex, but through *deprivation*. We won't give; we'll take away.

Entertainment needs an archetypal artist of old: a tormented, isolated, loveless, and hopeless young man or woman with the creative ability to justify his or her sad existence. This person would live according to an old maxim that is a foreign concept to many of today's greed-driven, fast-living "artists": no pain, no gain.

Thus, New Renaissance needs a lonely soul to take on the suffering of the world and turn it into masterpieces. This soul may find itself a victim of unrequited love, nervous breakdowns, overwork, isolation, exile, squalor, sickness, and mental illness, none of which would be experienced in vain.

As I'm sure you know, there have been beings like this, doomed souls who happened to be some of the greatest artists ever. Dostoyevsky, Zola, Keats, Coleridge, Browning, Poe, Dickinson, Toulouse-Lautrec, Rilke, Kafka, Woolf, Joyce, Mann, Lowell, Plath, Robinson, Lardner, Lawrence, Pound, Toole, Berlioz, Beethoven, Schumann, van Gogh, Munch, and Rothko are the names that immediately come to mind. True artists lend themselves to suffering without the help of "experiments" like I'm proposing. If we choose the right person, our manipulations will likely be superfluous.

We will select someone who appears destined for a tortured artist's life anyway, thereby keeping your meddling with his life to a minimum. I am only asking you to provide our Renaissance Man with constructive pain in the most humane and beneficial ways. This means doing three things: (1) Keeping the artist lonely, (2) Keeping the artist inspired, and (3) Keeping the artist creating. The specifics shall come as we go along.

And to clarify, in no way will any of us personally capitalize on this project. You will not make public any accounts of this project. You will sign a vow of secrecy if you accept this job.

Finally, for every misdeed you commit toward this artist, you will help him in another way. The artist will always have food and shelter. The artist will have you to talk to about his troubles and to guide his career. The artist will have an invaluable education for free. And the artist will not die under our watch. These are all guarantees that might otherwise be unavailable. And unlike many tortured artists, this one will see his works actually reach the public. He will likely find great pleasure in sharing his gift with the world. Your job will be to make sure the artist doesn't get too confident or content with his situation.

I know you were a student of history before your expulsion from college, so here is a final speculation for you to consider: What if Adolf Hitler had been accepted as what he truly wanted to be—an artist? Oh, the things that art can do, and the death and destruction a good agent or manager could have prevented.

I swear to you that I am doing all of this to create a better world. Please help me.

Confidentially,

Foster Lipowitz

P.S.—Should you decide to deny a dying man his wish for your assistance on this project, I would advise you to never breathe a syllable of any of this to another soul as the repercussions would be irreparable.

—A letter that Foster Lipowitz sent me

31.

I called Sylvain and told him I'd take the job. I realized if I didn't take advantage of this extraordinary opportunity, I would have no choice but to get a real job and lead an average life. I didn't want my existence to be reduced to a collection of due dates. I didn't want to perpetually be working on my résumé. I wanted to do something that mattered, and after Lipowitz's letter, I could hardly think of a good reason to refuse his offer. Except for the moral issue.

I told Sylvain I would take the job under one condition: I could never be asked to do anything to this kid if I hadn't experienced it myself in some way. In explaining myself, I told him about how cops in training are required to have mace sprayed in their face to know what pain they'll be causing their victims.

Sylvain ran this by the three other people who knew about our scheme, Lipowitz, Richard Resnick, and Drew Prormps. Resnick was Lipowitz's longtime lawyer, a millionaire who was also intensely disenchanted with the entertainment industry. Prormps was a marketing executive at IUI/Globe-Terner whom Lipowitz had handpicked to be the vice president of New Renaissance. The three men agreed to my terms.

Unfortunately for Wynona, I once had a dog that was run over by a car.

32.

One of my earliest memories was dwelling on death as I looked out the car window on a family vacation. When my mom, dad, brother, and I were cramped in the car together speeding down the interstate to Disney World, I imagined what it would be like if one or all of them died. Someone probably said, "Harlan, you sure are being quiet," but I couldn't snap out of it. I made myself sad.

Death is huge to me. There is no getting around it. It is bigger than any thing or idea and twice the size of life. Every action of every animal and human is indirectly controlled by death. They spend their whole lives trying not to die. They can only enjoy a pathetic fraction of the physical world because of the limitations that death imposes upon space and time. Religions arose to justify death by hyping the hereafter. Death is the ultimate limit but can also serve as the ultimate motivation.

So it bothered me when I learned that Vincent didn't take death as seriously as I. He treated death like it was nothing. He played with it, much like the writers of *Blood Lust*.

Beginning with his second year at the New Renaissance Academy, I kept in close contact with Vincent's teachers and talked to him on the phone once a week, placing calls from St. Louis to Kokomo and charging them to the company. I checked on him to see what he'd been learning, what he'd been writing, and especially what had been going on in his personal life. Vincent's writing instructor said Vincent already possessed highly developed writing skills and a firm grasp on symbolism and irony. However, he brought to my attention that nearly all of Vincent's stories ended the same, with the protagonist dying in a playful, ironic way.

He wrote one story about a talking pencil who died of lead poisoning. Another was about a turkey starving to death on Thanksgiving. With Christmas approaching, Vincent wrote about a male tree ornament who grew long hair in hopes of being promoted to the angel tree-topper.

When he was instead demoted for looking effeminate, he killed himself and became a real angel named Stupid the Cupid.

Speaking on behalf of his superiors as he gave me my orders, Sylvain convinced me that to not teach Vincent a grave lesson about the greatest theme of all would do his career and his future audiences a great disservice.

33.

"How you plan on doing it?" asked Veronica, who had successfully killed her fetus since the last time we met. She now had short blond hair.

From my coat pocket, I pulled a little white envelope full of powder.

"Arsenic trioxide," I said.

"What's that?"

"Rat poison. It would be the cleanest way, I think."

"I don't want it to hurt her," said Veronica.

"I'll mix it in really good with her food. You can even do it yourself if you want."

"Hell no. Why you gotta do it so close to Christmas? This is gonna ruin our holiday."

"It's gotta be now. Vincent has to be the one to find it, and he'll be home from school in two hours. Plus, the Christmas thing adds to the overall effect, don't you think?"

"I just don't know about this."

"Sorry, but these were my orders. You promised your cooperation, Veronica."

I thought about how in movies, usually action movies, a cheap way of getting the audience to invest in the plot is to endanger the life of a dog. There can be fifty men graphically terminated by machine-gun fire or an entire building full of workers destroyed, but no one will stand for a cute little dog being killed. And almost always, the dog's life is spared to the relief of the audience.

"Fine. Here's her bowl."

Veronica handed me the bowl, and I quickly mixed the powder with Alpo. I thoroughly mashed up the meat with a knife and fork, causing it to congeal into a mass of brown poison.

"Heeere, Wynona!"

34.

Wynona pranced in daintily and licked her lips. Veronica didn't want to watch, so she gathered up her kids and went to Wal-Mart.

"Vincent's going to need somebody to talk to when he gets home," I told her.

"Then talk to him," said Veronica.

"I'll talk to him later. I can't be here when he gets home. He's a smart kid. He might suspect something."

"Well, I'm not staying around to watch it, and neither are the kids."

"Yeah. Okay."

Veronica picked up the terrier and hugged it.

"I love you, Wynona baby. I'm sorry."

She kissed the dog and set it down.

"See you, Harlan. I guess leave the door unlocked for Vincent."

"Okay. Sorry about this."

"You just keep those checks comin is all I got to say."

I set the doggie bowl down on the sticky kitchen linoleum. Wynona looked up to me with wide eyes as if to say thank you and eagerly commenced her last supper. She ate like she was starving.

I don't know what The Thing Called God is or looks like, but I envision It as a gigantic rotating orb of light that generates equal amounts of warmth and coolness. As I saw the Alpo disappearing from that doggie bowl, I imagined this perfect orb floating farther and farther away from me. It was getting smaller and smaller, and then it was a dot, and then it was a speck, and then it was gone.

I watched the convulsions and wild eyes and waited for the conclusive thud. When it finally came, I laid Wynona's limp body underneath the Christmas tree and left the front door unlocked for Vincent, just as I had been instructed.

IV. BRITNEY

35.

The summer after Vincent's third year at the academy, Veronica presented the world with a fifth child, a brain-dead baby girl named Britney. Vincent was nine, and by then had become well-read, was capable of writing detailed movie critiques, and had heard and analyzed every single Beatles song.

I had still been phoning Vincent on a weekly basis. Since the death of his pet, his life had been uneventful, until one August afternoon when Vincent saw his mom shaking uncontrollably on the floor and called 911. Paramedics rushed his mom off to the hospital. By the time I called him, it had been three days since Vincent or his siblings had seen their mother. Their food supply had dwindled to cottage cheese and Fruit Roll-Ups.

I called the Kramden hospital and learned that Veronica's labor was not a success, that the baby was not healthy, and that the mother was in serious condition. I caught a flight to the airport in Evansville, Indiana, drove a rental car to Kramden, picked up Veronica's children, drove them to Burger King, and then took them to the hospital. I figured someone needed to do this. I also reasoned that Vincent needed to spend more time in hospitals.

"Are you Foster Lipowitz?" squealed Vincent's younger sister, Sarah, out of the blue as I was driving them to the hospital.

"No. I'm Harlan Eiffler. I'm Vincent's manager. I've told you all that three times already. How do you know Foster Lipowitz, anyway?"

"She don't," said the oldest boy, Dylan, who was about eleven. "She just heard me talkin 'bout how he was mom's and Vincent's boss and how he kills people for a living."

"Where'd you get that?" I asked with a laugh.

"I seen it in one of my mom's supermarket magazines. It said Foster Lipowitz was in good with the mob, and if he didn't get his way, he'd have somebody killed, but he was so far up that they couldn't ever catch him."

"Those supermarket magazines are full of lies," I said.

"I'm just telling you what it said," replied Dylan. "Who the hell are you anyway?"

"I'm Harlan Eiffler!" I turned on the stereo, hoping to quiet them. I shook my head, marveling at the stupidity of Vincent's siblings. Then I remembered Veronica's habit of turning her womb into a test tube for illegal chemicals. I looked over at Vincent and thought, Damn, son. You're a miracle.

Vincent's brothers and sister whined about the tape I had playing.

"Please shut up," I told them. "You need to be exposed to music like this."

"Who the fuck is it?" asked Dylan.

"Frank Black."

"Never heard of him," he said with contempt.

"I'm not surprised. They don't play him on the radio or MTV."

"That's 'cause he sucks," said Dylan. "He don't get on the radio 'cause he ain't good enough."

"No. It's the opposite. He's too good. He's not on the radio 'cause he's not bad enough."

"Turn it to 96, dude. They play D-Prayvd."

"Yeah. Turn it!" added four-year-old Ben, the youngest of Veronica's specimens.

I looked over and smiled at Vincent, who rolled his eyes. I turned my tape up louder and louder still to drown out Dylan, who Ben now joined in cussing.

36.

I knew equally trivial amounts of information regarding the two men at the paramount of the New Renaissance hierarchy. Both were enigmas whom I assumed I would never meet. Remembering that I worked at the St. Louis Public Library for a year as a teenager and never met the library director, I accepted that I would likely never shake hands with the CEO or VP of an important company like New Renaissance, despite being a dedicated employee.

From talking to Sylvain and searching the Internet, I had gleaned minimal background facts about Foster Lipowitz. I knew that as a teenager with not a nickel to his name, he unceremoniously turned in an application to work in the Globe Books mailroom. This commenced decades of hard work, ingenuity, and, perhaps later on, treachery, as he furiously tugged the top of the corporate ladder toward his direction. I knew he was loved by some, hated by others, but respected by all, which likely led to those tabloid legends. And I know that he had an exalted sense of what entertainment meant to the world, and believed that he had the power to shape culture for the better. For the sake of doing my job in good conscience, I believed in him.

As for vice president Drew Prormps, I only knew that he was in his thirties and, according to Sylvain, "a real go-getter." A couple of teachers at New Renaissance mentioned his name and commented on how devoted he was to making quality entertainment, as well as how strikingly handsome he was. I knew he was a Harvard graduate and started out in marketing for an independent record label. He later became a marketing executive for IUI/Globe-Terner, and he seemed to have become Mr. Lipowitz's right-hand man with relative ease.

37.

"Are you the father?" asked the doctor.

"No. I'm a friend of the family. Is the mom going to be okay or what?"

"The mother is going to be okay, but I'm afraid her daughter never will be."

He went on to explain that Veronica had overdosed on methamphetamines, which caused premature labor. Her brand-new child had severe brain damage and was underdeveloped in sickening ways. I pictured a face that even a mother couldn't love.

I returned to the waiting room where Vincent sat quietly while his brothers and sister tore up every magazine from *Highlights* to *Vogue*. His sister, Sarah, literally devoured *Entertainment Weekly*, almost choking on the pages.

"Is she going to die?" asked Vincent after I sat down next to him. He looked straight ahead as he spoke.

"Your mom or the baby?"

"My mom."

"No. She's doing a lot better now. She's going to be fine."

"What about the baby?"

"She'll die if she's lucky. She's not at all healthy."

"I don't want her to die, though."

"Well, I don't *want* her to die, but she won't have a life worth living if she lives. She doesn't have any arms or legs, Vincent."

"She can still have a good life. I'm going to be rich someday and give her everything she needs. Mom says I'm going to get us all a big, nice house when I sell my movies and songs."

Apparently, with help from his mother, Vincent had gone from not valuing life to valuing life in terms of valuables. I had known thoughts like these, wanting to be gagged with a silver spoon. I would have to adjust Vincent's thinking on this topic someday soon.

"A big house isn't going to make her life better," I said. "Her brain is showing."

He turned to me, his sad eyes meeting my own. He still hadn't grown into those big, sad eyes.

"She's still my sister."

"I know. I know that. I'm sure you'd be a good big brother to her. But even if you lose her, you have to accept it. You can use that pain for your work. Remember what I told you when Wynona died?"

"That which does not kill us only makes us stronger."

"Right. Especially for you, because you're a writer."

Vincent's brothers were wrestling each other. His sister was sticking a pen down her throat. Vincent focused a troubled gaze on his untied generic tennis shoes.

"What's wrong, turkey?" I asked.

"You have me thinking about Wynona. I miss her."

"I'm sorry." It had been a year and a half since Vincent found his dog dead.

"Did you know what my mom said when she died?" asked Vincent.

"No."

"She said not to worry about Wynona dying, because if she had been someone else's pet, like the coolest kid in school or someone like Ben Affleck, she probably would have liked them better than me."

"Your mom is an idiot. Wynona wouldn't have liked them. They wouldn't have been as good to her as you were. And you two had been through so much together."

"I thought about the same thing with my mom. If she had a really good-looking kid who was good at baseball, wouldn't she like him better than me? Would she trade me in if she could?"

"I would apply my same argument," I said. "Are you a good son to your mother?"

"Yes. I think so."

"Then she wouldn't like anyone else better. I know she doesn't always show it, but she loves you and wouldn't trade you for anyone."

"Even if I didn't have any arms or legs?"

"Sure."

38.

I later deduced that there was good reason for Foster Lipowitz to embrace Drew Prormps. After familiarizing myself with his work, I saw that there was likely nobody in the entertainment industry more skillful at selling unexceptional products to the masses. He was responsible for the success of some of the most untalented acts of the day, such as pop singer Kristina Gomez and my favorite band, D-Prayvd. I always assumed some performers sold their souls to become famous, and now I knew who did the buying.

Lipowitz picked Prormps for New Renaissance because he knew that his fledgling company would have many tough sales ahead and that the public would need convincing. Prormps would do the convincing with his savvy marketing, and now he would be marketing quality entertainment instead of helping pollute the world. And by hiring Prormps, Lipowitz not only acquired an asset for his cause, but he also decreased the force of his competition.

Sylvain said Prormps was thrilled to have the opportunity to work for New Renaissance. An intellectual who appreciated high art, he had been unhappy marketing multimillion-dollar products full of bad grammar and butts. He had been waiting for something like New Renaissance to come along and give his career a higher purpose, and like most of us in the company, he was grateful to have a chance for renewal.

39.

Veronica specifically asked to see me, which I could tell saddened Vincent. A frumpy nurse led me to her room, where she lay pallid and frazzled but still gorgeous. She now had long, wavy brown hair with highlights.

"What's up?" she moaned.

"Hey, Veronica. How are you feeling?"

"I feel good as long as they got me full of drugs." Her voice sounded desperate and shaky. There was a spooky quality to her as she looked around the room with floating eyeballs.

"I brought the kids. They were worried about you. At least one of them, anyway."

"Have you seen Britney?"

"Who's that?"

"It's the baby."

"No."

She attempted to focus her eyes on mine and shook her head like she had a dose of sour cough syrup in her mouth.

"She's so ugly. She's so gross. They handed her to me and I just started crying. I didn't want to hold her. I wouldn't take her. I don't wanna look at her or touch her. I don't want her. She's so ugly. I don't want her."

"Well, you shouldn't have been doing drugs when you were pregnant."

"I know. But I didn't think she'd make it."

"She might not still," I comforted her.

"What am I gonna do? I mean, she didn't even look human."

"You created a monster."

"Shut up! You are ass-like!"

"Sorry. I don't know what to tell you, Veronica. You ruined your kid's life before it even started. You're not getting sympathy from me."

"Oh, man. I don't want your sympathy. Everything you say is a comedy of drama."

"Then why did you want to see me?" I asked.

"I don't know. Oh yeah—while you was here, I wanted to ask you something. Come here."

Her index finger motioned me toward her bed. She propped herself up with her elbows and had a sexy look on her face.

"Why wouldn't you do me?" she druggily pleaded.

"What?"

"Why wouldn't you do me at the hotel?"

I laughed but then paused when I saw she was completely serious and wanted a serious answer.

"Because I didn't think it was right," I answered.

"But why?"

"Lots of reasons. For starters, you're Vincent's mother."

"So?"

"So why are you asking?"

"Nobody had ever said no before."

"That's another reason why I didn't do it. Let me go get your kids and bring 'em in here."

"No!"

"You haven't seen them in days."

"I don't wanna see them! I don't want them to see me! I don't want any of this!" She pounded on the hospital bed with both fists.

"Would you cool it?"

"You didn't see what came out of me! It was gross! I feel so dirty! I want out of this! I want out of this, dude! This sucks!"

A plump, blond nurse with teddy bears on her shirt rushed in.

"What's going on here?" she asked.

"She's hysterical," I replied.

"Shit! Shiiiiit! This sucks a ball's ass!" wailed Veronica.

"Sir, I'm going to have to ask you to leave," said the nurse as she prepared a syringe.

"No, no, no, no, no, no," sputtered Veronica. "Don't make him leave. I'm okay. I'll be good now. I'll be good."

"It's time for your shot, anyway."

"Give it to me. But let him stay."

Veronica coyly accepted the tranquilizer.

"May he stay?" she asked, pouting seductively.

"Well, okay. Five more minutes. You need to rest. Don't get her all worked up like that," said the nurse to me on her way out.

"I wanna move," said Veronica, now subdued and somber.

"Do you now?"

"Yes. I would like to move to California."

"Why? Let me guess—you want to be an actress. Or maybe an intern for someone's tongue?"

"I want to start over. I don't want to be here anymore. You could move me there and use it against Vincent. He'd never get over it."

"What about your other kids?"

"What about them?"

"Would you take them with you?"

"Yeah. If you pay for the move and everything."

I considered it for five seconds.

"It's too much," I said. "I'll assume it's the drugs talking."

"It's me talking. Drugs don't talk."

"Go to sleep. And you're welcome for taking care of your children."

"I'm welcome. Think about it. California. New start. Will you sign my Achilles' tendon, Miss Veronica? Yes, I will."

She fell asleep but her blabbering continued. Her dreams sounded like nightmares with bad melodies and poorly written dialogue.

40.

"Do you think she was serious?" asked Sylvain.

"I think so."

I called Sylvain from Veronica's house after we got home from the hospital. The kids, including Vincent, were playing outside.

"She's a whore," I continued. "And whores, especially small-town whores, tend to think that the answer to all their problems is moving to a big city, usually New York or L.A."

"That's true," said Sylvain. "I grew up in Wisconsin."

"She doesn't even know what she wants. Well—I take that back. She knows she wants a clean slate. And I'm sure she's thinking she can become an actress and get famous. Again, she's a tremendous whore. I know how these people think. She wants to be famous or at least to be

sleeping with someone famous. She probably thinks that it would be better to be famous and miserable rather than unknown and miserable."

"Or even unknown and happy," said Sylvain.

"Exactly. You know what I'm talking about."

"Of course I do, jack-rear."

"So what do you think? This isn't anything we should touch, is it?"

"I don't know, bro. I'm thinking we could really do something with
this. I think it might be a good opportunity we should take advantage of."

"I think we'd be doing Vincent a favor by getting that woman out of
his life," I replied. "He might be more likely to get inspiration if we *don't*
send her away."

"Tell you what. Let me run this by Prormps and see what he thinks."

By this time, Drew Prormps was playing an active role in our project.

"Okay," I said. "I gotta go."

"Yeah. Me too. I got a date with Judith Light in an hour."

I turned off my cell phone as Vincent came inside. He looked upset
and lay down on the floor. He stared at the ceiling and picked at his scalp.

"What's wrong, scrub?"

"I don't know," he snapped back, which was uncharacteristic for the
normally nebbish boy. For a brief moment of paranoia, I wondered if he
had heard me talking to Sylvain. He's so sensitive; maybe he could hear
people's cell phone conversations in his head. Maybe he was already on
to us, only two years into our project.

"Actually, I do know. I don't like playing with them," he said to my
relief.

"I've always been the same way," I said. "Never played with the
neighborhood kids growing up. Despised recess at school. You're lucky. At
your school you don't have to go to recess if you don't want to. You don't
even have to do group work. Your school encourages individuality."

"All kids seem to like it outside so much. But not me. I don't like the
outdoors at all."

"I'm the same way. Everything I love is indoors. My books, my music,
movies, TV. Everything I need. All that's outside are a bunch of bugs and
allergants."

"Yes. I like the indoors better, too," said Vincent. "Someday, I'm
going to have a great big house that'll be so awesome that I'd have no

need to ever leave it for outside."

"Sounds good. But, you know, we shouldn't be that way."

"I don't like the sun, either," said Vincent.

"Why not?"

"You can't even look at it. I prefer the moon. You can look at *it*."

"Have you ever noticed that the man in the moon looks sad?" I asked.

"No."

"Remember that the next time you're looking at it, okay? He's frowning and his eyes are turned downward in sorrow."

"Okay. But Harlan?"

"What?"

"Also, you can get a sunburn, but you can't get a moonburn."

I laughed.

"That's true," I agreed. "Hey—did you know that Neil Armstrong was the first man on the moon because he was the dispensable one?"

"No."

"The other astronauts were the ones who knew how to get back if something went wrong. He didn't know how. So it wouldn't have mattered if he died."

"He still got to be the first man on the moon."

"That's right. But you know that famous line, 'one small step for man, one giant leap for mankind'?"

"Yes."

"He screwed that line up. He meant to say 'one small step for *a* man.' What he said was redundant, but no one seemed to care."

"Why are you telling me all this?" he asked.

"Why am I telling you this? I'm telling you all this because it's the truth. I think you should know the truth about everything. Don't you think you should know the truth?"

"Yes, but your truth always seems to be ugly."

"Yep. The truth is ugly. For instance, I don't want to bum you out, but every man, woman, and child you see, no matter how beautiful, are skeletons underneath. And skeletons are ugly. Big black eye sockets, animal mouths, those jerky movements. Picture them when you see them on the street. Walking skeletons, everywhere. There's meat, flesh, and brain attached, but when you get right down to it, they're just skeletons. Pretty creepy, when you think about it, isn't it?"

Vincent nodded.

"And look at the world around you. Some people will say things like, 'Oh, but this world is so beautiful. Just look around at the earth's natural splendor, the trees, the water, the grass.' Have you ever thought about what's underneath this beautiful earth?"

"No."

"Corpses. Billions and billions. More like trillions. They don't just disappear, you know. They're all right there, underneath us. Rotting bodies. More skeletons. What's the beauty in that?"

"I don't know." He got up and looked out the window at two dirt patches. Under one was his dog, Wynona. Under another was a skunk he named Athena. He befriended the skunk and attempted to domesticate it after Wynona died, but one of his mom's boyfriends shot it.

"Everything is ugly underneath," I said. "Don't you forget that."

"Excuse me." He turned from the window and headed for his bedroom. He left with a contemplative gaze with worries behind it, the same gaze he would wear as an adult who could never remember where he left his keys.

I peeked in and saw that he was lying down, his face in his pillow. I thought about uplifting him with my more positive theories, such as how, as an artist, he had the ability to create alternatives to this world, things both gorgeous and pure, works that expose ugliness and illuminate truth and so forth. I thought about telling him my belief that the artist is the world's redeemer who gives meaning to a sad, short, retrograde existence, who takes a stand against time. Instead I went back to the living room, turned on the big-screen TV, and watched an episode of the critically acclaimed *Sex and the City* in which the lead protagonist accidentally passes gas while having sex with a stranger.

41.

Sylvain called the next day and told me not to send Veronica to California. He had passed the idea along to Prormps, who was all for it. Prormps then relayed the idea to Lipowitz, who thought it was too harsh and forbade it. Veronica was to stay in Vincent's life, for better or worse, and she would continue to assist us in our cause.

That same day, Veronica was released from the hospital. She didn't
come home until late that night after her kids had gone to bed. I had been
left to baby-sit all day for the second day in a row. When she returned in
a car with bass-booming speakers, I was watching her *Blood Lust 4* DVD
to see if it was as bad as I thought. It was.

Upon Veronica entering her shack, I was expecting to meet Britney,
but I instead encountered her latest boyfriend, Kyle. He had marijuana
eyes and wore an Abercrombie & Fitch shirt, baggy pants, and lots of jew-
elry. His hair was short and bleached.

His favorite musician was Eminem, his favorite TV show was *The
Man Show,* and his favorite movie was *Friday.*

"What up?" he said in an accusatory tone.

"So pleased to meet you," I said unctuously.

"That's my son's manager that I was telling you about," said Veronica.
"He's going to get me to Hollywood."

"What up?" the twentysomething tough guy repeated, this time with
a quick nod and less disdain.

"Where's your baby?" I asked.

"It's hooked up to some stuff at the hospital. They're gonna keep it for
a while."

"It nasty!" said the gangsta.

"Are you the father?" I asked.

"Heeell nah."

"So are you gonna help me move?" asked Veronica.

"I don't think this is something we should discuss openly like this," I
said, motioning my head toward Thug Life.

"What up," he said.

Veronica sat down next to me. She also had marijuana eyes.

"Kyle, go outside," she said.

"Aight, but I'm smokin up a hooter," he replied as he left.

"Charming young man you have there. Has young Kyle impregnated
you yet?"

"Shut your mouth. Are you gonna help get me outta here?"

"So you were serious about that?"

"Yeah."

"What would you do in California once you got there?"

"I've always wanted to be an actress."

"Of course you have. You know, I don't want to preach, but my mom always said life is as good as you make it no matter where you live. I ran off to California once, and it just made things worse."

"I don't know. I think I'd be happy there. I've just always seen myself there being like the famous people you see in the *National Intruder* magazines in those pictures where they didn't know their picture was being taken. You know, like there will be this celebrity couple and they're usually in like a grocery parking lot and they're wearing sweatsuits with their jackets tied preppy-like around their waist and they always wear sunglasses and they're drinking bottled water. They look so happy."

Her favorite musician was Justin Timberlake, her favorite TV show was *Will and Grace*, and her favorite movie was *Titanic*.

"You could do that here," I replied. "You could even take up Scientology like the stars do."

"I hate science. Are y'all gonna help me move or not?"

"No. We're not."

"Why not?"

"We're going to need you in the coming years. Besides, we can't take a boy's mother from him, even though you're not much of a mother."

"He's off at school most of the year."

"But then there are your other kids. You're wanting to uproot them and move them across the country like it's nothing. You still have one of them in the hospital, for Christ's sake."

"We'll just move anyway."

"Good luck. You won't be getting our checks if you move."

"This sucks. Oh, well. I'm gettin stoned."

42.

I got a flight back to St. Louis that night and was able to follow the in-flight movie without headphones. The following week when I made my usual phone call to Vincent, an unfamiliar voice answered his phone.

"What up?" The voice was cool and hard, like a rapper's.

"May I speak to Vincent?"

"He ain't here no more."

"Oh. May I speak to Veronica?"

"She ain't here either. Who this?"

"This is Harlan Eiffler, her son's manager."

"Mothah fucka." Hard breathing followed his profanity.

"Ouch. Was it something I said?"

"Was it something I said?" He was mocking me. Of course, this was coming from a man whose entire persona relied on mimicry, from his haircut to his wardrobe to the attitude he learned from rap videos. I hoped we could help young men like this someday.

"More like something you *did*, bitch," he continued.

"I'll assume this is one of Veronica's skanky boyfriends."

"You know me, bitch."

"Oh, yeah. Is this that Kyle guy?"

"K-Kwik, mothah fucka."

"Well, K-Kwik, what is it exactly that you think I've done?"

"All I know is that Veronica was saying you was gonna move her to Hollywood, and now she's gone. Left a week ago without saying good-bye to me or her kids or nothing."

"Where are the kids now?"

"Cops come and got 'em. What'd you do with her? That ain't cool."

"I didn't do anything with her. I told her we wouldn't help her move. I had nothing to do with it."

"Bullshit."

"Do you know where I can find Vincent?"

"No."

"Listen. I need to talk to him. I—"

He hung up.

43.

Vincent later explained to me that two days after I left Illinois, he awakened to find that his mother wasn't around. Neither were her clothes, makeup, or hair dyes. Days passed and the only person to return was Veronica's boyfriend, who liked to smoke there. Then one day a doctor from the hospital called to inform Veronica of Britney's death. Dylan told the doctor his mom was gone for good, leading the doctor to call the police, who called social services, who put in an emergency order to find the four Djapushkonbutm kids a foster home. They had no relatives to turn to; Veronica's own mother had left town herself long ago.

I had been instructed by Sylvain, who had been instructed by Prormps, who had been instructed by Mr. Lipowitz, to track down Vincent and explain to the authorities that he was due back in school in a week and that we'd take care of him as we were contractually obligated to do. I showed them the necessary documents, and freed Vincent from the foster home. I ended up not having to use the bribery money I had been given.

"But what's going to happen to my brothers and sister?" asked Vincent in my car.

"They'll stay in that home for a while, I guess. They might find foster parents if they're lucky."

"Will I ever see them again?"

"I guess so, if you seek them out. Would you even *want* to see them again?"

"I want to make sure they're doing as well as I am. At least I know I'm in good hands."

"That's sweet of you. I wouldn't miss those kids."

Vincent missed his siblings enough to base characters on them in TV shows and movies he later created.

I was driving on that narrow country road to Vincent's childhood home for the last time. He wanted to go back to collect the possessions he had accumulated throughout his first nine years. He would then take these possessions to his new home, a tiny student apartment back at the New Renaissance Academy in Kokomo.

"So listen. If you want to talk about your mom or anything, here I am."

"I don't suppose there's anything to talk about," he said. "She's gone."

"Do you know why she left?"

"She didn't love us. I had suspected it all along."

"Does that hurt?"

"Of course it hurts. Our mother hates us."

"I'm sorry. She didn't deserve a kid like you. With a mother like that, I don't know how you've turned out as good as you have."

"You've helped me."

"No I haven't."

"Yes you have. You've given me a future. Mom probably wouldn't have stuck around as long as she did if it weren't for you and the opportunity you've given me. I'm very fortunate."

"Don't say that. You aren't fortunate. Your life almost entirely sucks."

"It could always be worse."

"Oh, it will be. Besides, this isn't about being fortunate. You deserve the opportunity we've given you. People like Pamela Anderson whose career began because someone saw her on the Jumbotron at a football game—those people are fortunate. Healthy movie stars who were born with good looks are fortunate. You're not fortunate. Don't ever let me hear you say you're fortunate again."

"Okay."

We finally reached the end of the road, though there was nothing to see there but the yard that Vincent hated playing in, with its deflated swimming pool and animal graves. His home had been reduced to a black pile of indistinguishable rubbish, leaving him nothing to come back for.

44.

"I've never set fire to anything before," I told Sylvain on the phone the day before I rescued Vincent. "At least nothing that big."

"There's not much to it, chief. Just throw some gasoline around and light a match. Any idiot can do it. Lots of idiots have."

"But what if I get caught?"

"You said it's the only house around for miles, right?"

"Yeah."

"Then don't worry about it. It's no big thing."

"It kind of *is*, though. Have you ever burned down a house?"

"Shoot. I've burned down three or four."

"Three or four?"

"Yeah. *Blood Lust 2*. And *Blood Lust 3*, come to think of it."

"But those are stupid movies."

"Look. The man wants the house burned down, so you had better burn the house down. He's paying you well, and you haven't had to do anything big since the dog thing."

He was right. I was being paid very well. I would soon be able to buy my mom her dream house. I could also now afford to live in a hotel room, something I had wanted to do since childhood. I loved the concept of having room service and maids cleaning up for me seven days a week. I stayed at the Hyatt inside of St. Louis's Union Station and could even afford the pay-per-view movies and items from the minibar.

"I don't really see the point in doing this," I said.

"It's symbolic, bro. If you take away his house, he has nothing. No home, no mother, no family, nothing. Just his head. That's what we want. Just him and his thoughts, you know? And now he'll have to live on campus year-round, and we can keep tabs on him better."

"I think his mom's boyfriend might be living there. What do I do about him? Just ask him to step aside while I burn the house?"

"Eiffler, man, you just don't get it yet, do you?"

"I guess I don't. Enlighten me."

"You're not thinking like us. This boyfriend is inconsequential. A piece of trash like that could be bought for five hundred bucks, probably less. If he's there, tell him you'd like to buy the house. Pay him extra to vacate the premises immediately. Pay him extra to never mention seeing you. Whatever it takes. It doesn't matter. Money isn't an issue for us. It *is* an issue for everyone else, though, and that's how we can do pretty much anything to make this project work."

"What if he won't agree to take the money?"

"Raise the amount until he does."

"You make it sound so easy."

"Trust me. It really is that easy."

It ended up being even easier. Not only was Kyle absent, so was nearly every item in the house, even the big-screen TV. There wasn't much to burn except the house itself and the keepsakes, toys, and books that Vincent wanted to recover.

I felt funny about buying big jugs of gasoline, so I bought five pints of whiskey instead. As it turned out, I only needed three because the house was so tiny. I poured the whiskey on the floors and tabloid-covered walls, which I actually enjoyed quite a bit. Then I stood outside the opened front door, lit a couple of matches, threw them in, waited a moment to see if the fire would spread, hopped in my new Saab, and sped away.

45.

The next day, after feigning shock over Vincent's house, I told him I'd sit in my car since he probably wanted a moment alone with his debris. He walked all around the wreckage, searching for salvageable items, though there were none. I was a talented arsonist.

He paused in front of the mound under which Wynona was decomposing and bowed his head. He patted the spot where Athena the pet skunk rested and then got in my car. As I backed out of the gravel driveway, he stared at what was left of his house. Admittedly, I had not personally experienced such a fire. I justified my actions by considering the fact that I had lost my childhood home when my mom banned me from living there after my California escapades.

"They were just things," I said as I accelerated back toward town. Vincent didn't reply. He just picked at his scalp.

"Just things," I continued. "Things don't matter. At least you or your family weren't in there."

"I have a feeling that's why it was burned down. They knew no one was living there."

"Oh. You think that someone caused the fire?"

"Definitely. The furniture and TV had been taken. Someone was up to something. Did you do it?"

"Me?!"

"Yeah. You can tell me if you did."

"Vincent, why the hell would I burn your house down?"

"I don't know why, but I could smell whiskey all over the place, and you have two bottles of whiskey in the backseat."

"You know I like to drink."

"My burned-down house smelled like your breath does sometimes."

"Come on, Vincent. I didn't burn your house down."

"Do you swear?"

"I swear. If it was actually burned down by someone, it was probably that Kyle guy or one of your mom's other boyfriends. Nobody else even comes out to your house, do they?"

"No. So should we call the police?"

"I don't think so. It wouldn't really make any difference. You're going to live in Kokomo now. Your brothers and sisters have the foster home. If we called the cops about this, it would be a whole lot of trouble over nothing."

"But what if mom decides to come back home? Where will she go now?"

"I really doubt she'll be back."

"Why do you say that?"

"I don't know."

"Yes you do. You're not telling me something."

"Okay. You're right. I'm not. Remember that day at the hospital when she asked to see me?"

"Yes. I was mad because she didn't want to see *me*."

"Well, she told me then that she desperately wanted to leave town."

"Did she say where she wanted to go?"

"No," I lied.

"Why'd she want to leave us?"

"I'll tell you why. But now listen very carefully, and don't ever forget what I'm about to tell you because it's crucial, okay?"

"Okay."

"Your mother left you because she is selfish. In general, that's what people are in one word. Selfish. Your mom was unhappy with her life, especially after giving birth to a deformed baby. Selfish people don't like being unhappy. Selfish people will do whatever it takes to get happy, even if it means abandoning their morals as well as their responsibilities and obligations to everyone around them. Your mom thought that running away would make her happy, so that's exactly what she did. She did exactly what she wanted to do. Do you know what a hedonist is?"

"No."

"A hedonist is someone who just wants to have fun. They devote their lives to seeking pleasure and avoiding pain. Your mom is a hedonist. She only wants pleasure. She only wants sex, partying, fame, and money, all of which can be really fun. You and your brothers and sisters were basically just inconveniences to her. Walking, talking inconveniences. I thought you were more important to her than that because you'd make her some money someday, but I guess she lost her patience. That's another thing about hedonists. They are weak and have no will."

Vincent stared straight ahead, worry plastered on his face.

"Do you have any other questions?" I asked.

"Not right now."

"Just remember that you're not like they are. You're not going to be selfish. You're not going to run away to an endless party. You're going to take the losses handed to you and use them. And between your mom leaving, your baby sister dying, and your house burning down, you've got plenty of losses to use."

"That's a trade-off that leaves me feeling kind of cheated," said Vincent.

"Don't feel cheated. Someday you're going to make a lot of people happy with your work. And remember, that which does not kill us..."

"That which does not kill us only makes us want to die."

That was the first time it became undeniably clear that Vincent had The Sadness. All the greats had The Sadness. But unlike all those troubled souls before him, this sad young man had a devoted manager and a few other conspirators who would ensure he experienced no pain in vain. As with any child, the most difficult years loomed ahead for him, but he had at least gained a valuable new family to nurture his career. And I use the term "family" quite literally, because with Veronica's disappearance, a clause in our contract became pertinent, that clause which said in her absence, New Renaissance becomes Vincent's de facto guardian.

The artist, as he was referred to in the contract, was now in our complete custody.

PART TWO

V. DAPHNE

46.

I'm a sensitive guy who can feel when he's being videotaped and sympathize with urinal cakes. At least I've got grace in this homemade pair of contact lenses composed of pure love. With the artificial vision they provide, I can see all the girls wearing Freudian slips underneath their dresses, wrapping their bra straps around moonlit skyscrapers. I can also see what they look at instead of me. It is a handsome boy who has never had a worry in his life. He fingers his belt buckle with one hand and arm-wrestles with the other, grunting and struggling to reduce his opponent to barbecued pulp. Neither he nor she honors me with the time of day, yet I allow them to pace hand in hand around the inside of my head. And me, I stand off to the side with my back to the wall, thinking to hold her would be an apocalypse in my arms. I'm left with words, for better or worse, to stuff into bullets or wad in my purse, but I can't help but feel like an air traffic controller with delusions of grandeur, safely landing suicide missions on paper runways, turning my future hair prematurely gray, thinking wordy thoughts, accomplishing so much but not getting out nearly enough.

> — *A sample of Vincent's writing at age sixteen. He later adapted these lines into a song that became a hit single for a singer known as "Chad."*

47.

For the years following Vincent's becoming orphaned and homeless, there was little need for a finagler like me to provide him with inspirational hardships. Mother Nature, impudent strumpet that she is, wreaked her special brand of sabotage on Vincent's body and brain, subjecting him to the biological torture of puberty and the painstaking mental process of growing up.

Throughout his early teenage years, I served as Vincent's confidant and motivator. I had become more available for these purposes since my superiors had decided I should live in the same town as our most important client. Residing in a nearby Kokomo Days Inn, I regularly dropped in on Vincent to check on him and his work.

Vincent's writing ability was advancing steadily. He could now effortlessly work in the proper format for movies and television and had become proficient at writing dialogue. Some of the things he had written between the ages of ten and fifteen were far better than what the mainstream was offering, but I assumed his best work was yet to come.

Not surprisingly, Vincent's favorite sound had become the laughter of girls. But still small for his age and growing more awkward, he lacked the self-confidence and initiative to actually date a classmate. He preferred to admire girls from across the room and embraced the assumption that they would reject him, as they probably would have.

Once when he was fourteen or fifteen, I asked Vincent to tell me what a good day for him would entail. As if he had asked himself the question many times before, he gave me a long, detailed answer:

"I'd wake up feeling rested. I'd walk into my first class and receive smiles from three beautiful girls. They'd say 'hi' and call me by name. Then Mr. Barron would put in a video, and no one would be expected to talk because the video would be playing the entire class. After class, my favorite girl would stupidly flirt with me. I would play it cool but still make her laugh. Virtually the same situation would occur in Mrs. Thurman's class, except the perfect opportunity for humor would arise, and I'd make the entire class laugh. Then my favorite girl would linger around for me again after class and ask me to lunch. We'd somehow escape school and eat at Chick-Fil-A. Then we'd skip the rest of our classes and go back to her place to watch TV. We'd make fun of a bad soap opera or talk show. I'd go home later and write things that even I would like, and that night in bed I'd have a dreamless sleep. Not even a nightmare."

By the age of sixteen, Vincent had already established himself as one of the more troubled and alienated young men at his school. He had no close friends, and the few friends he had made as a child had grown apart from him. He was painfully introverted and said that sometimes at school he forgot what his voice sounded like. I would often ask him, "What did you learn at school today?" He would answer with a laugh, "How to hate myself."

Believing that Vincent held the perfect social position for an artist, I did not encourage him to make friends or leave his apartment. Instead, I bought him an electric guitar and an amp and taught him to play. I suggested that he write songs about the things he was going through. I hoped to make him more comfortable and productive in his solitude, since he would have it for years to come.

"You know, there is only one letter's difference between lonely and lovely," I told him once when he was down.

"There's only one letter's difference between loner and loser," he retorted.

"Stop talking like that and just trust me. You're better off alone."

"You always say that, Harlan. Why do you always say that?"

"Because it's the truth. You better listen to me. You know why?"

"Why?"

"Because there's only three letters' difference between prodigy and protégé."

At least I think Vincent and I had that conversation. It may have just been dialogue from a screenplay he had written based on our relationship. I can't remember which.

48.

When I think of Vincent as a teenager, this is the image my mind projects: a cramped little room with wooden floors and no window, completely darkened except for the light emanating from a twenty-one-inch television. Basking in the glory of that television glow is a scrawny, half-dead figure with big, round, bloodshot eyes and oily black hair, parted on one side, waving across the opposite side of his forehead. He lies on his threadbare couch, wearing the outfit he usually wore from his mid-teens to early adulthood: a heavily wrinkled, long-sleeved white dress shirt, a black undershirt, dark gray slacks, and socks that had once been white.

He sniffs and coughs frequently because of his ceaseless allergies. He flips through the channels, all seventy since he has cable, allowing the TV rays to soak into his flesh, receiving a television tan, which is actually not a tan at all, but rather a sickly pastiness punctuated by acne. I associate this image with Friday and Saturday nights.

"Don't you feel like a lazy American right now?" I asked the limp figure illuminated by the TV.

"You know I write all week," he said in his usual tired but warm voice. "It takes a lot out of me. If this is how I want to spend my weekend, then why don't you let me enjoy it?"

"I will, but do you really enjoy it? There's nothing but crap on TV. Especially on a Saturday night."

"You've taught me to learn from the crap so I won't repeat it, haven't you? Isn't that what my education has been based on?"

"Yeah. Okay, smart-ass. I just don't think it's healthy. I think the TV screen has become your only window to the world. That's not good for a writer."

Vincent let out a tired sigh.

"But I don't feel like doing anything. I don't feel like getting out."

"Why not?"

"I don't know."

"What's wrong?"

"I don't know."

"Believe it or not, I understand. I was the same way when I was your age."

"I know I'm a loser lying in front of the TV, but I find it comforting. Something about having the TV shining in the dark feels like home."

"Do you miss home?"

"I miss having one."

I wanted to comfort him but didn't know how. I couldn't say "things will get better" or anything of that nature. So instead, I said nothing and watched him flip through the channels. I noticed that he always stopped on the shows with girls, sometimes keeping it on their channel, sometimes not, but always pausing at the sight of the opposite sex.

"Are you searching for cleavage?" I asked.

"No. Just for girls in general."

He found one, an attractive young woman dancing in a bikini on MTV.

"I love how you can look at girls on TV without them knowing it," said Vincent. "You can stare at them all you want, but they can't look back."

"If they *could* look back, they wouldn't," I said. "Once you make it to that side of the screen, you tend not to care about what you left behind on the other side. It's a one-way relationship at best."

"Yes. Those TV girls don't give a damn about me."

"They don't give a damn about anybody."

Vincent slowly nodded, as if to say, "Ain't that the truth."

"What about the girls who *can* look back?" I asked.

"What about them?"

"Do you like anyone at school?"

"Of course I do."

"Who?"

"You won't tell anyone, will you?"

"Who would I tell?"

"Okay. Right now, I'm infatuated with a girl named Daphne."

"What's she like?"

"I'm not sure. I had never had a class with her until this semester. She's kind of exotic, and she's so gorgeous. I think she's the prettiest girl in school, for what that's worth."

"Is she hotter than those chicks off of *Hee-Haw*?" I asked. Vincent laughed one of those lazy laughs that merely exert air out the nose, not mouth.

"I'd say so. I'd say she's got the face that could launch a thousand spaceships. I like the way she dresses, too."

"Have you ever talked to her?"

"Yes. She actually sat next to me in the library yesterday. It was great."

"She sat next to you?"

"Yes."

"That's a good sign."

"I know, but I'm not going to read too much into it. Her liking me would be too good to be true. I try not to get my hopes up with girls. I try not to get my hopes up with anything."

The very next night, Daphne gave Vincent a call, bless his heart.

49.

As it turned out, Vincent's customs of isolating himself from his peers and dressing like he didn't care are what afforded him the attraction of Daphne Sullivan. Vincent was a curiosity to Daphne, and what was really social inadequacy she perceived as aloofness and mystery. At least that's what she told him the first time she called.

This phone call granted Vincent a happiness that I had never before witnessed in him. He couldn't conceal his giddiness and proved that he could be hilarious when he wanted to be, talking in funny voices and calling me "grandma." I decided to postpone terminating his newfound happiness for as long as I could.

"Remember how you feel right now," I told him after he informed me that Daphne had called. "Savor it. Suck on it. You won't get this feeling very often."

It had been ages since I had experienced the exhilaration of a new relationship. I was now thirty-seven and hadn't found anyone worth dating in years. But I still remembered how it felt when you made a connection. I still remember what CDs I was listening to when those old girls called for the first time. I listened to the same CDs when the deals fell through.

I told Vincent he should be writing. I knew from experience that artistic conditions would be riper than usual since the girl was not yet his but within reach. I knew he had to be salivating for love, and I told him to yearn through his pen, to not ask out his muse until she gave him something.

She gave him several heartfelt songs, one of which deserved to play through stereo speakers from coast to coast. The song was called "All Out for You" and was the best thing Vincent had written up to that point. It was slow and had a sad, haunting melody, as if he knew the romance that had inspired it was doomed. Here was its chorus:

I've taken the liberty of giving us a full moon.
I've arranged for all the stoplights to stay green.
I've made some phone calls to make sure you keep smiling.

I've reserved the space underneath our feet.

I've gone all out for you, so why won't you go with me?

Vincent had recorded himself singing the song while playing guitar and reluctantly surrendered the tape to me. He refused to play anything live, though he probably could have made a good performer. Of course, this was irrelevant to New Renaissance, which pledged to spare its artists the troubles of fame, not to mention its privileges.

New Renaissance itself had become a bit less privileged a year after the burning of Vincent's home. Foster Lipowitz's health forced him to retire from his CEO position at IUI/Globe-Terner. Steven Sylvain assured me this would in no way prevent New Renaissance from reaching its goals. Over the decades, Mr. Lipowitz had accumulated dozens of powerful allies in the entertainment industry, and although he retired, his name alone had considerable pull.

Furthermore, Lipowitz's retirement from IUI/Globe-Terner had positive effects. He could now focus all of his attention on New Renaissance, of which he would remain CEO. Also with his departure, Lipowitz declared New Renaissance an independent company, free of any formal affiliation with the IUI/Globe-Terner empire.

I had more faith in my company than ever before. I proudly FedExed Vincent's tape to Sylvain in Los Angeles immediately after "All Out for You" gave me chills.

50.

After several more nightly telephone conversations, Daphne asked Vincent if he wanted to "hang out," which led to his first date. He was able to afford the date because of the meager advance I had given him for half the publishing rights to his song. I let him borrow my new Volvo to take Daphne out. He had recently acquired a driver's license but until then had seldom put it to use.

"Tell me everything about it," I said.

"It went surprisingly well. Nothing bad happened," said Vincent as he sat on his couch with the TV off and his stereo on. At the time, he was in love with the Clash, whom I had introduced him to.

"Where'd you go?"

"I took her to the Waffle and Steak for dinner. I like to watch the funny people that go there. Not that we made fun of them. I mean, I'm sure they thought I looked funny, too, with my dumb outfit."

I presume Vincent was referring to the fact that in public, he normally wore black suspenders.

"Then what?"

"Then we went to the movies."

"What'd you see?"

"That new Halle Berry movie."

"Was it bad?"

"It was bad, but I'm thinking she might be right for the lead in the screenplay I'm working on now."

"So then what?"

"Then we went back to my place and talked until about two in the morning."

"Did you kiss her?"

"She kissed me. I was kind of nervous about it, but she took care of it. It was nice. It was like an awkward love scene from a John Hughes movie, but it was nice."

I noticed Vincent had a sweet smile. He had thin, dark lips that looked soft and effeminate, and when they curved upward his smiling muscles caused the top half of his face to droop. His long eyebrows made near-perfect diagonals that accented his lean, long face.

"Hey, Harlan?"

"What?"

"How do you know if you're in love?" he asked bashfully. He blushed. With such pasty skin, the redness in his cheeks was unconcealable, sometimes giving him a rosy, girlish complexion.

"I'm the wrong guy to ask. I don't think there's any such thing."

"That's sad."

"Not really. I save myself a lot of trouble."

"But it's a good kind of trouble. It's a risk you should be willing to take. Don't you want to be in love?"

"Nope."

"I want to be in love. I'm ready to throw a dart at a map to figure out where Daphne and I should run away to."

"You're such a romantic. I'm sorry to tell you this, but you'll soon find out that all anyone cares about is fucking and shopping."

"Not Daphne. She's different. She'd have to be different to be interested in me."

"That's true."

"She's already asked if she could come over again today."

He was falling for her, which was acceptable. But now it appeared that she might be falling for him, which was not.

51.

I discussed my plans with Sylvain, and he got me the OK from Prormps and Lipowitz. I hoped that my first plan would work so I wouldn't have to resort to the second. Plan A was to research the social career of Daphne and then present Vincent with the more unsavory details. I remembered several instances in high school when I was heartbroken and repulsed by lovers whose lecherous pasts were revealed at the lunch table. Considering that Daphne was supposedly the prettiest girl in Vincent's school, I was confident her moral record would be thoroughly blemished.

I also deduced that Daphne's beauty translated to popularity, which would make my dirt-digging easier since everyone would know her. I was correct; Daphne's filth was unearthed after one short conversation.

I sauntered into the New Renaissance Academy's cafeteria after school, searching for students of approximately sixteen years of age. I approached the first table I saw, where two teenage boys sat, one a neo-hippie with long hair, the other a prep.

"Excuse me, guys. Do either of you know a Daphne Sullivan?"

"Oh yeah," said the long-haired boy after a mischievous laugh. "We both know Daphne."

"Are you friends of hers?"

"No. She's no friend of ours," said the other boy.

"Do you two mind if I ask you a few questions?"

"What's this about?" asked the hippie.

"Oh, I'm sorry. My name is Mr. Carraway. I'm the new guidance counselor. Daphne's teachers have reported her exhibiting some troubled behavior, and I'm just trying to form a profile of her before I get to know her myself, so I'm interviewing some of her peers. May I sit with you?"

"Yeah," they answered. I sat down and pulled a notepad and pen from my dad's old brown sports coat.

"So please tell me anything at all you know about Miss Sullivan."

"She's an incredible 'ho,'" said the prep.

"Yeah," agreed the hippie. "She's legendary."

"Really?"

"Really," said the hippie. "Anytime between classes, if you're in any given hallway, there's at least five or six guys in that hallway that she's had sex with. Maybe even a girl or two. She's a fiend."

"She'll probably sleep with you if you ask her," said the prep.

"I'm happily married," I said. "Tell me more."

"She used to leave school during the weekend to go sleep with thirty-year-olds," said the prep.

"She exchanged sex for drugs," said the hippie. "And this was when she was, like, fourteen."

"At a party once she just stayed in the bedroom and did one guy after another," said the prep. "I didn't see her leave the bedroom once the whole night."

"Jesus. I didn't know you New Renaissance kids were so decadent."

"Most of us aren't," said the hippie. "She mostly does older guys that don't even go here. But she has corrupted quite a few of us with her one-night stands."

"Anything else?"

"No, not really," said the hippie. "Her being a big-time 'ho' and a party girl is pretty much the crucial part of her identity. There's not much else to her."

I returned my pen and pad to my coat pocket.

"Gentlemen, thanks so much for your time and cooperation."

"Don't mention it, dude," said the hippie.

I arose from the lunch table.

"Oh—just out of curiosity, what do you know about a student named Vincent Djapushkonbutm?"

"Don't know him."

"Never heard of him."

52.

I conducted two more interviews with New Renaissance students, one with a boy and one with a couple of girls. After hearing identical testimonies from everyone, I could officially declare Daphne Sullivan sexually promiscuous, physically reckless, and morally deficient. I invited myself to Vincent's apartment, which had been uncharacteristically straightened, and told him to sit. I told him I had talked to a few faculty members at school and that Daphne's name came up. I went on to give him a full report on the extracurricular activities of the girl with whom he was falling in love.

"I already knew all of that," he claimed after I was done dumping the truth.

"Did you really?"

"Her ass looked suspicious. I listened for the gossip. It's a small school, and she *is* legendary. But I'm over it, and I don't care."

"You don't care that your girlfriend is a whore?"

"*Was* a whore. And I wish you wouldn't call her that."

"Sorry. I just thought you were smarter than to date a girl like that."

"A girl like what?"

"A girl who lives for partying and sleeps with everyone she meets. I thought you valued love so much, and you're with someone who obviously doesn't. You're just another warm body to her."

"But I'm not. I haven't slept with her."

"You better keep it that way if you don't want VD."

"Please stop talking about her like that. She said she had been the way she was because nobody gave her a chance. All the guys just treated her like an object. But I won't. Now she has someone who will be good to her and actually love her."

"How could you love her?! I'm telling you, she's going to break your heart like it's nothing. I know girls like this. They use their bad home life to justify bad behavior, but they don't know what true pain is, so they cause other people pain without any remorse. They hop from boyfriend to boyfriend and from bed to bed. How could you waste your love on her?"

"Maybe if someone like me had wasted their love on a whore like my mom, she wouldn't have left us."

Vincent hadn't mentioned his mom in years. I bowed my head and waited for him to continue.

"I have to believe that people can change. I might be wrong, and I probably am, but I have to believe that to make sense of everything. Otherwise, there would be no point in my writing, and there would be no point in a thing like New Renaissance."

"Okay, Vincent, but I've warned you. You're likely to get horribly screwed over by this girl. People like Daphne are barely human. They're just vaginas or penises surrounded by a big mass of flesh, and it just so happens that the flesh forms a person."

"I told you to stop talking like that." His face tensed and turned red.

"I'm just looking out for you."

"I realize that, but why can't you just let me be happy for once in my life?"

"I can't say why. I just can't," I said with a laugh.

"Then maybe you should leave me alone."

He arose and opened the door for me, and we parted without good-byes. I then called Daphne on my tiny cell phone.

53.

That night, Steven Sylvain called my hotel room and gave me the star-tling news that Kristina Gomez was seriously interested in recording "All Out for You." At the time, Gomez was as ubiquitous as a celebrity could get. The previous year, she had the number-one album in America (*Passionate*) and at the same time starred in the number-one film (*Takes One to Know One*). The Latin-American enchantress was an industry unto herself with her own clothing line, her own perfume, her own record label, her own movie production company, and her own restaurant. Like many of her entrepreneurial celebrity friends, Gomez was a true "renais-sance man."

Sylvain's news didn't thrill me because I had despised Gomez for many years, not only for her omnipresence in the entertainment world but also for her stereotypical Hollywood behavior. She had married twice by the age of twenty-five, neither marriage making it past that impossible six-month mark. She was a fixture in the tabloids with her never-ending love affairs. And she proudly referred to herself as a "diva."

Further lowering Gomez's worth in my eyes was the fact that her initial popularity could be directly traced to her belly. Always wearing her trademark midriffs and belly button rings, Kristina's well-toned stomach deserved more royalties than the person flaunting it. The stomach burst onto the scene as part of the latest teen pop craze. Like all of her contemporaries, once Gomez reached her twenties, she became driven with the desire to "grow as an artist," which simply meant wearing even fewer clothes and singing even more about sex.

But despite my disaffinity for Kristina Gomez, I decided she would be an ideal guinea pig in learning if New Renaissance could work. To my knowledge, this would be the most noteworthy deal a New Renaissance artist had achieved to date. By this point, about a dozen New Renaissance projects had materialized, though most of them had failed to make a widescale impact. Several of our artists were working with prominent producers and agents, but none as powerful as Gomez.

When Sylvain was shopping Vincent's demo around as a song publisher, he discovered that he had twice slept with a girl who had gone on to become Gomez's publicist. After exploiting this opening, Sylvain gave her the tape. She played it for Gomez, who was in need of new songs for an upcoming album, which would coincide with an upcoming movie, which would coincide with an upcoming marriage.

54.

Daphne had blond hair, large breasts, and good posture. She also possessed an unusual, half-classy, half-trashy fashion sense that hinted at the artist within her. When I met her, she was wearing skin-tight corduroy pants and a neon-green blouse. I must admit she was dazzling.

I had called her the previous day to make an appointment to meet with her, claiming that I was a manager interested in her career. I told her my name was Jack Burden. She agreed to meet me at Denny's, where we both ordered coffee.

"You look so familiar," she said as she lit a cigarette.

"Do I now?"

"Yeah. I don't forget a handsome face."

"Actually, the boy you're currently seeing probably showed you a picture of me. I'm Vincent's manager."

"You're Harlan!?"

"Yeah. Harlan Eiffler."

"But I thought you said your name was Jack."

"I lied. I don't want Vincent to know we ever met. If he asks, I want you to tell him you met with Jack today."

"He talks about you all the time. He idolizes you."

"That's ridiculous."

"No, really. He loves you."

"Listen, you don't have to do that. I'm not interested in being your manager. That was a lie, too."

"Then maybe I should leave."

She scooted across the booth.

"I can still get you a lucrative deal, though."

She stopped scooting.

"New Renaissance students aren't in it for the money. They teach us that from the beginning."

"Save it, kid. I know all about you. You're not New Renaissance material. You're famous."

"Shut up. What's this about?"

"It's about Vincent."

"What about him?"

"Do you love him?"

"Not really."

"Well, I think he loves you."

"Cool."

"I want you to stop seeing him. I want you to completely cut off all contact with him without giving him an explanation. If you do this, I will pay you on a monthly basis. If you tell Vincent or anyone else about this and I find out, you will no longer receive payment, and you will be in breach of the contract that you are about to sign."

"Why are you doing this to him?"

"It's for his work. I'm afraid you're interfering with his writing time. This is just something that managers have to do sometimes."

"But I can't just brush him off for no reason."

"Oh. I guess you've never done that to a boy before?"

She gave me a malicious look that only girls are capable of, a hot-blooded glare full of sex and brutality that causes its recipients to instantly teem with regret.

Her favorite band was Phish, her favorite TV show was *Wheel of Fortune*, and her favorite movie was *The Breakfast Club*.

"Well, consider this. Were you honestly planning on staying with Vincent?"

"Yeah, okay, I *was* thinking about leaving him alone. He's so nice and sweet. I was thinking I wanted him as a friend. I wouldn't want a relationship to ruin our friendship."

"Of course. So now you'll be getting paid to do something you were likely going to do anyway."

"How much money are we talking about here?"

"$2,500 a month. For really doing nothing at all."

"How long would you pay me?"

"Two years. You'll probably leave the academy by then, and you and Vincent will go your separate ways."

"I don't know about this."

"Daphne, just think about all the places you could go with that money. In a few months, you could leave this life behind. You could fly off to any country in the world. I'll send you the checks wherever you go. You'd be set."

I was counting on the idea of traveling abroad to seal this deal. The promiscuous girls that I had known in my time seemed to jump at the chance to stay in a foreign country.

"Can I think about it before I give you an answer?"

"No."

"Why not?"

"If I don't have you sign these contracts today, how do I know you won't tell Vincent?"

"Oh."

"Tell you what, Daphne. I'm going to go to the restroom. I'll take my time, and you sit here and sort things out."

"Okay."

I snatched her car keys off the table.

"Just in case," I said, shaking her keys.

After pacing around the Denny's restroom for exactly five minutes, I returned to my table where Daphne agreed to sign the necessary papers. She signed quickly, snubbed out her cigarette, and slid out of the booth without looking up.

"I can go now, right?"

"Certainly. You'll be getting your first check next week. Thanks very much for your cooperation."

"Thanks for the coffee."

"Oh, and you do realize this will be the last time you ever speak about this topic, right?"

"I understand."

"If you tell anyone about it, trust me, we *will* find out."

"I wouldn't want to tell anyone about it."

"Okay. Good-bye, then."

"See ya."

At the front of the restaurant, I got in line to pay and hollered at Daphne as she was exiting.

"Hey, Daphne! One last thing."

"What?" She walked over to me.

"Were you really attracted to Vincent?"

"Yes. I really, honestly was."

"Do you mind me asking what you saw in him that the other girls didn't?"

Daphne paused and pushed her hair out of her face.

"I could tell that he was special. That's all."

"He *is* special. You're lucky to have known him."

"You're telling me," she said, waving her copy of our contract.

55.

It was obvious that all Vincent could think about was Daphne. He was sullen and lethargic and had a far-off look in his eyes, even while watching TV in the dark. It had been less than a week since Daphne stopped calling Vincent, stopped exchanging looks with him during class, and stopped walking with him in the hall after class. After two days of this,

Vincent cornered her at her locker and asked what was wrong. She told him not to worry about it and that she would call him. This call never came, and by the end of the week, Vincent witnessed Daphne latched onto another boy after school.

"I know why you're so down," I said upon a Saturday-night visit to his apartment. "You can talk to me if you'd like."

"I don't want to talk about it," he mumbled.

"That's fine. I understand."

"How could she be so heartless?!" he blurted.

"I wish I knew," I said. "But you better get used to it. She won't be the last."

"Everything was going so well. I was ready to pick out names for our kids. I figured we'd make up a new name together, something like Puja or Brampton. But she just cut herself off from me out of the blue."

"She was leading you on. It's just something people do. It's happened to me plenty of times."

"Last week she said she'd have me over to her apartment this weekend. I had never even been there before. But she hasn't even returned my call."

"You called her?"

Vincent blushed.

"I wasn't going to just give up without even trying. This afternoon I left a witty message on her machine. I had written it in advance. But she hasn't called me back."

I remembered doing the same thing before I had given up on women. I would draft an answering machine message, something sincere but not eager. Since my tongue was prone to knots when talking to girls, I practiced the delivery aloud. I thought even if the girl had no intention of calling me, if my message was creative and funny enough, she would surely change her mind. After leaving the message, I stayed close to the phone and checked the caller ID after each time I left the room to urinate.

"I bet I know what you're thinking right now," I said.

"What?"

"That she still might call and change the complexion of your evening. That any second now she'll salvage what's left of the night."

"The thought had crossed my mind." He sighed.

"She won't call. She's got a busy body, and busy bodies come with hectic schedules."

He said nothing and looked catatonic for a while, mindlessly picking at his scalp.

"I keep thinking about how my voice inside her answering machine is the only part of me that will ever be in her apartment," said Vincent. "It's probably in there right now, but here I lie on my couch."

"Hey—that reminds me. I talked to Sylvain yesterday. Kristina Gomez already has some people lined up to work on an arrangement of your song. She'll be recording it soon."

"That's nice. I'm sorry about all this."

"About what?"

"You were right about Daphne. Sorry."

"No need to apologize. I only knew because I've experienced it myself. But that's when I would pick up my guitar and my pen and write my head off. That girl is worthless, but if you don't get some songs out of this, she wins."

"I know. But I just want to lie here tonight."

"I don't blame you. You take it easy and relax tonight. But you write tomorrow, you hear me?"

He nodded and picked up the remote control from the floor, sighing pitifully as if it took all his strength. As he flipped through the channels, we saw several girls, including Kristina Gomez on two different channels.

"She's so beautiful," he said. "I guess I'm better off with those TV girls after all."

56.

A month later, Vincent's ninth year at the New Renaissance Academy came to a close. One of Vincent's female teachers at the academy had talked me into volunteering to chaperon the school's year-end dance. I in turn persuaded Vincent to go so I wouldn't have to endure it alone. Neither of us had ever been to a school dance before.

Vincent and I stood outside the dance floor with our backs against the walls, watching the teenagers dance in their suits and dresses. I thought about how people look so stupid dancing, especially boys when they're dancing fast.

"See, this isn't so bad, is it?" I asked.

"Yes. I hate it here."

"Why?"

"Look at all those happy couples."

"But they can't write like you."

Since Vincent's heart had been broken, it became apparent that Lipowitz's so-called experiment could work. With some fresh, palpable pain, Vincent's artistic output was not only copious; it was amazingly good. In a month, he had written an album's worth of songs that included some of the best lyrics he would ever create. Meanwhile, Daphne kept receiving her checks, though now I had to send them to Paris.

"Look at them," said Vincent. "Everybody just finds each other. They get together so easily. Why can't that happen to me?"

"I've asked myself the same question many, many times." Strangely enough, I was already on the path that would lead me to meeting the love of my life.

"Have you ever been in love, Harlan?"

"Sure I have."

"How many times?"

"Three. But all three didn't love me back."

She was out there, alive and well, and she was going to love me back.

"I hate the word 'unrequited.' What an ugly-sounding word," said Vincent.

"Not as ugly as 'gonorrhea.' What about you? How many times have you been in love?"

"Twice, I guess."

"With whom?"

"I guess with Daphne, and I've never told anyone this since it's kind of gross, but the other was a cousin when I was little."

"That's weird."

"I know. I didn't know any better. I'd still pick her over Daphne, though."

"Yeah. Daphne's probably done half of France by now."

"How did you know she was in France?"

"Oh, one of her teachers told me. So do you have your eye on anyone else?"

"No. I'm not ready to be hurt again yet. Besides, I've been doing a lot of good writing without anyone. Between Mom and Daphne, there's a lot to dwell on."

"Get used to it. There are a lot of cruel, thoughtless people out there."

"I know."

"I know you know. You've always known it. Hey—remember the first time you were interviewed by New Renaissance?"

"No."

"Well, we asked you to complete the sentence, 'I write because (blank).' This was to see if you were creative and to see if you were creative for the right reasons. And you don't remember what you said?"

"No."

"You said, 'I write because you wrong.' I liked that a lot."

"Now it would be, 'I write because she left.'"

I laughed.

"Still a genius. Would you excuse me for a minute?"

"Sure."

From my blazer pocket I pulled a rough mix of Kristina Gomez's upcoming single and handed it to the DJ, along with twenty bucks. I then hid behind some decorations and watched Vincent as "All Out for You" came on. Gomez's version of the song was surprisingly tasteful, even beautiful. It was soft, romantic, and dreamlike, complete with a string section.

Vincent smiled and looked around the room for me. I felt bad that he couldn't find me, so I stepped out and waved. I did some goofy dance moves, and so did he. I pretended like I needed some punch but continued to watch him from across the room.

He walked around the dance floor, looking uncharacteristically refined in a suit I had bought him. He moved slowly with his hands in his pockets, smiling with what I assume was pride. As he looked at all the lovers slow-dancing, the smile faded. The lovers seemed to be lost in his song, embracing and whispering to one another, swaying so finely as Vincent stood in the background not knowing what to do with himself except stare at the entire picturesque scene. In another two months, the soundtrack to this moment would be the number-one single in the country.

VI. KARI

57.

After the artistic and commercial success of the Kristina Gomez single, Mr. Lipowitz became eager to release more of Vincent's music. Thanks to Daphne and myself, Vincent had a surplus of songs written and on tape, songs so excellent that I couldn't imagine making them part of the vapid fodder that is radio, yet this was our goal.

It was decided by my superiors that rather than divvying out Vincent's songs to dozens of different performers, only a few would receive his material. This decision was a reaction to the hit single–oriented state of the record industry. The average mainstream album included approximately one quality song while the rest of the tracks served as filler. By putting a batch of Vincent Djapushkonbutm originals on one product, we would create a consistently strong album for several performers, and be fair to their audience.

The difficult part in bringing our plan to fruition would be choosing these few worthy singers or bands. Thus, I was elected to stay in L.A. for part of the summer and help Steven Sylvain find the best possible fits for Vincent's songs. Unlike my last stay in L.A. nearly twenty years before, I wouldn't have to spend futile days searching for a record deal and wasteful nights performing music that no one cared about. I would be the one making the deals this time, and I didn't have to sleep on anyone's floor either.

Meanwhile, Vincent remained in Kokomo, where he decided to get a summer job since he had grown tired of being unmoneyed. True, his living expenses as a New Renaissance student were paid, but he had no funds of his own, and he wouldn't be seeing any royalties from Kristina's hit single until fall. His desire to work pleased me; I reasoned that employment was a crucial part of existence that he should experience.

While I found a place to live at the Renaissance Hollywood Hotel, Vincent found a place to work at a Kroger supermarket near his apartment. He chose the position of stock boy/bag boy, assuming it would require little interaction with the public. The job required interaction with other employees, though, which is how he became best friends with an eighteen-year-old named Neil Elgart. The boys established a rapport after Vincent heard Neil quoting a Replacements song. They shared identical taste in music, as well as disgust for the same popular musicians and actors of their day.

Neil was a senior at a public high school where he didn't get along well with his classmates and sported haircuts that would have been derided had he not been so willing to fight. He was a poor student but not unintelligent, and he didn't participate in extracurricular activities at school, in favor of playing guitar at home. Neil was a good friend to Vincent while I was off making friends of my own for him in California.

58.

The night I arrived in L.A., Sylvain met me at the hotel bar, where we discussed the possibilities for Vincent's songs over a few rounds of Scotch. We concluded that we needed newcomers to record his music, preferably young males who could actually play instruments. A musician with no previously released records seemed logical; having established popular performers suddenly playing creative, unique music wouldn't make sense. Critics were puzzled by Kristina Gomez's sudden improvement with "All Out for You," especially considering how the rest of her new album was her standard lowbrow sexual fare. Of course, no one bothered looking in her CD's liner notes at the name in parentheses: All Out for You (V. Djapushkonbutm).

Sylvain and I also decided Vincent's last name was too lengthy and awkward to bring up at meetings and that a shorter, less ethnic name might better promote our cause. Sylvain had his heart set on "Jablonski." We threw around names before I decided Vincent should have a say in the matter.

We then formulated a plan for getting Vincent's demo to the right people. We assumed our initial step would be to scout bars and clubs until we found the perfect performers. But therein lay a problem. The ideal performers of Vincent's songs would be those with a mentality similar to his, as well as those who shied away from a commercial sound. Paradoxically, anyone fitting this description would likely be insulted by an offer to record someone else's material. This led us to the option of taking the demo to record labels to find the best place for the songs, assuming they would have at least one or two talented, deserving acts within their stables.

We decided Sylvain would pass the demo to Prormps, who would give it to Mr. Lipowitz. Lipowitz would distribute copies of the demo to the presidents of all his former Terner Bros. record labels. We would then meet with whoever could do the most with the songs. Sylvain suggested that in the meantime I should consider buying a new suit.

59.

After returning to my suite and fixing myself another drink, I called Vincent and asked him what he would like to change his surname to.

"Do I have to change it?" he asked. I could tell by his voice that his nose was stopped up.

"You don't have to change it legally, but we think it would be good for your career."

"What difference does it make what my last name is?"

"It doesn't really. So why don't you go ahead and change it?"

"What about my mom?"

"What about her? It's not even her name. It's some foreign guy's that left her in a month."

"But how will she know I'm the one writing the stuff if I change my name?"

"Vincent, you know the general public doesn't care who writes things. They just want to be entertained. Do you really think your mom would check to see who writes what?"

"She might since she expects it of me."

"Fine. So you want to keep Djapushkonbutm?"

Vincent's sigh floated across the country.

"Well, I hate to go against you," he said. "What would you want it changed to?"

"Whatever you want. You can keep it the way it is if you want."

"No, that's okay. You're right. Did you have any ideas?"

"How about Vasari?" I suggested.

"No thanks. If we're going for alliteration, how about Viscosity?"

"That's horrible."

"I think it's a beautiful word. Hey, Neil, what do you think I should change my last name to?...Neil suggests Vas Deferens."

"Neil sounds juvenile. What are you doing hanging out with him?"

"He was just kidding. Got any other ideas?"

"I don't know. Jablonski?"

After half an hour of this, we compromised on "Spinetti," his mother's maiden name.

60.

A week later, Prormps reported to Sylvain that the demo had been sent to all the label executives, and their reaction was unanimous. None were at all interested in the songs. The consensus was that the songs were definitely good but too difficult to market. Frustrated and impatient, Lipowitz made a personal phone call to the head of the biggest Terner Bros. subsidiary, Continental Recordings, and demanded that he meet with Sylvain and me, the songwriter's publishers. Sylvain was designated as my copublisher since he was more familiar with negotiating than I.

An appointment was scheduled for that afternoon. Sylvain and I sat in one of the many sterile waiting rooms of the Continental tower, where hundreds of platinum records I hated hung on the walls. We both had suits on. Like my old suit, my new one was form-fitting on my lean frame. But now, my coat had no patches on the elbows, and I had matching pants. As always, I kept my shirt's top button unbuttoned, my tie was loosened, and I still wore my scratched-up black wingtips.

"So do they know anything about New Renaissance?" I asked Sylvain.

"I don't think so. It's been kept under wraps pretty well so far. But now we're getting to the point where the kids are getting stuff made, so we can't keep it a complete secret from the suits."

"So what do I tell them about it?"

"Nothing much. Tell them it's a management company based in Indiana or something. Don't get specific about what we're trying to do. Might scare 'em off."

"What else shouldn't I say?"

"Don't worry about it."

We were called into a large, posh office with black décor where we shook hands with four handsomely dressed white men of varying ages and sizes. They expressed curiosity in why the movie star Steven Sylvain was there, so he explained that he now worked for a management company called New Renaissance that published songs for the writer in question.

"I'm sorry, but I have to ask. Will you say it?" said one of the younger men. "Will you say, 'I get off on this shit'?"

Sylvain turned his back to prepare himself. He spun around and yelled his line.

"I get off on this shit!"

Everyone except me laughed and applauded. We declined an offer of coffee and took seats around a long glass table. The attention turned toward me.

"So tell me, Mr. Eiffler, who else have you represented that I may have heard of?" asked the oldest man, a tan gentleman with shiny white hair.

"I just have the one client, Vincent Spinetti."

"Just one client?"

"Just one."

"Who'd you have before him?" asked another.

"Nobody. I've been working with Vincent for nine years now."

They were stifling laughter.

"Oh. I guess you're used to guys who represent forty acts at once and don't give enough attention to a single one of them and then drop them at the first sign of trouble. That's not how we do it."

An awkward silence followed in which I was stared at as curiously as if I were an amputee. I was being honest; each New Renaissance manager only had one New Renaissance client. It was the manager's job to work with a producer or agent in order to get a project made. I was provided with a special agent, Sylvain, who was privy to the tortured artist project.

"What Harlan means to say is that New Renaissance looks at its artists' careers from a long-term point of view, you know?" said Sylvain. "I'm sure he'll add more clients soon, though. We expect big things from Harlan."

He patted me on the back, which irritated me deeply.

"I see," said the white-haired man, who I assumed was the label president since the others followed his lead. "Well, Foster Lipowitz demanded that I meet with you, Harlan, so I know you must be doing something right. But the thing is, we really don't know exactly what to do with your client's songs."

"And why exactly is that, may I ask?"

"The thing is, Harlan, the music isn't genre-specific, and we really don't know what demographics we would push it toward. Lyrically, it's kind of, how do I put it…out-there, and I really can't picture this kind of music getting much radio play."

"But that's the idea. We don't want his songs to resemble any crap on the radio. In fact, that's the last thing we want."

"Do you think that he might be open to, kind of…retooling the songs to make them a little more accessible?" asked a middle-aged man. "Because I'll be honest, I really don't see the music getting anywhere as is."

"Let me ask you this," I said. "Did you listen to the demo?"

"One of my assistants e-mailed me a full report on it," he replied.

"Did any of you actually listen to it yourselves?"

They didn't answer. Sylvain jumped in.

"Forgive my associate. He's new to this. What we want to make sure you realize is that the demo your people heard was just a rough cut of our writer singing along with an acoustic guitar. It's just the basics, and we'd build on that. We'd get a hot producer, and it would be much more accessible by the time it's done."

"Right," said the leader. "I'll tell you what. I know that Lipowitz has faith in this project, so we'll see what we can do."

"We realize we're asking you to take a risk on songs like these, but with Lipowitz *and* Prormps behind it 100 percent, we think the risk is evened out," said Sylvain.

"Prormps is behind it, too?" one asked.

"One hundred and ten percent," said Sylvain.

"What does your guy look like?" asked another. "Do you have any head shots?"

"Is that really an issue?" I asked.

"Naturally, we'd like to know what we're buying looks like."

"But he's just the songwriter," I said. "He's not going to perform at all. Nobody will ever even see him."

"Oh. I see. I didn't realize that. Was that in the memo?"

"I don't think it was," said another.

"Yeah, Vincent is strictly a writer," said Sylvain. "We were hoping you could just hook us up with some hip new performers to play his material. Somebody young, something you could sell."

"I see," said the leader while the others nodded.

61.

We concluded that Vincent's material would indeed have a home in Continental Recordings, and the company's A&R department would immediately begin searching for candidates to record the songs. In accordance with Lipowitz's wishes, these candidates would then be presented to Sylvain and me, and we would have the final say. I was dreading seeing what underwear models they would dig up to screw a marketable facade onto Vincent's music, but I consoled myself with the belief that his songs were brilliant enough that their substance would glow through any stylistic trash dumped on top.

The difference between Vincent's music and everything else on the radio was that I could tell he put a lot of thought into each verse and chorus of every song. They were carefully crafted in all aspects, whereas most current songwriters would apparently accept any melody that popped in their head, just so their uninspired lyrics would fit.

Vincent's songs were melodic, but not so much that they were sappy and saccharine like most pop tunes of his time. He loved using unpredictable chord progressions with lots of minor chords. The lyrics were intelligent but not pretentious, poignant but not profound, sometimes puzzling upon first listen but ultimately insightful. Some of the song titles were: "The Poetic Urge," "The Thanks I Get," "Baby Has Anthrax,"

"Fifteen Flaws," and "The Boy Who Didn't Get Mail."

The bittersweet songs were catchy and often dealt with unrequited love, loss, and The Sadness, topics that Vincent had become well acquainted with. But talking to him throughout that summer, I sensed The Sadness was ascending. I attribute this to him finally finding a close friend. He now had a peer to commiserate with, someone else dissatisfied with life, who hated all the same things. And they even had fun together. Unhappy in his broken home, Neil often visited Vincent's apartment, where they made fun of television, listened to music, played guitar, and watched old movies. They even drank beers, though Vincent had not yet learned to like the taste.

I regularly asked Vincent what he had been writing that summer, but he said he hadn't been able to write as much as he should have. His job took much of his time, and when he came home after five, he was too tired to be creative. We agreed he would stop working once school started. I told him that no matter how bad things were looking, he was fortunate that his creativity would spare him from a more laborious future. Vincent agreed he was fortunate and from then on held a deep admiration and sympathy for the clock-punching masses. He always felt guilty for not having a "real job," even though his own vocation would cause him to suffer from overwork and exhaustion, since his mind did enough heavy lifting as a writer to herniate his brain.

62.

For the next month, July, I had little to do except wait to see what acts Continental could find. For the first week of this wait, I mostly stayed in my hotel room ordering room service and reading. By the second week, I became restless, which prompted me to ask Sylvain if I could meet Mr. Lipowitz. As unlikely as it was, I wanted to meet the man who had given me a future ten years before. But Sylvain couldn't get me an appointment with Lipowitz, nor with Prormps.

Noticing my boredom, Sylvain entertained me by taking me to his favorite clubs, where he talked to women while I got drunk on a barstool. He never asked the women to go home with him, probably because he was afraid of how they would react to his missing leg, though this didn't stop him from flirting every chance he got.

I was hung over the day I met with the record executives again. Sylvain and I returned to that sophisticated black office and were introduced to Chad Carter, a goateed twentysomething to whom Continental wanted to give Vincent's first lot of songs.

"What's up?" Chad said to Sylvain and me. When I offered my hand, he grabbed it and hugged me with his other arm, which made me uncomfortable. He did the same thing to Sylvain, who didn't seem to mind.

"Man, I love your shit, Mr. Sylvain."

"Call me Steve."

"You were just a rough draft. Consider yourself proofread," quoted Chad from *Blood Lust*. "I love it, man. I said that all the time when I was little."

"Thanks, bra," said Sylvain.

We sat down on black leather chairs in the office's sitting area. Chad sat with one leg underneath himself. We declined drink offers, except for Chad, who asked for a frappuccino.

"We think Chad could take these songs to a whole new level," said the leader. "He's got next big thing written all over him."

"I don't know about all that," said Chad. He wore tight blue jeans that were faded on the thighs, a little T-shirt that said Phys-Ed, and motorcycle boots. Both his arms were so covered in tattoos that the drawings ran together into one vast, colorful inkblot like a second skin.

"We had signed Chad awhile back to be a part of a multi-ethnic vocal group we had formed," said the leader. "What was the name of that group, Bob?"

"Maintain," said Bob.

"Right. Maintain."

"Those guys were a bunch of fags," said Chad. Everyone laughed except me. He ran his fingers through his shoulder-length hair, which was half-brown and half-blond, all stringy and tousled.

"Right. So then we discovered that Chad could play guitar and had a great voice, too. He was definitely the breakout artist of the group, so we decided we could do more with him as a solo act."

"He's really an amazing guitarist," said one of the men. "Awesome singer, too."

"I'm decent at best, man," said Chad.

"The only thing he's missing is enough original songs to make up an album," said the leader. "So that's where your guy's songs would come in. I think Mr. Lipowitz will be happy with Chad."

"Sounds good," said Sylvain.

"Do we have a deal, Mr. Eiffler?" asked the leader.

"Well, may I ask Chad a few questions?" I asked.

"Fine by me," said the leader.

"Shoot," said Chad.

"What do you do for a living?"

"I'm a party planner."

"Do you mind playing songs that someone else has written?"

"I don't know, man. The way I see it, I'll make 'em my own."

"What are your thoughts on the current state of radio?"

"It's all right."

"You don't think it's at all horrid?"

"That's twice now you've badmouthed radio, Mr. Eiffler," interjected one of the middle-aged men. "What is it exactly you have against it? After all, you're a part of it now."

"Well, rather than telling you what I have against it, could I *show* you? Is there a radio in here?"

"Yes," said the leader. He picked up a remote control and pointed it at a cabinet across the spacious room. The cabinet's doors smoothly slid back to reveal a stereo and two monolithic speakers. He turned the radio on, and a hair-loss commercial was playing. "Press this to go through the stations," he said as he handed me the remote.

"I don't think this is necessary, Harlan," said Sylvain.

"No, please," said the leader. "I'd like to see this."

I stood up and pointed the remote at the radio. I faced the men like a professor presiding over his class.

63.

"First of all, half the stations will be on a commercial, but I realize there's not much we can do about that...A waterbed commercial...Two deejays that are not funny but who think they are. Listen to them provide their own laugh track. They think they tell it like it is, but they never mention the fact that they're corporate henchmen who are forced to play the same twelve songs all day long...Wow. An actual song. Is it country or is it pop? The only thing that sounds remotely country about it is his accent, which is probably fake. I bet he's from Canada. And I swear, the lyrics to country songs must all be written by the same person. He likes writing nostalgically about his past, especially about his home and its front porch, his mom and dad, his truck, summertime, how great his girlfriend is, how he has a wild streak, how he works hard but cuts loose on the weekend...Oldies. I'm sure this song will end up on the charts again someday when some uncreative band covers it and it ends up being the only decent song on their album...A boy band. Who is allowing this shit to get on the radio!?"

"Okay, Harlan," said Sylvain. "They get the idea."

"No. Let him talk," said the leader. "We might learn a thing or two. Please, continue."

"Listen to that prissy melody. There's nothing interesting about it. It's weak. It's not the least bit catchy. And I've seen these guys on MTV. They're not even that good-looking. In fact, they're kind of homely...Oh, Jesus. Rap. Just listen to this. That's a Police song he's using. Does it bother anyone else that rap relies on blatantly stealing other people's music and talking over it? Listen to that. He's attempting to sing. And listen to the instrumentation. It sounds like a child playing a Casio keyboard... Ahh, Led Zeppelin. Classic rock stations have decades of music at their fingertips, yet they only play about four different bands. At least they've played Ozzy more ever since he got a TV show...McDonald's commercial...Oh my God. Someone I actually like. Billy Joel deserves better than the radio...Another commercial...Hip-hop. Some girls singing about their bodies with a sample of a Motown song in the background. Are you all hearing this? Those lyrics are appalling. And by the way, every song we've heard so far rhymes crazy with lazy or world with girl...Bill Withers. See, there was once good music...I don't know who this guy is, but he should be paying Dave Matthews royalties. That's another thing. For every act that's a hit, you're guaranteed half a dozen imitators...Budweiser commercial...A new rock song. Listen how they cleverly go from loud metal, to a soft, boring melody. Bands like this always have lyrics like, 'You can't save me,' and I tend to agree. And everybody uses that voice nowadays…News. Something about terrorism…Another rock song. This one's not as bad as most. Oh. It's a Sprite commercial…And now I must be at the far left of the dial. Classical…Jazz. Good stuff that no one ever listens to…And it's those girls singing about their bodies on another station."

I turned off the radio, and the men stared blankly at me. They were probably responsible for half the songs I had chastised.

"In short, there's not a single original idea on the radio today," I continued. "So Chad, I really hope you can improve upon that."

"I hear that," said Chad.

"That was quite a demonstration," said the leader with a grin. "I hope Chad will meet your standards."

"I'm actually playing tonight at the Troubadour," said Chad. "Why don't you come down and check me out, see what you think?"

I agreed. I hadn't been to the Troubadour since my own band had played there for a crowd of eight.

64.

His stage name was simply "Chad," and he already had quite a following, mostly college-age females. He played an acoustic set by himself, and I concede, he had talent. He showed off adroit guitar playing and a strong, distinctive voice. Furthermore, he had excellent stage presence. I was not at all surprised when he became a superstar the following year, or when he was named one of VH-1's "Sexiest Artists of All Time" right behind Kurt Cobain.

I would fault Chad, however, for only playing cover songs. At least they were antiquated songs by quality singers like Elvis and Sinatra who, coincidentally, didn't write their own songs either. He did play one new song for an encore. It was called "The Poetic Urge," written by "a kid in Indiana," as he told the audience. Judging by their reaction, the crowd approved.

As soon as I returned to my suite, I phoned Vincent, who was playing guitar with Neil. They were flirting with the idea of starting a band tentatively named American Lesion.

I told him about Chad and how I felt he might actually do his songs justice.

"What's he like, though?" asked Vincent.

"He's kind of a hipster. Dresses in vintage clothes. I wouldn't call him a prettyboy, but he is kind of pretty."

"But, I mean, does he seem like a good person?"

"I don't know. I guess. I didn't really talk to him that much."

"Can you find out if he is or not?"

"I don't know. Maybe. Why?"

"Because. If he gets famous singing my songs, what good would it do if he's just going to be a typical heathen rock star? I don't want to have done all that work for a guy who's going to be a bad influence on kids. He could end up making New Renaissance counterproductive."

I hadn't even considered this issue before. It was a valid argument. I thought about how a few years back, millions of teenage boys changed their hairstyle to emulate their hero, an outspoken rapper/actor who constantly pleaded guilty on weapons and drug charges, who was quoted in an interview saying, "When scripts get to me, well, I don't like to read. That's like the worst thing in the world for me to do. You know, sit down and read something. I hate reading."

The next day, I called Sylvain and had him track down Chad's number. About four days later, Chad finally answered the phone and agreed to meet for a drink.

65.

Chad arrived fashionably late at Dragonfly, the club of his choosing, though "fashionably" is debatable. He wore thong sandals, a T-shirt showing a screen-printed photo of his own smiling face, and blue jeans with the pockets turned inside out. He said, "what up," pulled out a chair, and folded both legs underneath himself with maximum aplomb.

"Sorry I was late, man. I was smokin a bowl and lost track of time. You know how that goes."

"Actually, I don't. I've always been partial to drinking. It smells better." I was on my fifth Scotch of the evening.

"Cool. Sorry if I was out of line."

"That's all right. I like your shirt. Is it supposed to be funny, or are you conceited?"

"Both. Nah, it's a joke. I thought it was funny."

"You'll probably have real T-shirts with your face on them soon. Will you wear those?"

"No way, man. I'm not that lame. Hey, I was meaning to tell you, that was cool what you did with the radio at the office. Those fuckers didn't know what to say."

"Thanks. I enjoyed doing it."

A young redheaded waitress approached.

"Hi. What can I get you?"

"Bust me up with a kamikaze."

She laughed.

"Okay. Could you bust me up with your ID?"

"I could, but I'm afraid I don't have it on me. But check it out, I can prove I'm at least twenty-one."

"Oh, really?"

"Really. I've had the seven-year itch three times."

She laughed again.

"All right. That'll work. And another Lochgar for you?"

"Yes, please," I answered. "That was pretty smooth, Fonzie."

"Thanks, man. That was too easy."

"Aren't you twenty-one?"

"Oh, yeah. I'm twenty-three. My license got revoked a while back for driving coked up. Plus, I don't have a place for my wallet. Check this out."

He stood up to show me all of his outwardly turned jeans pockets, including those in the back.

"Yeah. I noticed those when you came in."

"I think this should be like my trademark. It's kind of like the hobo look, only cooler, you know? What do you think?"

"I think it's pretty stupid. It'll probably catch on."

"Yeah, right. So why'd you want to see me?" He sat back down and ran his fingers through his carefully messed-up hair.

"Well, Vincent, the writer of all those songs we plan to give you, he just wanted me to get to know you a little better before we sign his material over. His songs are really important to him. So thanks for meeting with me."

"No problem. That dude can really write a tune, man. Tell him to have no fear. I really think I can add a lot to those songs."

"I think you can, too. You put on a great show the other night. I meant to tell you afterward, but you weren't around."

"Ah, yeah, sorry I missed you. I took off with some Asian groupie after the show. Bitch told me she was sixteen after we were done having sex."

"Is that something you do a lot?"

"What? Hook up with fans?"

I nodded.

"Yeah, I'll just come out and say it. Pussy is my weakness. I can't resist. And when you're a performer or somebody important like that, it's so easy. Like, I remember I started getting ass when I was in the Little League World Series. Then I eventually got into music, which led to tons more ass. It's crazy. Those girls don't even care about me as a person, you know? They just want the guy onstage, the image, and that's it."

His favorite musician was Jimi Hendrix, his favorite TV show was *ESPN Sports Center*, and his favorite movie was *RoboCop*.

"Doesn't that bother you?"

"It did at first. But you know what? You're only young once. Work hard, play hard. Life is short, and this won't last. Nothing lasts."

"But the music on your CDs will last. Isn't that worth something?"

"True, but you can't fuck a CD, man. Actually, you can. I tried boning a Shania Twain CD once. It was lame." He laughed. I rolled my eyes.

"So what happens if you become famous? Do you see yourself changing?"

"Man, I know this sounds lame, but I would not let fame change me one bit, man. I'm not into that celebrity stuff, like having an entourage and shit. I would behave exactly the same."

"That's what I was afraid of."

"Whoa. Step off, man. What's with the sudden disrespect?"

"Well, Chad, now *I'm* going to say something that may sound lame."

"I don't care. Just so you show the love."

"I'll show the love. But what I want to say is that I hope you realize that if you become a celebrity, you'll have a tremendous amount of power, especially over the young, impressionable people who look up to you. What you do and how you behave will influence what they do and how they behave. It's stupid, but some of them have no one else to turn to but celebrities."

"I know about all that, but I'm not a role model, man. I'll just come out and say it. My morals are flexible."

I buried my head in my hands.

"You'll be a role model whether you want to or not," I groaned. "I'm not suggesting that you stop doing drugs or sleeping with teenagers. But could you at least stay at home when you're doing it?"

"No way, dude. I hate staying home. But just chill. I'll stay out of trouble. I'll be nice to people as long as they show me the love."

"Whatever you say, Chad. I was just thinking that since the songs are so different that maybe the rock star could be different, too. That's all."

"Dude, I am different. Did you not see my hobo pockets?"

66.

"You know I can't just walk in their office and say Chad cannot use these songs because he's a whore."

"I realize that," said Vincent. "So just say he's not talented enough or something."

"But he is talented. I'm afraid he's as good a candidate as any to record your stuff."

"How about just letting Neil and me play them? All we need is a drummer."

"Vincent, you know that's against New Renaissance policy."

"I know. Could just Neil sing them?"

"Is he somewhat good-looking?"

"Not really."

"Then probably not."

"But he's a good guy."

"Give him some time."

"What's that supposed to mean?"

"It means don't get too close to your friends because they'll screw you in the end. You ought to be writing instead of wasting time with him."

"I'm not going to write anymore if my stuff is going to end up going to idiotic sluts."

"I thought you already knew there was a strong possibility of that happening. You suffer and create, and they indulge and perform. That's how it works."

"I know. I trust your judgment, Harlan. I'm sorry to be like this, but I'm just not too happy about the situation."

I paused for a moment.

"Well, neither am I. I'll talk to Sylvain."

Sylvain, as I expected, scoffed at our complaint. He argued that musicians and actors can't be hired on the basis of what they do in their personal lives. If such were the case, he said, there would be no entertainers at all. I demanded to run our complaint by Mr. Lipowitz. Sylvain refused but promised he would pass the word on to Drew Prormps.

The following day, Sylvain relayed a message to me from Prormps. This message was Prormps's reply to my complaint: My work in L.A. was done for now, and I was to return to Indiana. I asked Sylvain for Prormps's number.

"I'm not going to let him just brush me off like that without me talking to him first," I said.

"He's a busy man, and my job is to talk to you so he and Lipowitz won't have to. Forget it."

"I'm asking you as a friend," I said. "Not as a business associate but as a friend who isn't really asking much. Please give me his number."

"Oh, hell, Harlan. If you're gonna put it that way…"

67.

"Ah, Mr. Eiffler! So nice to finally speak to you."

Prormp's voice was affable and gentlemanly. His secretary had put me on hold ten minutes prior.

"You too."

"I must say, you have just been doing a superb job with our artist. Let me tell you, there's already some serious buzz on him. People are talking about this unknown genius hiding in the forest of the Midwest. He's going to be hot. This kid is going places, and I want to thank you in advance for getting him there."

"You're quite welcome. It's been an interesting job, to say the least."

"I bet it has. So what can I do for you today?"

"Well, did Steven tell you the idea that Vincent and I had?"

"Yes, he did. And what idea was that?"

"We were thinking that New Renaissance should consider hiring performers whose personal lives won't have a negative influence on the public."

"Oh, right. Yeah, Steve did mention that. I hear where you're coming from. Of Kierkegaard's levels of existence, Chad Carter doesn't exactly embrace the ethical over the aesthetic."

"Right," I hesitantly replied, irritated that he had read something I hadn't.

"The problem with that, Harlan, is that at the end of the day, in show business, we can't judge artists by their personal lives. We have to judge them by their work. In fact, as you know, bad behavior can actually be a positive for us because it tends to increase a performer's popularity. The bottom line is that we pay the artists to render a service, and as long as they deliver, we'll work with them, even if they like to get crazy after hours. That's just the way it is. I don't like it either, Harlan, but my hands are tied here, and I'll tell you, this Chad kid, there's some serious buzz on him as well. I really think we can get him to the top. He may not choose despair like Kierkegaard would want him to, but he's going to be hot."

"My argument is that the main goal of New Renaissance is to improve culture, right?"

"No doubt. But the thing is—"

"So if we're providing well-written works of art to a bunch of whores and assholes, then wouldn't we be helping to make culture even worse?"

"I don't look at it like that at all, Harlan. I think the art will speak for itself. I trust that the public can separate the art from the artists. And New Renaissance is all about the art. Not what goes on outside of the art. Besides, we're not in the role-model business. We're in the entertainment business, and as far as that goes, I really think Chad gives the industry hope. This is all about the passion and music inside of him."

"Music that Vincent wrote."

"Exactly. There is no division between his music and his life. His songs are the very essence of him at the moment he sings them." I wasn't sure who he was talking about at this point.

"It's just something Vincent and I were really concerned about."

"I appreciate your concern, Harlan. But look at it this way. While Chad may like to party and such, at least most of his energy goes into his music. He could be doing a lot worse with that charisma of his. Look at Charles Manson. He failed an audition for the Monkees and then decided to make himself a youth culture guru. Look at what happened."

"Do you think I could talk to Mr. Lipowitz about this?"

"Sure you can. But I'm certain he'll tell you the same thing I have."

"Could I have his number, please?"

"I believe he's out of town this week."

"Could I have it so I could call him next week, please?"

The number Prormps finally gave me sounded familiar. I tried it immediately after hanging up.

Sylvain answered. I had called his cell phone.

68.

Disenchanted and worn out, I booked a flight back to Indiana. I would no longer resist allowing Chad the songs, not that my resistance mattered at all. Continental bought Vincent's song rights from Sylvain the next day, and the papers were signed without me.

Sylvain said that Prormps had pulled that bit of telephonic trickery once before when someone asked to speak to Lipowitz. He explained that his cell phone was technically the correct channel through which one could reach Lipowitz, though he always directed any calls for Lipowitz back to Prormps. Supposedly, Lipowitz had become increasingly reclusive in his poor health and didn't want to be bothered.

Before returning to my old hotel room home at the Kokomo Days Inn, I stopped by Vincent's apartment, where I met Neil. He looked like someone I would have been friends with in high school. He wore a bedraggled pair of high-top Chuck Taylors, a perennial favorite of young American outcasts, as well as khaki pants torn off below the knees, and a Misfits T-shirt featuring an intimidating skull. His dyed-black hair shagged down in his eyes, giving him a detached, voyeuristic demeanor as he tilted his head back and peeped from behind his coif. He could be interpreted as either punk rock or poor. Factually, he was both.

As Vincent later told me, Neil was both tough and vulnerable, someone who proudly carried a chip on his shoulder but who also carried a reservoir of tears behind his eyes. He declined to shake my hand upon our introduction, waving at me instead.

"Neil doesn't believe in shaking hands," said Vincent.

"Sorry," said Neil.

"Believe me, that's fine. I shook enough hands in California to last me a decade."

The three of us sat on the couch, Vincent in the middle.

"So Neil," I said. "Has Vincent told you what New Renaissance is all about?"

"Yeah."

"What do you think about it?"

"Honestly, I'm sorry, but I think it's kind of dumb. I was telling Vincent, there are tons of great movies and bands out there already. People just don't know about them because they don't bother looking."

"You're exactly right, and that's why New Renaissance is necessary, because people don't bother looking. What we're doing is serving mainstream audiences good pieces of entertainment on a silver platter. But I'm guessing you don't want to be served like that, do you?"

"Nah. I don't need any help."

"Neither do I. But you and I aren't the audience that New Renaissance is after. That's not to say we won't benefit from it. Can you imagine getting in your car and turning on your radio and hearing a pop music station playing good music?"

"It *would* be nice," said Neil.

Vincent and Neil were watching an old Don Knotts movie when I arrived. They had developed a strange fascination for the man. I told Vincent to resume the tape. I observed how he and Neil laughed at all the same things.

They were best friends. They called each other if they saw something funny on TV that they wanted the other to see. Neil made Vincent mix tapes full of obscure acts like Slim Cessna's Auto Club, the Low Budgets, and Kentucky Prophet. Vincent taped Neil's favorite TV shows for him since Neil's mom couldn't afford cable.

Neil's favorite band was the Ramones, his favorite TV show was *The Tom Green Show*, and his favorite movie was *Fight Club*.

I hadn't had a friend in ages. The idea of a couple of guys actually caring about each other and not talking about work had become foreign to
me, which would make it easier for me to break up their friendship.

69.

As we had agreed, Vincent quit his job at Kroger's when his tenth year at
the academy commenced. At such a small school, it didn't take long for
the news to spread that a New Renaissance student had written a hit song
for Kristina Gomez. The name Vincent Spinetti was now in common circulation among his peers, though he received no special treatment for his
accomplishment. If anything, Vincent had become the object of even
more jealousy and ridicule. For the first two months of the semester, rarely
did a day go by in which Vincent didn't hear someone mockingly singing
the chorus of "All Out for You." While his recognition at school
increased, his social situation worsened; I could not have asked for our
project to be going more swimmingly.

Vincent gained no new friends at school. The other kids assumed his
life was privileged and perfect, and no one mentioned his years of suffering before selling a measly pop song. Neil remained Vincent's only friend,
and they continued to see each other every weekend.

In October, Vincent finally received his royalties for the Kristina
Gomez single. It wasn't a life-changing amount of money, especially since
Sylvain and I shared 50 percent of the royalties as the song publishers,
Gomez received 10 percent as the recording artist, and the lawyer,
Richard Resnick, received 5 percent for business affairs. Also, income
taxes took a considerable slice, and New Renaissance received 25 percent
on any alumni sales. Giving 25 percent of their royalties was how New
Renaissance alumni reimbursed their company for the "free" education.
However, it served another purpose in keeping the writers hungry, so to
speak.

It would have been enough money, however, to help relieve Neil's
worsening home situation. Neil's mom was in serious danger of losing her
house. His dad had left his mom, his little sister, and him when he was
five, and now the family was on the verge of going hungry, literally. But
Neil refused to accept any money from Vincent, not even a loan. He

appreciated it, he said, but he had seen the strain Vincent put himself through in writing, and he didn't feel right about taking his friend's hard-earned pay.

So Vincent sent all but one thousand dollars to his siblings in Kramden, Illinois, whom he regularly wrote and occasionally talked to on the phone. He would continue sending them the majority of his royalties for the rest of his writing career.

"Why would you give them all that money?!" I asked once. "They were so mean to you."

"It's not just for them. It helps me absolve my guilt."

"What guilt?"

"I've been given this great opportunity. I make money from writing. It makes me feel bad for everyone."

70.

The newfound prominence of Vincent's name at school did, however, lead him to meet an attractive, freakish ninth-year student named Kari DuBrow. The rebelliously dressed girl with the holey skirt approached Vincent one day during lunch as he sat huddled in the corner of the lobby reading Charles Bukowski. He often skipped lunch in favor of reading alone, which spared him the social horrors of the cafeteria but did little to improve his skinny physique.

Kari introduced herself and congratulated Vincent on the success of his song. She said that it was cool despite being a pop song, and he instantly developed an intense crush on her. She was a songwriter herself and was impressed that he could write something that was playable on the radio yet not awful. He instantly assumed they were soulmates.

Vincent had always noticed Kari in the halls, with her daring haircuts and political T-shirts. It was a dream for him that, for the next two weeks, she spoke to him at some point every day. It was also dreamlike but a bit nerve-wracking when she asked if he'd like to join her and her friends in the cafeteria for lunch.

Perceptive as always, Vincent soon realized that Kari intended to be his platonic friend. Nevertheless, he clutched onto the hope that their friendship could lead to more. As with Daphne, the possibility of romance allowed Vincent the fluke of happiness.

So when Vincent asked Kari if she wanted to do something and she said yes, I asked him if this would hurt Neil's feelings since they usually hung out on the weekend. After all, considering his home life, Neil needed a friend now more than ever.

As with most things I told him, Vincent took these comments to heart. That Saturday, he invited Neil to his apartment along with Kari. Vincent said the three of them had a good time listening to music and watching TV. He also said having Neil there put him at ease since it obviously wasn't a date. Most important, he said that Neil and Kari got along just fine.

71.

Sylvain and I agreed that paying off Neil probably would not work. He had firmly rejected Vincent's offer of money and would likely do the same toward any unethical proposal of mine. Also, he seemed to genuinely care for Vincent. Sometimes he called Vincent during the week just to see how he was doing, and he wasn't even getting paid to do so.

Paying off the girl held potential risk as well, because at some point, she would be tempted to tell Neil about me, and he would likely tell Vincent even if they were estranged from one another. I decided to save New Renaissance's money for a change and try a more creative scheme, one which easily earned the approval of my employers.

My scheme felt like something from a bad sitcom, but it seemed like the easiest, safest way to go. In my hotel room on my laptop, I typed out the following letter:

"Hey! I am your secret admirer. If you would like to meet me, please come to Shoney's at 7 p.m. on November the 9th. Have a seat in the waiting section up front. Let's keep this a secret, please. I want it to be just you and me versus the world. I can't wait to see you. Also, I promise I'm not a psycho and/or a pervert."

Immortal Beloved

I sent one copy of the letter to Neil and the other to Kari. At the designated time, I sat in my car across from the Shoney's parking lot. Neil arrived first in a dilapidated Honda Accord with punk rock stickers on the bumper. The young girl I presumed to be Kari arrived shortly there-after in a Mercedes. She was a cute, diminutive rock chick wearing a plaid skirt, T-shirt, and fishnet stockings. Her hair was short, spiky, and multi-colored. She strutted into the restaurant without hesitation.

Her favorite band was Rancid, her favorite TV show was *The Simpsons*, and her favorite movie was *Taxi Driver*.

I had been in love triangles several times before and knew all too well that they could never end up equilateral. Someone had to be the odd man out. I was betting that Kari could fall for Neil for the same reasons she likely *didn't* fall for Vincent. Neil was older and tougher. He had a bad-boy mystique that might appeal to a girl who had been going to an elite private school all her life. Meanwhile, Vincent was smart and sensitive, but such a worrier that he constantly feared his internal organs would spontaneously stop working or that his apartment would explode.

The worst that could happen would be for Neil and Kari to be noth-ing but confused by the letters and to leave the restaurant separately. Instead, they didn't leave the restaurant until after eight, at which time they both departed in Neil's car.

72.

Vincent called me up crying. His voice was shaky and nasal.

"You were right," he said quietly. "Neil's been seeing her."

"Oh, geez. I'm sorry."

"I want to cut them."

"Don't cut them. Is there anything I can do?"

"Would you want to come over?"

"I've been drinking too much to drive," I said. "But you're more than welcome to come over here if you feel like walking."

Ten minutes later, Vincent was sitting on the edge of one of my hotel room's twin-sized beds, picking his scalp with both hands, bouncing one of his legs like an anxious kid who would soon have to give an oral report to his class. It had been a week since I had seen Neil and Kari together. Since then, Vincent had noticed strange behavior in both. Neil didn't call. Kari didn't notice him at school. Neither showed any interest in wanting to be with Vincent. He confronted Kari at school, and she was kind enough to give him the truth.

"I'm sorry, but I warned you about those girls," I said, lying on the other bed across from him, staring up at the blinking red light on the fire alarm. "When there was only one man and one woman in this world, the woman went and found a snake."

"But what about Neil? How could he do this to me?"

"I told you. Fucking and shopping. People are selfish."

"Love is what's selfish," Vincent replied.

"I know it feels awful, but look. We'll make 'em all your slaves some-day. Forget 'em. Let them rot away with whichever sexual partner they think they're in love with at the moment. In the long run, the highlight of their lives will have been knowing Vincent Spinetti. Their only signif-icant contribution to this planet will be that they served as inspiration for something you wrote."

"He said I was his best friend."

"And he probably meant it at the time. But talking is just air. Circumstances change with the weather."

"I had never had a best friend before."

"Trust me, you don't need friends. Just someone else to use you. You have to do everything on their time. You're supposed to be able to talk any time they call, but you can never seem to catch them at the right time. They only call when they want something. Sometimes they'll call just to get the number of another friend. They're not there for you. Where were they when my dad was dying? And they will always, *always*, choose a girl over you. Indefinitely. I've done it myself. Love, I mean, sex is just too powerful. And when they have a girl, you're little more than an inconvenience to them. No sir, you don't need friends at all, Vincent."

"You say all that, but aren't you my friend?"

"No."

"Then what are you?"

"I'm your manager. I thought you knew that. I'm not here to be your friend. I'm here to help your career and provide you with guidance."

"Then give me some guidance," said Vincent.

I got up from the bed and walked over to the dresser to my bottle of whiskey. I dropped ice in a cup and poured him a drink.

"Here's your guidance," I said as I handed him the cup. Then I walked over to my stereo, which I kept on a table in the corner. I looked through my heaps of CDs and found one of my favorite heartbreak albums, *Lincoln* by They Might Be Giants. That night, instead of fussing, we got drunk and listened to my favorite records, one after another.

"No, you don't need any friends, Vincent," I boozily mused as the night progressed. "I don't have any friends. The closest thing I have to friends are business associates, and they're all in California, and I just don't know about California sometimes."

Vincent nodded as he sucked down whiskey and gently swayed to the music. The Dead Milkmen's *Soul Rotation* was now playing.

"Did you ever think about how, when man went west, his values started, like, spilling out of his soul?"

Vincent shrugged his shoulders. He was now keeping a beat with one foot.

"Way far East, man was peaceful and spiritual," I continued. "But then he lost more and more on the way across Europe and the Atlantic, and past the Mississippi, and finally to get gold in California. But then again, once he was in California, there was nothing between him and the East but the Pacific."

Vincent was no longer listening. I shut up and joined him in concentrating on the music. We listened together until we fell asleep at around 4 a.m., and it remains my favorite memory of Vincent Spinetti.

VII. JANE

73.

"It shouldn't make any difference, but Friday and Saturday nights are the worst. They're the worst because the loneliness is magnified. The best you can do is hope that there is someone else like you out there, but if there is, you will never meet this person because she doesn't get out either. So you're left with your thoughts, and your thoughts are living people in your brain who call and hang up and lounge around like armed security guards who happen to be beautiful. In between these thoughts, you think about what's going on out there. The girl of your dreams is being ravaged by a man who doesn't have a care in the world. Just to hear her voice would make you happy for a week, but he gets to spend the day and night with her and thinks nothing of it. Somewhere across town there is laughter and fun and something that resembles kindness and love. There are people having a good time, not watching the clock, not wanting to sleep. Sleep is all that feels good. Sleep feels like a little death. Those tiny hours in the morning when everyone is asleep are the only ones that don't feel lonely. But for right now, there are boyfriends and girlfriends, people in love, wide awake. They hang out. They hang out. They hang out. They do nothing worthwhile except each other. Friends, friends, friends. Fiends. Inside jokes. There are so many stupid conversations going on right now. You could be having a meaningful conversation with a taxi driver. You could talk to him about how Travis Bickle's taxi was a metaphor for his loneliness. You are not missed. If you aren't being thought of by a single mind on Earth, do you really exist? Chad will always exist. They make plans so easily. They don't debate over dialing numbers. Bleak house. You have a gray tint on your contact lenses. But you have your work. They don't have that. They are cowards. Everyone seems so afraid to be alone. It takes strength to lie there alone and take it. They just want to copulate, and that's their biggest concern of the night. You want a tragedy. An assassination. A massacre. An earthquake. A city falling to the ground. Something to get the people on TV to be on the same page as you."

—An e-mail Vincent wrote me when I was staying in Los Angeles again

74.

Thoroughly heartbroken by Daphne, Kari, and Neil, Vincent became increasingly isolated in his final year and a half at the academy. He concentrated on his work, writing more songs, a couple of movies, and entire seasons of TV shows. By the end of his eleventh year, there was little left for him to learn at school. All of his teachers agreed he was more than ready to quit the academy to write professionally.

The summer after Vincent graduated from the New Renaissance Academy, I returned to L.A., this time to help Sylvain pitch Vincent's television shows since I was so familiar with the material. I had asked Vincent if he would like to join me, but he declined, saying he "just didn't feel like going anywhere, let alone California." So he endured a self-imposed exile in his new apartment, which he was able to afford with his 10 percent of Chad's CD royalties.

Chad's CD, which he personally titled *Self-Titled*, was released when Vincent was seventeen. By the time Vincent turned eighteen, Chad was heralded as the savior of the music industry. He was talented, his music had substance, and with the help of his smoldering good looks, charisma, and the bad behavior that kept him on tabloid covers, his revenue was phenomenal.

Chad was a typical celebrity, but his music was different and creative, and the masses accepted it. Around the same time, other New Renaissance alumni saw their work reach the public thanks to the hard work of New Renaissance publishers, agents, and managers such as myself. About half of these works were successes. I found a good portion of the material to be pretentious. Nevertheless, New Renaissance as a whole was working as planned.

Vincent continued to live in Kokomo, as there was nowhere else for him to go. He considered moving back to Kramden to be closer to his siblings but decided they didn't want him there. They rarely replied to his letters. So he chose to live in a cheap one-bedroom apartment in Kokomo that was slightly smaller than his student apartment.

Vincent's new apartment had white carpets and white walls, and the front door opened to a living room in which the thrift-store furniture was directed toward the television. On the floor were a stereo and piles of CDs and books that Vincent had accumulated through the years, many of them purchased by me.

Connected to the living room was a kitchen that Vincent seldom used. He preferred ordering pizzas and fast food over cooking. His bedroom was next to the kitchen but was also seldom used, since he slept on the living room couch, which is also where he wrote.

After I read all of Vincent's TV scripts, I decided it was time to return to California. Television was notoriously devoid of quality and intelligence, two virtues Vincent's TV shows had more than enough of. With Vincent moved into his new apartment, I once again booked a reservation at the Renaissance Hollywood Hotel. Since I didn't know how long I would be gone, I bought my client a surplus of alcohol before I left, a purchase recommended by my bosses.

75.

Sylvain and I were called into another sophisticated office with black decor, this one in the IUI/Globe-Terner skyscraper. We were on the tenth floor, which was headquarters to Empire Television, IUI/Globe-Terner's largest TV company. We were supposed to meet with the head of Empire, as well as the heads of Empire's cable channels. Lipowitz used his lingering clout to get us a meeting with these men, his former employees.

I expected the process of getting Vincent's television material to the public would be easier than releasing his music, as performers of television aren't as consequential to their product's success as the performers of music. Most TV actors aren't as famous as the characters they play. Carol Brady was more famous than Florence Henderson. Archie Bunker was more of a household name than Caroll O'Connor. Kramer was more popular than Michael Richards. As long as the writing was good, which Vincent's was, the actors would be superfluous.

Sylvain and I shook hands with seven white males. By this time, it was common knowledge in the industry that Sylvain had become an agent, but he still had to talk about his old vocation of doing *Blood Lust* movies. He didn't seem to mind.

After we all sat at a long glass table and finished small talk, the men asked me about Vincent's shows.

"The best one is a one-hour drama, but it has comedy as well. I would rather not use the word 'dramedy,' but I suppose that's what it is. It would take place in a supermarket and be aptly titled *Grocery Store*."

The men snickered.

"Yeah, I guess I deserve that, but hear me out. Historically, TV dramas have either been crime shows, law shows, or hospital shows. I checked the *TV Guide*, and twenty-one out of the twenty-eight current prime-time dramas fit into these categories. That's three out of four. I don't think there's any need for another of these supposedly exciting shows full of life-and-death situations. So if you're just looking for another show full of dead prostitutes, then maybe I should just stop talking right now."

"We're listening," said the middle-aged man at the head of the table, presumably their leader.

"So my client, Vincent Spinetti, wanted to use a less exciting occupation, something common and thankless, even banal. That's why he made the setting an average supermarket, with the ultrabright lights and automatic doors and shopping carts and everything. I think it's a refreshing concept—a working-class drama filled with ordinary problems. It will let the average viewer know that he's not alone."

"So what happens at this grocery store?" asked one of the suits.

"The workers suffer through their work week. They toil through their shifts and hate their lives, but at least they have camaraderie. Normal things happen. Some of them get fired. Some new people get hired. Some of them steal. Some of them fall in love. There's a love triangle. There are problems with the customers. And the boss is the villain. The workers organize a strike. And we see their home lives sometimes as well."

"People watch TV to get away from all that stuff," said another. "Why would anyone want to watch it?"

"Because the writing is so good. I acknowledge the premise might sound dull, but the premise doesn't do the writing justice. That's why I brought copies of the pilot for all of you to read."

As I passed around the scripts to the unimpressed men, Sylvain added to my pitch.

"Another thing is that it would have a wide appeal to all different sorts of demographics, you know? All ages are represented. There's a teenage bagboy, and then there's an elderly bagboy. There's a middle-aged black woman cashier. There's twentysomething girls working in the meat department. You could cast hot girls for their parts to pull in the male viewers. You could get established actors to play the managers. And you could have celebrity cameos for the shoppers."

"What do you think, Brad?" asked the leader.

"I'll take a look at the script. Doubt I can do anything with it. Sounds like the biggest plus would be that it could attract the supermarket chains for advertising."

"Wait a minute," said one of the younger men. "Forget supermarkets. This concept has some major product placement possibilities. Can you think of a better setting for product placement than a grocery store? Half the things advertised on TV are sold at the supermarket, especially if it's one of those superstore type deals, like Super Wal-Mart. Is it one of those type stores?"

"No," I answered. "It's just a regular supermarket that's not even doing good business anymore thanks to places like Super Wal-Mart."

"We could tweak it," said another. "If it's a hit, just think how many advertisers would pay to have their products prominently displayed on the show. We could have, like, special displays in the background for the advertisers that pay the most, maybe even announcements on the PA"

The leader seemed to be deep in thought. His hands were in a pyramid shape with all the fingertips touching.

"I figured we'd just use fake name brands," I said.

"No way," said the young guy. "Look at how big product placement in movies has become. Every car in *Extremers 5* was a BMW. Why shouldn't we use real groceries in a grocery show?"

"The fucking commercials could have characters from the TV show in them!" suddenly exclaimed the leader. "The commercials could be a fucking part of the show and advance the plot! Then everybody would watch the commercials. Lipowitz was right about this kid. He's a mother-fucking genius!"

76.

I pitched another of Vincent's ideas, but the men were so excited about *Grocery Store* that they didn't care. My second pitch was a parody of sit-coms called *Situation Comedy*. It featured several innovations, my favorite being its unique laugh track. Instead of having an entire audience laugh, the laugh track on *Situation Comedy* would consist of one man with an obnoxious chuckle. Also, the set would have a fourth wall on the pilot, but through a contrived mishap, this fourth wall falls. In subsequent episodes, viewers would still see the wall lying in ruins on the front lawn.

The men failed to see the humor in this.

"Let's just focus our energy on *Grocery Store* for now, and if it goes over, we'll take it from there," said the leader.

After another meeting was scheduled for the following week, Sylvain and I were dismissed. Until then, the contracts would be drawn.

"Looks like we just sold one big hour-long commercial," I said to Sylvain on the elevator.

"Yeah, well, at least we sold it. And it sounds like they're gonna give it a big push."

"We can't let them do this to Vincent's show."

Sylvain said nothing. We walked off the elevator and into the humongous lobby with its black-and-white marble floors and walls.

"Don't you agree!?" I yelled.

"Agree about what?"

"That we can't let them do that to Vincent's show."

"Sure I agree. I'll talk to Prormps about it."

"Screw Prormps. I don't even think he's on our side."

Sylvain shrugged his shoulders as we left the building. He lit a ciga-rette as soon as his dress shoes touched the sidewalk.

"Then again, I doubt Lipowitz would stand for this," I said. "You should talk to Prormps about it so maybe he'll talk to Lipowitz. I guess

Lipowitz is our only hope."

"Whatever. I'm on it." Sylvain was going to limp off without saying good-bye.

"Wait," I said. "Would you want to do something tonight? Maybe go over some of Vincent's other TV ideas?"

"Can't do it. I'm meeting with a guy. Sorry."

"Oh. I guess you're meeting up with your coke dealer."

"Shut the fuck up."

"I'm right, aren't I? You're back on drugs. I know you've been acting funny."

"Don't tell Lipowitz, or I'll kill you."

"Okay, Steven Sylvain of *Blood Lust* fame. Don't worry. It's not like I'll ever even talk to Lipowitz. How's he doing, anyhow?"

"He's okay for now, I think. Heard he's been in remission for a while. I gotta go, man. I'm sorry. I'll see you at the meeting or whatever. Laters."

Since there was nothing else to do, I called Sylvain the next day to talk to him about his drug problem. He said his relapse could be traced back to Chad. Upon Lipowitz's insistence, Sylvain checked in on Chad's recording sessions from time to time as a measure of quality control. At the recording studio, Chad had little trouble in enticing Sylvain. Chad thought "it would be cool to get messed up with Johnny Lane from *Blood Lust*."

Sylvain claimed that initially his problem was under control and that the only time he used was at the studio with Chad. But then Chad became the hottest music act in America, and word got around that Steven Sylvain had played a role in getting the pop star signed. With his name rising back toward the A-list, Sylvain found himself being invited to more parties and became reacquainted with some old friends. He was soon hooked again, and he even found a new dealer named Raoul. Sylvain had been introduced to Raoul by Raoul's lover at the time, Drew Prormps.

77.

For the next week I mostly stayed in bed in my hotel room, disgusted by everything, sickened by existence, questioning my profession. I watched TV day and night, I drank my meals, and I thought about asking Sylvain for some drugs. I didn't call Vincent because I didn't feel like talking. The only productive thing I did was plan out how I would handle the *Grocery Store* deal. I was going to arrogantly deliver an ultimatum to the executives because I didn't care anymore.

After waiting for him in the IUI/Globe-Terner lobby for ten minutes, I called Sylvain on my cell phone.

"What are you doing?" I asked.

"Just crashin, bro. Killer party at Leo's last night."

"Are you not coming to the meeting?"

"What meeting?"

"The meeting where we sign Vincent's TV deal."

"Oh, yeah. The thing is, I brought home a friend last night, and she's still with me, you know? You can handle the meeting without me, can't you?"

"But you're the agent. I'm just the manager. Isn't it California law that managers can't negotiate deals?"

Sylvain laughed.

"Technically, yeah, but managers make deals all the time anyway. Don't worry about that. Go ahead and sign everything. Laters."

I was led into the office and took a seat. I noticed there was a woman sitting with us this time, though no one bothered to introduce us.

After I was done thoughtlessly perusing a contract, I pushed it aside and said nothing.

"Well?" asked the leader.

"It all looks great. But Vincent and I have decided that we will not sign over *Grocery Store* unless you agree to not use your product placement idea."

"Forget it. That's the main reason we want it."

"Then, I'm sorry, but I can't in good conscience sign this contract."

"That's quite all right, Mr. Eiffler. We can quickly develop our own supermarket show."

"No you can't. I always copyright Vincent's ideas."

"Well, we could easily create our own show called *Department Store*. That isn't an issue."

I had anticipated this.

"Fine. *Grocery Store* is yours. But only under one condition."

"And what's that?"

"Vincent has an idea for a new cable channel. We want it on the air by the time *Grocery Store* is televised."

"Mr. Eiffler, we're buying an entire season of your TV show, and in exchange you're asking for an entire channel. You're being ridiculous."

"Hold on, now. It's not as bad as it sounds. His idea is called Art TV. Art TV would turn an ordinary television set into a picture frame, and in that frame would appear works of art from antiquity to contemporary. They'd change every two minutes. There'd be no talking, just classical music in the background. At the bottom of the screen would appear the title of the painting and the artist. And because it requires no actors or studios, it would be dirt-cheap, which means few or no commercials."

"That's all there is to it?" asked one of the men. "Just pictures?"

"Yes, but I'm sure there will be more content in two minutes of a Dalí painting than an entire hour of *Survivor*. I think it would be the best way to expose the average American to art. People who have never set foot in a museum will be exposed to art for the first time because they'll be able to see it from their couches. They'll be flipping through, and maybe a painting will catch their eye, and they'll stop on it and wait for the next painting. They might learn to love art, or at least appreciate it. And it's something you could just leave on the TV when you're not really watching it. It could be part of a room's decorations. It could be a good conversation piece at parties, even."

"I don't think it would work, Mr. Eiffler," said the leader. "People want to be entertained. It's not entertainment."

The men nodded.

"It's just pictures," said another. "Trust me. The average viewer wouldn't care."

"It's not entertainment," repeated another.

"But that's just it. I don't think TV is even entertaining. I think TV has little value outside of being something that you can make fun of when you're bored. It makes stupid people stupider. And now you're telling me that with all the trivial, brainless channels out there, none of you are interested in putting actual art on the air?"

"It's boring," one of them muttered. I sighed as loudly as possible.

"May I be so bold as to turn on that TV?" I asked, pointing to the plasma flat-screen TV on the wall.

"Go right ahead. Why?"

"I've got a point to make."

The leader slid a remote control from his end of the table to mine. I stood up, turned on the TV, and switched to channel two.

78.

"Please, just humor me. I want to show you that something like Art TV would be a serious improvement. Look. Commercial, commercial. Here's a show. I've watched this before. It's directly ripped off from a thing that Jay Leno does. Can someone tell me how it's possible that Leno always beats Dave in the ratings? Doesn't that tell you something about our country?...A dating show. I guarantee you that at some point on this show, that girl will say something like, 'Tell me why I should pick you,' and then the guy will say, 'Well, instead of *telling* you why, why don't I *show* you?' and he'll proceed to kiss her pornographically...A commercial, a cartoon, a commercial, a soap opera with hot young Latinos... Commercial—here you go. QVC. There's a shopping channel, yet you don't want an art channel...Commercial. Can we please stop having commercials where you hear someone in the background having an orgasm only to discover that they're actually eating a candy bar or washing their hair?...Discovery Channel. Discover Christopher Lowell talking about bedspreads...*Jeopardy!* One of the few shows on TV that rewards intelligence instead of who can eat the most horse rectums or lie the most or be the biggest whore, like on a reality show. I deplore anyone who has ever appeared on a reality show, although I probably shouldn't say that. At this point, chances are someone in this room, or any room in America at any given moment, has appeared on a reality show."

One of the men raised his hand. "*Temptation Island*," he said.

"Sorry...An Olsen twin sitcom on the Family Channel. I don't know why you aren't more interested in Vincent's *Situation Comedy*. Sitcoms deserve to be made fun of. Nearly every sitcom on television is ridden with clichés. They always take place in New York. They have so many stock characters. There's always a sex-crazed, promiscuous character that makes every sentence a double entendre. There's usually an intrusive next-door neighbor or a flighty, eccentric receptionist, depending on the setting….Commercial, religious channel asking for money, ESPN, ESPN 2…On TNT we have an episode of *NYPD Blue*, groundbreaking because it shows peoples' butts…Commercial, VH-1. Probably the dumbest channel on television. Look at this. They're showing *Showgirls* for the tenth time this month. A movie known for its pertinence to music…Condom commercial, a news network, commercial, a whole channel devoted to animals. Another channel devoted to animals—MTV. The only music it plays is in the background of its reality show orgies…Commercial, another news network, another news network, commercial. Oh, here's what passes for an American Movie Classic nowadays. *Predator*. Not Fred Astaire being elegant. Not Jimmy Stewart being a gentleman. Just a California governor shooting at a monster…E!—something about how great Jennifer Aniston's life is. Usually they're showing a *True Hollywood Story* of a porn star since they ran out of drugged-out actors. Either that or the top two hundred sexiest feet. They're always making lists on these stupid entertainment channels…Sci-Fi Channel, commercial, Cartoon Network. Some of the prime-time cartoons like *The Simpsons* and *South Park* have the sharpest satirical writing on TV. That's pretty sad when our most intelligent TV shows are cartoons…Travel Channel, Home and Garden Channel, Food Channel, another shopping network, commercial, another news network, commercial, an entire channel devoted to golf, an entire channel devoted to soap operas, commercial, an entire network devoted to video games, commercial, and that's it."

I turned off the TV.

"That is what TV has to offer us. Maybe you're right. Maybe art has no place in television. It truly is a vast wasteland. I just thought you might be willing to take a chance on putting something of worth on TV screens, even if it's boring. But none of you are willing, so I guess that's that."

"I am."

All heads turned toward the speaker. It was the woman.

"Miss Watkins?" asked the leader.

"Yes. Excuse me, but I'm willing," she said quietly. "I like his idea. I agree with everything he's said, actually."

"Thank you," I said.

"You're welcome."

"What do you like about this idea, Miss Watkins?"

"I like that he's actually pitching something of value. It's something that might have a positive effect on audiences."

"Would you like to take on this project yourself?" he asked.

"I'd love to."

"Do any of you guys have a problem with that?"

They mumbled no.

"Very well, Mr. Eiffler. Miss Watkins here will be in charge of Art TV. We'll add a clause to the contract and buy the art channel in addition to the grocery show. We'll give you a call when the contract is ready to go."

The meeting adjourned. I smiled at the woman before I exited the office, and she smiled back.

"Mr. Eiffler," someone yelled at me from down the hall. I turned around and the woman was running to me.

"Mr. Eiffler, what you did in there, that was—well, I loved it."

"Thank you. Would you call me Harlan?"

"Yes. I'm Monica." She offered her hand. "I'm new here. That was the first time I ever spoke out loud at a meeting with those men."

"Thanks for doing so. I really appreciate it."

"I hope you don't mind my taking over your project. It sounds like a great idea."

"I don't mind at all. I'm sure you'll do fine with it."

The men filed past us as we talked in the middle of the hall.

"Also, I was wondering—Harlan, is it?"

"Uh-huh."

"I probably shouldn't do this. I normally wouldn't do something like this, but I was wondering if maybe you would like to get together with me some time. I'm new in town, and—well, it wouldn't be like a date, but—"

"Yes."

"I thought maybe we could talk about the art channel, and if—"

"Yes."

79.

Monica Watkins was the love of my life. It took me thirty-nine years to find her, but only an hour or so to fall for her. We ate at an Italian restaurant and ended up not talking business at all. I wanted to know everything about her, every joy or heartache she had ever experienced, what she was like in high school, what a typical day for her entailed.

She was thirty-four and had grown up in Kentucky. She had acquired a master's degree in business, but her true love was art. After failing to find an art job, she worked in New York for eight years for one of Empire's cable divisions. She was eventually promoted to vice president of Empire cable development, which required her to be transferred to L.A.

She couldn't remember the happiest day of her life, though she'd later say it was the day she met me. The saddest day of her life was when her dad died of a heart attack when she was a teenager. She was a shy outsider in high school and loathed cool kids. A typical day for her mostly involved working on cable channels she cared little about, being pitched things like reality shows featuring dogs in bathing suits. At night she liked to stay at home with her cats and read or listen to music.

She had straight, brown shoulder-length hair and the most adorable face I've ever seen. I couldn't ever tell if she was wearing makeup or not. She looked much younger than she was and had a perfect smile. She was petite and looked good in any outfit. She had brown eyes.

After dining, we went to my hotel room and talked until 3 a.m. Then she left without us having touched.

Her favorite musician was Bob Dylan, her favorite TV show was *Sanford and Son*, and her favorite movie was *Cool Hand Luke*.

The next day I called Vincent as I felt the need to tell someone about Monica. But Vincent didn't answer, nor did he return my call. He didn't answer the next day either, and I started to worry.

Since Sylvain was supposed to sign the amended contract anyway, there was no professional reason for me to stay in L.A. As much as I hated leaving Monica, Vincent was my responsibility, and I decided to return to him, wherever he was. Monica saw me off at the airport, which was nice since I had always secretly wanted a woman to do so.

30.

On the flight back to Indiana, I tried calling Vincent several more times to no avail. At this point, I was scared I would find him lying on his couch dead.

I could feel my heartbeat in my head as I knocked on his apartment door. Fortunately, he was alive to open it.

"Where have you been!?" I asked as I barged in.

"I've been right here."

"Why didn't you answer the phone?!"

"Because I didn't want to talk."

"You worried the shit out of me, Vincent."

"I'm sorry." He plopped down on his couch and looked up at me with eyes so purple and ringed underneath that he looked like he had lost a fistfight. His hair was getting longer than usual. He always seemed to be on the verge of having long hair but cut it himself to avoid this distinction. As usual, his hair swept down across half of his forehead while at the same time waving upward. He needed a haircut and a shave. He also needed to eat. He had finally grown taller, which made him look even skinnier, like a malnourished zombie in wrinkled, stained clothes.

I sat down next to him.

"Why didn't you want to talk?" I asked.

"I'm sorry. I didn't mean to worry you. I was too ashamed to talk to you." His voice was as calm and quiet as an elderly person's deathbed.

"Why were you ashamed?"

"I haven't written anything since you've been gone."

I had been gone more than two weeks, the longest Vincent had gone without writing since he had been recruited by New Renaissance.

"You don't have to be ashamed. You've worked hard all your life. Taking a break for a couple of weeks won't hurt anything. Just so you don't get stuck in a rut."

"I've got this great gig while there are people twice my age who have been writing for decades and haven't sold a thing. All I have to do is write, but I can't even do that. It's got me down."

"Cheer up. I sold *Grocery Store* and the art channel. They said to hold off on everything else for now. They didn't want to buy them all at once."

"They liked *Grocery Store*?"

"Uh-huh. So what have you been doing?"

"Nothing. The most productive thing I did was writing you that e-mail. I kept waiting for your reply."

"I don't want to start an electronic relationship with you. Besides, I didn't think that e-mail warranted a reply."

"Oh."

"Still, it was definitely the best e-mail I've ever received. I saved it. Sounds like you've been down lately."

"Yeah."

"I'm sorry. I had a fit of depression myself in California. Is there anything I can do for you?"

Vincent turned away from me.

"Could you buy me some more booze?"

"You mean you've drunk it all already?"

"That's another reason why I didn't want to talk to you."

"Vincent, I bought all that beer and whiskey thinking I could be gone for months."

"I know."

"You drank it all yourself?"

"Yes."

"No wonder you didn't get any work done."

"I thought it would help me write. But it made it even harder. I'm sorry."

"That's okay, but I don't think I'm going to buy you any more."

"Come on, Harlan. You of all people should help me out here."

"Actually, I've decided to cut down on my drinking."

"Why?"

"I'm in love."

"Harlan! That's great! We've been waiting for you to like somebody since I was little."

I told him all about Monica, and he seemed sincerely happy for me. But I realized my improved love life did nothing to help his situation. Under the condition that he would try writing again, I got a half-full bottle of Scotch from my suitcase and gave it to him.

81.

A month later, Vincent still had not started writing. He often tried, but his days and nights were mainly occupied with drunken, melancholy musing.

"I don't know how I'll make it through another lonely winter without anyone," said Vincent as he clutched onto a bottle of Miller Lite. "I will probably never be in the Christmas spirit again for the rest of my life."

"But it's July," I replied.

My employers and I had apparently miscalculated the effect that alcohol would have on Vincent. We had foolishly deduced that drinking would make him an even greater writer, since the artistic growth of Fitzgerald, Faulkner, Hemingway, Kerouac, Verlaine, Lowry, Robinson, Thomas, Smart, Carver, Capote, Crane, Crane, Roethke, Melville, O'Neill, O'Hara, Lewis, Anderson, Parker, London, Dreiser, Lardner, Cummings, Jarrell, Wolfe, Berryman, Lowell, Cheever, Chandler, Brautigan, Sexton, Hammett, Williams, Steinbeck, and Poe was not stunted by alcoholism, but evidently encouraged.

But for whatever reason, the drink was not conducive to Vincent's creativity. Indeed, it appeared the opposite. He had completely lost his creative impulse, that impulse that gave him sustenance and a reason to live. I feared that bereft of this impulse, he would eventually consider committing another act of self-annihilation common to artistic types.

"I just don't know anymore," slurred Vincent as he drunkenly lay on his kitchen linoleum. "You know how they say beauty is only skin-deep?"

"Yeah."

"Well, I've been feeling pretty ugly lately. Pretty ugly. Pretty. Ugly. And I've been thinking, if beauty is only skin-deep, then ugly is only skin-deep, and why don't I just take a steak knife and cut myself wide open?"

A drunken stupor and stifling depression robbed Vincent's sense of urgency. I knew it would happen eventually, and I already had a plan that would give him a trait as common to old artists and writers as suicide, almost as common as alcoholism.

I insisted that Vincent see a doctor so that he might find help for his general malaise and to see if there was a physical source of his lethargy. With his willpower drained into his toilet bowl, he put up no fight and agreed to see a doctor. I took him to a general practitioner whom I had paid exorbitantly ahead of time to follow my precise instructions.

After his visit with the doctor, Vincent came out to the waiting room where I had been sitting. He had a strange look on his face, not a smile or a frown, but a puzzled, incredulous gaze. He clutched his suspenders and pulled them forward.

"Well?" I asked.

"He told me I have tuberculosis. The incurable kind."

82.

Historically, the correlation between TB and creative prolificacy is undeniable. From Keats to Kafka, the disease has hung over the busy minds of dozens of geniuses, urging them to get their work done while they could. But eventually, science halted the ailment, and the cases still appearing were curable, except for Vincent's fictional version. My justification for this scheme was that I myself had experienced my share of health problems, such as depression, social anxiety disorder, stomach ulcers, and high blood pressure.

In case Vincent's heightened mortality wasn't enough to inspire him to write again, I had the doctor prescribe him a medicine that would supposedly slow the TB's progress. It was actually five-milligram tablets of Dexedrine, an amphetamine that would boost his energy and enhance his focus and motivation. The doctor warned him not to drink much with this medication, which I hoped would discourage any more unproductive drinking binges.

Unfortunately for Vincent, the medicine made him almost completely unable to sleep. But the medicine and the deadly diagnosis both served their purpose. For the next six months or so, Vincent stopped drinking and wrote more than ever, especially since he now had the early-morning hours to fill.

"How's the TB?" I once asked him.

"It's okay. I still don't think I have it, though."

"Still in denial, huh?"

"I have none of the symptoms, and I'm not coughing any more than I ever did. I've always had bad allergies. But anyhow, I don't care. If I have it, I'm glad."

"Why?"

"For obvious reasons. It makes me want to live more."

"It's good for an artist to have an impending sense of doom, I suppose."

"Oh, sure. I've had one of those for ages. I've always had this roman-tic idea of how I'll die. I believe that the bullet that is intended to kill me has already been made. It's out there somewhere right now, sitting on a shelf in a box, waiting for me."

"You think you'll be assassinated?"

"That's the idea, I guess. I think things like, 'Where will they get me? My heart? My head? Or will it be my face? Will I suffer long? Will I die smiling? Will anybody notice? Will anybody care?'"

"But you're not famous. Only famous people get assassinated. We're not going to let you get famous."

"Maybe they'll get Chad instead," Vincent joked. We laughed. "But now that I supposedly have TB and might not live as long, I really hope that bullet isn't there."

83.

I talked to Monica every night. Sometimes I called her, sometimes she called me. I was terrified that she would find someone else while I was away, so I kept in close contact with her. She seemed to feel the same way.

I eventually decided that I wanted my relationship with Monica to be completely honest. I even planned to tell her about this tortured artist "experiment" someday. But for now, my honesty came in regard to my feelings.

"I haven't let my guard down in ages," I told her on the phone. "But I've decided I'm going to let it down just for you."

"Thanks for making an exception."

"I'm so tired of hating everything. I want you to know that I don't hate you in the least."

"I don't hate you, either."

We then came to the agreement that we would not see other people, which was no big deal since most of the population repulsed us.

Meanwhile, Vincent had become crazy for a girl named Jane. He met her at the 7-Eleven convenience store down the road from his apartment building. She worked the graveyard shift there, which coincided with the only time that Vincent left the house. He ran out of coffee one night at 3 a.m. and went to buy a cup. He immediately fell for the cashier girl, who was reading an Edgar Allan Poe biography. They quickly established a rapport, talking about their love of Poe and their insomnia. She managed to make reference to her boyfriend, which didn't stop Vincent from needing a cup of 7-Eleven coffee every night thereafter during her shift.

I reminded Vincent of the heartache that girls had given him, but he said that Jane was different. He said she was smart, she didn't appear to be heartless, and she was a risk he was willing to take. Eventually, she began visiting Vincent's apartment during the day, cutting into his writing time. Then one day, Vincent called me with the news that Jane had dumped her boyfriend. Vincent was ecstatic, especially since Jane had dumped this boyfriend to be with him.

Our artist had his first girlfriend. They did everything together. She got him out of the apartment. They ate at cheap restaurants, went for long walks, and hung around the mall to laugh at the shoppers who had their pants pockets turned inside-out. They spent Sundays lying around her apartment and even had fun doing laundry together. They were happy and chemical-free except for her antidepressants and his amphetamines.

Her favorite band was the Flaming Lips, her favorite TV show was *Freaks and Geeks*, and her favorite movie was *One Flew over the Cuckoo's Nest*.

I wanted to let it go. For once, Vincent and I were both happy. In fact, up to that point, his relationship with Jane was the single biggest sliver of happiness that had nicked his existence. For the past three months, Jane was his life, and so his life was good. But our theories were correct; without loneliness, Vincent's work suffered. Naturally, he preferred spending time with his love over writing. He said he was "happily uninspired" and stopped writing altogether despite my constant lecturing on the importance of New Renaissance's cause.

As always, I conferred with Sylvain about Vincent's situation. He relayed the information to my superiors, and they insisted that I do my job. So late one night, I too needed a cup of convenience-store coffee.

84.

Jane was a tall, plain-looking girl with curly black hair, pale skin, and bright red lipstick. She and Vincent made a cute couple, and looking back, she may have been the one for him. They had similar attitudes and were both writers. She had written a book and had an English degree that afforded her this job at the convenience store.

She was reading a bound manuscript when I placed my coffee on the counter.

"Dollar-five," she said without looking up. I placed the money in her outstretched palm.

"May I ask what you're reading?"

"It's my boyfriend's screenplay."

"Is it called *Somebody up There Owes Me?*"

She finally looked up at me.

"Yeah."

"Vincent hasn't given that to me yet. Maybe I should be jealous."

"Are you Harlan?"

"Yeah. Harlan Eiffler. And you're Jane."

"Yeah. Vincent talks about you all the time. How's Monica?"

I laughed.

"She's great. I wish we lived closer to each other, though."

"What are you doing out so late all dressed up?"

As usual, I wore a slim-fitting suit with the tie loosened. At this point, I had dozens of these suits, mostly dark brown or gray, and hundreds of ties. I had also begun wearing a derby hat on occasion, admittedly because my hairline was receding. I suppose it would've helped if I had stopped slicking back my hair, but this hairstyle had become an important part of my persona.

"These are my work clothes. I'm working. And I'm actually out to see you."

"Oh?"

"Yeah. I have a proposition to make."

"That sounds weird."

"I agree. It's going to get weirder, though. May I have a few minutes of your time?"

"I guess."

"Jane, I hate to ask you this. I really do, but I have to. To put it bluntly, you are sucking the creative spirit out of my client, and I want to ask you if you'd consider refraining from seeing him."

"What do you mean?"

"I'd like for you to break up with Vincent."

"Would you?"

"If you grant me this request, you will be handsomely compensated."

"Go to hell, you bastard."

"I deserve that, I suppose. But you should know that you can name any figure you'd like. I already have a contract with a blank space waiting for your price."

"You're ridiculous."

"It can be one lump sum or a monthly salary of any amount your heart desires."

"No, asshole."

"Very well. Here's my card. If you should change your mind for whatever reason, I want you to call me."

"I won't."

"As you wish. But please, I ask that you not tell Vincent about this."

"Oh, I'm telling him."

"Jane, please. I beg of you. I'm only looking out for him. It's my job to make sure he's the best artist he can possibly be. I swear that I care about him. I know I sound like a hypocrite, but I care about him. If you tell him about this, all you'll do is break his heart."

"I thought that's what you wanted."

"No. It's not what I want at all."

We heard the door swing open and turned to see Vincent entering. He was tightly wrapped in a long black wool overcoat and wore his usual brown work boots, the kind that an old-fashioned farmer would wear. It was 4 a.m. I had assumed he had already made his nightly visit, but his appearance happened to be convenient for my purposes.

"Hey," I said.

"What are you doing here?" he asked.

"I couldn't sleep, and I wanted to meet your girlfriend. I figured this is the only way I could meet her since you never have me over anymore."

"Oh. Well, Jane, this is Harlan."

"I know. Vincent, this man came in here and—"

"Jane, please," I interrupted. "Let me be the one to tell him. I just told Jane that I could easily get her manuscript in the hands of an editor at

Globe Books. All she has to do is give it to me."

"I told you he was the best," said Vincent.

"Don't say that," I said. "I'm the worst."

"No way. This man is the closest thing to family I have. He's been with me through it all." He patted me on the back.

Vincent headed over to the coffeepot. I gave the quiet signal to Jane. She rolled her eyes and nodded.

I hung around until Vincent was done visiting. I insisted that he let me give him a ride home, saying it was dangerous to be walking around so late.

"You aren't interested in my girlfriend, are you?" Vincent asked me in the car.

"Lord no. Why would you say that?"

"I sensed some weirdness in there."

"I was afraid you'd think something like that. I knew it had to be strange for you to walk in and see me. But, honestly, I just wanted to meet her. She's what you've chosen the last few months over writing, and I just wanted to see what was so special about her."

"Did you see what was so special about her?"

"Yes."

"What?"

"Like you said, she's different from other girls."

I stopped at a red light.

"Hey, you know what we should do?" I asked.

"What?"

"Let's drink some whiskey like we did that one time. I've got some back at the hotel."

"But I'm not supposed to drink with my medication."

"Oh. That's an old wives' tale."

"I don't really feel like drinking."

"Please? I get so lonely in that hotel room without anyone."

"Well, I know how that goes."

85.

I proceeded to get Vincent drunk. At my hotel room, I had a bottle of whiskey from which I had been drinking very little. After several whiskeys and water, Vincent's tongue loosened.

"I've been meaning to tell you something," he said.

"What's that?"

"I'm impotent." I laughed and then apologized when I saw he wasn't laughing with me.

"It's that medication," he continued. It must have been a serendipitous side effect I hadn't planned.

"So you and Jane haven't consummated your relationship?"

"No. It's pretty embarrassing. But at least I know she's genuine. She's stuck with me despite the fact that we can't make the beast with two butts. She's so great."

"Do you love her?"

"Yes."

"Does she love you?"

"I think so."

"Do you realize that she's caused you to lose your drive? I mean, when you found out you had TB, you were a finely tuned writing machine. You were writing entire seasons of TV shows two years in advance. Now you don't get anything done. Don't you resent her for that?"

"Not at all. She's what I had been waiting for. She's what I had been writing for. Isn't that what all men are working for? For love? Isn't that the goal?"

"No. More like sex."

"Is that what you've been working so hard for, getting my stuff out there in hopes of getting laid?"

"No. I was hoping the stuff I got out there would entertain whoever's not getting laid. Entertainment means more to the loveless, as I can tell you from experience."

We drank some more. I flipped through the TV channels for the next hour. At around 7 a.m., we were shocked to see that an entertainment news program had a story on *Grocery Store*, which would be debuting later that year. The cast was attractive and included Bruce Willis as the boss. But judging by the dialogue, it appeared that Vincent's ideas had been kept intact.

"This calls for a celebration," I said. I opened my bottom dresser drawer, pulled out a paper sack, and held it up to Vincent.

"Have you ever heard of absinthe?" I asked.

"Yes. They were always drinking it in a Hemingway novel I read. I didn't think it was sold in America."

"Sylvain sent me a bottle. He's in rehab and had no use for it. I don't know where he got it. But I've been saving it for a special occasion."

"I shouldn't drink any," said Vincent. "I know I shouldn't drink something that strong on this medication."

"Hey, don't worry. I'll take care of you. Have one cup."

The green goddess got Vincent where I wanted him. After one cup, his eyes had a happy-go-postal look, and he cussed like a rabid seaman. I gave him another cup, while I gingerly sipped on my first. He was soon all id.

"I want Jane!" he screamed into my face.

"Okay, Tarzan."

"Gimme some more absinthe."

"I don't think you need any more. You were right about your medication."

"Give it here, goddammit, or it's gonna be like the *Hindenberg* part two up in here!"

I gave him the bottle, and he took a swig.

"I want Jane! Now!"

By this time, Jane's shift was over. I gladly agreed to drop the maniacal inebriate off at her place.

"Here you are, Vincent," I said as I pulled up to Jane's house. "Go on in and have a good time with your lady. Call me if you need me."

I watched him stagger to her front door. She let him in, and I drove away.

My inspiration for this scheme came from an accident I experienced as a teenager in which I ruined a relationship with my drunkenness. There was a girl I had feelings for who invited me over one night to her apartment. I was very nervous to be alone with her and vomited my dinner beforehand. To abate my nerves, I added a copious quantity of whiskey to my empty stomach.

I had failed to consider that I had recently begun taking a medication for my anxiety and depression, a medication that apparently didn't coincide with excessive drinking. I had always handled my liquor well before, but this time I lost all control of myself. I even blacked out. The next day I was told I had been a scoundrel and had said things that I was astounded my own voice box could produce. I felt awful, and she never forgave me.

About an hour after dropping Vincent off, I called Jane.

"Hello, Jane. This is Harlan Eiffler. I was just wondering if you've given any more thought to my proposal."

"Come get your client. He's passed out on the lawn," she said. "And bring your stupid contract."

86.

Vincent hated himself. I told him that Jane informed me he went berserk. After Jane denied him a kiss, he threw a tantrum. She showed me the evidence: a kicked-in television screen, broken dishes, slashed stereo speakers, and marks on her arm where he grabbed her. He also verbally abused her, making vicious personal attacks that she considered unforgivable. She said she was afraid she had seen the real Vincent and could no longer look at him the same way. She wouldn't take any of his calls or reply to his long, handwritten apologies. A month later, she was living in New York City with a book deal on the table.

And so The Sadness came back for Vincent, dark as ever. He resumed his isolation in his sloppy apartment. For months, nothing fazed The Sadness, not the appearance of Art TV, not the numerous musicians who were making number-one hits of his songs, not even the success of Grocery Store. Critics overlooked the commerce built into the show since the writing was so sharp. Audiences overlooked the show's lack of action or excitement since the cast was so sexy.

Vincent was not sexy. Vincent was a malodorous wreck. At least he was now writing frantically and obsessively, mostly things inspired by Jane. But he was exhausting himself. I told him to stop working so hard, but he wouldn't listen. He was hell-bent on purging himself of pain. When he wasn't writing, he was making up chord progressions on his guitar that made him cry, playing them over and over.

After his scene at Jane's, he refused to take any more medication. He said he'd prefer to die. But so abruptly stopping the amphetamine likely caused even more depression. And even without the medication, he still had trouble sleeping. He said his brain wouldn't shut up.

He turned to drinking again. I refused to buy him alcohol, but he found that he could buy it himself without getting carded. His swooping, waving black hair had begun to turn gray. He looked old, beaten down, and grizzled, and alcohol became the only thing he spent his money and time on. The rest of his earnings continued to go to his siblings, who were likely leading much happier lives than he.

One night when I went over and watched *Grocery Store* with him, which I did every week, he suddenly picked up the shot glasses lying on the floor and threw them one by one at the wall.

"Why'd you do that?" I asked.

"I need to stop drinking. I wrote that episode when I was sober. I can't write that well anymore. I can't do anything anymore."

But the next time I came over, he was drinking shots of whiskey from one of his old pill bottles. Throughout that winter, this medicine bottle, an orangish brown one with the prescription label on it, was always within Vincent's reach. His trademark medicine bottle shot glass was at his side the night I found him lying unconscious on the living room floor, wrists bleeding, torn scripts scattered all around him.

VIII. CINDY

87.

"Vincent?..."

His purplish eyelids flickered and opened, and his weak brown eyes adjusted to the eerie hospital lighting. He languidly pushed his hair off his brow and raised himself up a bit on the half-reclined bed. He looked drained, like the fabric of his hospital gown was all that held him together. Seeing him like this made me feel sick. I wanted to vomit. I pictured myself on my knees with my sweaty head in a toilet, desperately expelling my insides, and I thought about how this position was my appropriate place in the world.

"Hey," I said, standing over him.

"Hey."

"How are you?"

"I don't know." He looked at the bandages wrapped around his wrists. "I'm sorry about this."

"Shh. It's okay."

He had been in and out of consciousness since I had found him the previous night. He was heavily sedated upon this visit the following evening.

"Why didn't I die?" His voice was hushed and shaky.

"I came over when you wouldn't return my calls, and I found you and took you here. You bled all over my car."

"Thanks for saving me."

"Don't mention it."

"Sorry about bleeding in your car. I guess I shouldn't have done it that way. I should have drunk something. But Malcolm Lowry drank a bottle of shaving lotion, and Billy Joel drank furniture polish, and it didn't work for either of them."

"Can I get you anything?"

"No."

"I should probably let you rest."

"No. Please don't go."

I sat down by the window in the big vinyl chair intended to serve as a bed for overnight visitors.

"Do you want to watch TV?" I asked.

"No. I'd rather talk."

"Okay."

We said nothing for two minutes. Vincent finally looked over at me and ended the silence.

"If I had owned a gun, I would've shot myself through the heart. Oh, wow. Who sent those flowers?"

There was a gigantic arrangement of white orchids by the window.

"Foster Lipowitz," I answered.

"Really? I didn't think he even knew of me."

"Sure he does. According to Sylvain, he's a big fan of yours, and he wants to meet you and me before he dies. That should be fairly soon."

"That's nice. But Harlan?"

"What?"

"Are you mad at me?"

"No. I'm mad at myself. I pushed you too much."

"No you didn't. I like being pushed."

"Well, I'm not going to push you any more."

Vincent tried to wiggle his index finger underneath his wrist bandages, presumably to feel the stitches.

"Can I ask you why you did it?"

"Typical reasons. I hated my life and such. I felt lonely and got to thinking about things. I couldn't even write. It all got me feeling worthless." He gave up on trying to get underneath the bandages and lay both arms at his side.

"You shouldn't be so down on yourself," I said. "Lots of people would love to have your life. You always have money coming in. You've been incredibly successful. Your writing has gotten to the public. You've entertained millions. You've even enlightened some. Your dreams have come

true. I never saw *my* dreams come true. I tried and tried but never got anywhere with my music. I never even got a single reply from my demo tapes.
I was convinced there was some postal worker out there who harbored a
secret grudge against me and that he was throwing away every tape I sent
out. Things never happened for me. But look at you. Look at all you've
done. And to be so young."

"I know all that. But you have a woman."

"Yeah, but it took me forty years."

"I might not have forty years in me."

"Sorry."

"At least I'll be able to write about this," he said, limply pointing to
his wrist.

A nurse told me that visiting hours were over, so I playfully messed
up Vincent's oily hair, which didn't feel right, so I straightened it, and said
good-bye.

"I'm so sorry about this," Vincent said as I was leaving.

"Stop apologizing. You know, Bertolt Brecht said, 'To be good is to be
suicidal.'"

"I guess I'm too good for my own good, then."

"Yeah, well, from now on you're going to have to be more like me.
I've been happy lately. And honestly, I'm no goddamn good."

88.

Vincent and I moved to Los Angeles a few days after he was released from
the hospital. We both decided he needed a change of scenery, perhaps a
sunnier climate. The relocation was also practical for business, and coincidentally, I would be closer to Monica. We left Indiana and never went
back.

"You denied me a chance to get to heaven, so the best you can do is
the City of Angels?" observed Vincent on the westward-bound plane.

"That's good. You should write that down," I said as I had said countless times before. "Are you serious about the heaven thing?"

"Yes. I think when you die you go to a place where you can instantly
recall any memory and relive it. You can relive something that happened
to you when you were two, even if you couldn't remember it when you

were alive. And also, you can relive other people's memories. You could be at any event in the history of the universe. You could be a spectator at Jesus' crucifixion. Or you could go to other planets and see their Jesus get killed."

He was getting excited. As his voice grew louder, the couple sitting across from us turned to watch him speak.

"And it wouldn't have to be just the past. You could watch what's happening in the present to all the living people, all at once or one person a time. It wouldn't matter because there would be no time. You could look a trillion years into the future. You could even see people's thoughts. But I guess you're too cynical for stuff like that."

"I don't know. How can you be so sure?"

"I always think about it like this. When I was little, I absolutely hated school. I had no friends. I was miserable there. The only thing that got me through was thinking about the summer, when I'd be home again. Of course, home wasn't that great either, but I got it in my head that once school let out, everything would be okay, and I'd feel fine. Maybe I was naive, and maybe I was just telling myself lies, but it didn't matter because it got me through. That's how I feel about heaven."

"How'd you feel when you came home for summer and your house was burned down?"

"I felt the same. Except from then on, I thought about home as being a girl."

I had once had similar thoughts on the way to Los Angeles twenty years before, when I left my mom and brother. I'd make it big, and then I'd be home.

"Do you believe in God?" asked Vincent.

"I wasn't sure until I found Monica," I said, slightly embarrassed. "Having her makes me want to believe It's entirely possible."

"You should write that down."

89.

When we arrived in California, I paid for Vincent's stay at Promises rehab in Malibu, where Steven Sylvain had been secretly staying off and on for the past year. Sylvain highly recommended Promises, as it was the best (or at least most fashionable) rehab center at the time. Such tortured artists as Ben Affleck, Diana Ross, and Robert Downey Jr., had convalesced at Promises.

Promises looked like a rich Californian's home and was like one on the inside with its gourmet chef. It was a large, Spanish-style stucco house with an orange-tile roof. When I dropped off Vincent, Sylvain was smoking a cigarette in front of the Promises house. A tendril of his hair waved in the wind. He wore a cow-print bathrobe, flannel pajama bottoms, and no shirt, exposing a tuft of gray chest hair and a faint scar. He limped toward Vincent.

"There's the man," said Sylvain, shaking Vincent's hand. "Vince, I'm so glad to finally meet my best client. I've heard so much about you."

"Thank you. I've heard so much about you as well."

Through the years, I had been telling Vincent all about Sylvain. He was also familiar with Sylvain's work. At school he had been instructed to avoid the action movie clichés that were so abundant in the *Blood Lust* franchise.

"You mean a lot to New Renaissance, you know?" said Sylvain.

"Thank you. It means a lot to me."

"I love that *Grocery Store*. And that new CD by Mahatmama. Beautiful songs."

"Thank you."

"Hey, Steven," I said.

"Oh, hey. What's up, Eiffler?"

"Not a lot," I said.

"Don't worry about your boy. I'm gonna show him the ropes and take good care of him and whatnot."

Sylvain winked at me.

"Vincent, why don't you go tell them you're here?" I said.

As Vincent dragged his luggage into the house, I pulled Sylvain aside.

"Listen," I said. "As far as I'm concerned, the project is over. It's already gone too far. Besides, it's obviously been a success already."

"I know. But that's not up to you or me, bro."

"I don't care. I'm not hurting him anymore. And I seriously want you to take care of him while he's here. Don't tell him to write. Don't tell him to do anything. Let him relax."

"Fine, but does he have some new stuff for you to be selling?"

"He had some new screenplays, but he ripped them up before he tried to kill himself."

"Doesn't he have them saved on his computer?"

"He's always written things out longhand."

Sylvain flicked away his cigarette. Vincent returned.

"My room's ready," he said.

"You know, I tried that myself, once," said Sylvain lifting up his sleeves to show Vincent the scars on his wrists.

"I'm sorry," said Vincent.

"I was sorry to hear about you, too. Glad you made it, though. Just wish those screenplays and shit would have made it, too. Why'd you rip those up, bro?"

I gave Sylvain a dirty look.

"For one thing, I wasn't happy with them," said Vincent. "But also, I didn't want a bunch of whores to profit off of them after I was gone."

I patted Vincent on the back, said good-bye, and watched Sylvain lead him into the stylish sanatorium.

90.

Vincent adapted well to the asylum of rehab. He enjoyed decompressing with the Pacific Ocean and the Santa Monica mountains in view, spending much of his long days in leisure and reading at night. He made his bed every day, always cleaned his plate at meals, and even socialized, mostly with his new friend Steven.

"It's amazing what you've done to him," said Steve. "You can tell he's so smart, but he's got this sadness to him. And that was a nice touch giving him the gray hair. He's like this, I don't know, like this tormented young man from Russian literature or something."

"Actually, I'd classify him as more of a Byronic hero. You've read Russian literature?" I asked.

"Yeah. The kid's turned me on to some really cool stuff. I wish I had gone to his school, you know? It's like he has a Ph.D. in everything that ever was."

Steve, in turn, exposed Vincent to cardio workouts. As they exercised, they talked about their unhappy, fatherless childhoods, how Vincent was repeatedly forsaken by heartless beauties, how Steve used to skip from one cover girl to the next, and how both were perpetual losers in the game of love, but with different styles of losing. Vincent pointed out a pattern in Steve's relationships with women: Most had ended with him indulging in fleshly pleasures with strippers, which made headlines, seen by whomever he thought he loved at the time.

"But he helps me understand myself better, you know?" said Steve. "One day when we were lifting weights he said, 'Steve, I think I figured out what your problem is,' 'cause I had asked him to figure it out. So I said, 'Talk to me,' and he asked me how long had I been famous, and I said about twenty-five years. And he said, 'Well, your problem is that you have not had an honest moment with another human being in twenty-five years.' And he's freaking right. I haven't."

Vincent later told me that he had read this line in a *Newsweek* article on author Zadie Smith, who was quoting Matthew Broderick, who was quoting Marlon Brando.

"So I told him, 'You're right. Let's you and me have an honest moment right now.' And Vincent said, 'How do we do that?' And I said, 'I guess we should say something honest and real that might hurt us to say aloud.' I made him go first, so he thought for a while, and then he said, 'I hate my mother with all my heart.' And I didn't even have to think about it. I pointed to my fake leg and said, 'I miss dancing.'"

91.

Whether rehab truly helped Vincent in the end, I do not know. It kept him away from alcohol and steak knives, but it didn't heal his heartache. Not helping matters was Vincent's therapist, a woman I never met, who diagnosed him as a manic-depressive and who rejected him once he developed a minor crush for her. Soon after this rejection, Vincent checked himself out of the rehab center that had been his home for a month.

Vincent's radio and television success allowed him to buy a new condominium in L.A., which was larger and more expensive than his apartments and which had a better view. Meanwhile, I bought a new apartment as well, which was much more spacious than my hotel rooms but less clean. Vincent and I lived in the same part of the city, an area that was not overtly tony but definitely safe.

As I had told Steve, I would no longer take part in inspiring Vincent the way I had in Indiana. Monica strengthened this conviction. She told me she couldn't love me if I continued torturing an innocent boy.

Indeed, I told Monica the true nature of my relationship with Vincent. That's how much I loved this woman. I revealed to her my contractually sworn secret, risking economic and perhaps even physical ruination, all for the sake of an honest relationship. I hadn't even revealed the secret to my mother. Monica was the only person I ever told. She was appalled by how I had been spending the last twelve years but said it wouldn't stop her from loving me, further proving I had found my mate.

Monica wanted me to be nothing but kind to Vincent, and I complied. She was exaggeratedly kind to him on the few occasions the three of us were together. She fawned over him and gave him motherly attention, which he loved.

I told Vincent to be a kid and have fun, but he said these were foreign concepts to him. He concentrated on screenwriting, and his screenplays were mostly inspired by his relationship with Jane. The best screenplay he had written up to this point was titled *The Best of Days Are the First to Flee* and perfectly mirrored their doomed romance.

By now, probably about half a dozen of Vincent's screenplays had made the rounds in Hollywood. But even with Lipowitz's name attached, few agents or producers had been interested in investing in any of Vincent's unique visions. As with his music and TV writing, his screenplays could best be described as bittersweet. Vincent could see the sadness of laughter. He melded comedy with drama, often within the same line of dialogue. The results were offbeat, thought-provoking screenplays that didn't have the sense of physical excitement that Hollywood was so obsessed with. Nor did any of his screenplays glorify criminal behavior or have cool, likable villains. At best, two of his screenplays were optioned but didn't materialize.

By the time Vincent came to Los Angeles, the power of Lipowitz's name was waning. Making matters worse was his deteriorating health.

Around the time Vincent left rehab, Mr. Lipowitz left the isolation of his mansion to live out his final months at a nursing home for the elite. Sylvain told me Lipowitz would be requesting my and Vincent's presence "any day now."

Nevertheless, Vincent's name was on the rise, and Sylvain was able to get the attention of the producers of our choosing once they knew they were dealing with the creator of the wildly successful *Grocery Store*, not to mention the mind behind some of the best albums of the past three years. Of particular interest to producers was his connection to Chad, *People Magazine*'s latest "Sexiest Man Alive," who was also making headlines at the time for performing oral sex on two fifteen-year-old prostitutes, thereby cheating on his latest fiancée, Kristina Gomez.

92.

Nothing came from Steven and me meeting with these producers. The consensus was that Vincent's movies were too quirky and smart to be successful. In marketing terminology, quirky movies like Vincent's are called "tweeners." Because of their uniqueness, they fall in between marketing categories and are therefore harder to sell.

Several producers recommended that we pitch the movies to independent filmmakers who would be more likely to take a chance on "different" material. I didn't bother explaining to them that marginalized independent film audiences weren't what New Renaissance was after, and that our mission was to infiltrate the mainstream in an effort to improve the mind of America, a mind largely composed of the vacuous images and sounds of radio, television, and cinema.

Half a year passed without any progress in selling Vincent's screenplays. New songs of his were constantly surfacing on the radio, brilliant songs made hits by sensuous singers. Sexy actors and eager advertisers kept *Grocery Store* going strong, and Vincent had already written its second and third seasons. Art TV was still on the air and praised by one critic as "the best thing that has ever happened to television." And some of Vincent's other TV shows, including *Situation Comedy*, were now on the air. Yet he couldn't seem to write a sellable screenplay.

He became angry at himself, but more important, he became frustrated with the film industry. I assured him that Sylvain, Prormps, and I would continue trying to get his movies made and that he should continue writing new screenplays, if he could.

"But I've written so much that I'm starting to run out of inspiration."

I had been dreading hearing him say something like that, since it would normally be my cue to call Sylvain and discuss what devious stringpulling I could do next. But lately he seemed healthier and free of The Sadness; even his allergies had improved since moving to California. And I couldn't do anything that would depreciate my value in Monica's eyes. So I let it slide and hoped more traditional muses would assist Vincent.

"I know that can't be true," I replied. "You'll just have to delve deeper into your experiences. And I know you have enough experiences. You're the prince of unrequited love. You have TB. You had a horrible time at school. You had a horrible home life. You left home for good when you were nine. You've had a rough time ever since I've known you, all the way back to your dog dying."

"Poor Wynona."

"Yeah. Wynona. I always want to call her Toto."

A few seconds later, Vincent formulated the idea that would make more money than all of our other deals combined.

93.

I loved his idea. Steve loved his idea. Prormps and Lipowitz loved his idea. The idea worked on several different levels at once and could satisfy business and artistic types, lowbrow and refined audiences alike. Vincent had the screenplay written in two months, at which time Lipowitz managed to get Steve and me a lunch meeting with Bob Kuntzweiller, an old partner of his and the head of Dead Line Pictures. We had already unsuccessfully pitched *The Best of Days Are the First to Flee* to Kuntzweiller, but Lipowitz asked him for this one last favor.

We met at the Grill, a meeting place for the Hollywood elite that happens to serve food. Sylvain and Kuntzweiller ordered expensive wines, and I asked for water. The waiter listed options for bottled waters with foreign names before I clarified that I wanted regular water.

Sylvain and Kuntzweiller talked about old times; they had done sev eral movies together, including the first two *Blood Lusts*. They also talked about upcoming films on Dead Line Pictures, all of which had titles beginning with gerunds, such as *Taking Back Omaha* or *Seizing Stephanie*. Eventually the conversation led to my pitch.

"Well, let's face it," I said. "Hollywood is out of ideas. It has been for years. The majority of films this past summer were either sequels, adaptations of comic books and TV shows, or remakes of old movies. But it doesn't matter because unoriginality sells, and it sells well. So with this in mind, and with the state of Hollywood in mind, we would like to do a remake of *The Wizard of Oz*."

"It's been done. Remember *The Wiz?*"

"Exactly. All these new movies have been done before, and that ties in with the theme of Vincent's screenplay."

The waiter brought us our drinks, saying their names as he set them down. He proudly said "Chassagne Montrachet" and "Savigny Les Beaune" but made it a point to say "tap water" with utter contempt. I laughed and continued.

"Vincent's already figured out all the details. The casting is crucial. We want Kristina Gomez to play Dorothy. Colin Farrell will be the Scarecrow. Justin Timberlake will be the Tin Man to show off his dance moves. Russell Crowe will play the Cowardly Lion. And the Wizard of Oz *has* to be Puff Daddy."

"I like it. Sounds doable. Tell me more," said Kuntzweiller.

"Tell him about the witch," said Steve.

"Well, this is some bold casting, but you'll just have to trust Vincent and me. We want the Wicked Witch to be played by Julia Roberts."

"That's crazy, but I'm lovin it. And you know, the special effects possibilities are endless."

"Right. We want Toto to be completely computer-animated."

"Sounds great, guys. Sounds like a sure thing. I'm seeing the green light already."

"Okay, but there are a few other things you should know about Vincent's vision of this film," I said.

"Give it to me."

"Vincent sees this entire project as an extremely expensive piece of social commentary. He wants the movie to reflect the state of American culture and to satirize the type of entertainment that influences our culture."

"You lost me."

"Here's an example. Dorothy has her cleavage showing in every scene of the movie."

"Hmmm…A sexy *Wizard of Oz*. This could work."

"Exactly. That a sexy *Wizard of Oz* could even be made and released is Vincent's way of showing how mindless our culture has become. In a similar vein, we'd have a gangsta rap remix of 'Somewhere over the Rainbow.' The other songs would be horrible pop songs. And Dorothy falls in love with the Scarecrow, Tin Man, and Lion, which would warrant at least three sex scenes. And we want ridiculously long action scenes. You know that scene where the talking trees throw apples at Dorothy and the Scarecrow?"

"Yeah."

"We want that scene to last twenty minutes. It'll have some *Matrix*-like special effects. And things will explode periodically on the Yellow Brick Road for no reason. The poppy field scene will be full of drug references. And Dorothy and the Witch will have a violent fight that will end in a lesbian kiss. Basically, we want it to be so full of clichés and excess that it will be the Hollywood blockbuster to end all Hollywood blockbusters."

I didn't tell him that this is literally what we were hoping for.

"It could be social commentary for some people," said Steve. "But at the same time, at the end of the day, it would be a rear-kicker of an entertaining movie."

"Exactly," I said. "It would be pure, unadulterated entertainment. No values, no substance. Just entertainment."

"Hey," said the producer. "That could be the tagline."

94.

After we sold *The New Wizard of Oz* screenplay, my financial security was cemented. Further strengthening my income was my cut of Vincent's TV sales and CD royalties. Vincent's songs could be found on nearly twenty CDs, and as copublisher, I still received 25 percent of music royalties. From TV and movie sales, I received 15 percent commission as manager.

By law, Steve's cut as an agent was limited to 10 percent. The New Renaissance lawyer, Richard Resnick, was given 5 percent and as always, 25 percent went to reimbursing the company itself for the academy education it provided. After income tax, this left Vincent less than 45 percent, the majority of which he continued to send to his siblings. Had his mother still been in the picture, she would've been entitled to 5 percent of Vincent's royalties. But New Renaissance had heard nothing from her since she disappeared.

With such economic stability, there was no reason for me not to get married. So one night, I took Monica to the Los Angeles International Airport, the most romantic location I could think of, telling her I wanted to watch the people. We watched the people and planes come and go, and as one plane took off, I suddenly assumed the position on one knee, produced a ring, and said, "Monica, I've waited my whole miserable life for you. You are the smartest, funniest, most compassionate woman I've ever met, and I love you. Won't you marry me?" She said yes and cried. I almost cried as well. We agreed to marry the following year.

In the meantime, Vincent turned twenty-one. His birthday was in April, around the time *The Wizard* went into preproduction. My gift to him was a stained-glass picture of Garth Brooks playing Minor League baseball. To celebrate, I took him out to eat and to the Roxy to see the Strokes, one of his favorite bands. Afterward, I took him to an upscale bar, the Buffalo Club, where he had his first drink since his suicide attempt.

"So, how does it feel to be twenty-one?" I asked.

"The same."

We sat at the bar and stared at our drinks.

"Hey, there's something I've been meaning to ask you," I said.

"Okay."

"I was wondering if you'd be my best man."

His eyebrows slanted quizzically, and he smiled.

"You really want me?"

"Of course I do."

"It would be an honor."

"All right then."

"There won't be that many people at the wedding, right?"

"Right. Hardly any at all. Monica's family, a few from my family, and that's about it."

"Good. I'm so excited for you," said Vincent. "Monica seems like a genuinely good person."

"She is."

"And she's pretty, too." Vincent twirled his stirrer around in the ice cubes. "Do you think I could have another drink?" he asked coyly.

"Sure. But only because it's your twenty-first birthday." I signaled the bartender for another round. I noticed Vincent's eyes looked sadder than usual.

"Are you okay, Vincent?"

"Why do you ask?"

"You look kind of down."

"Will you still do things with me after you get married?" he asked.

"Always. Don't worry about that. Hey—why don't we find *you* someone while we're out?"

"There's no one for me. And even if there were, I couldn't trust her. All my angels have been centerfolds."

"What about that girl cattycornered from you? She's alone. I saw her looking at you."

She had long blond hair and a low-cut dress and a form that could inspire a lustful grunt from even the most prudish of construction workers. Vincent waited a moment and then discreetly looked at her. She smiled at him, and he reflexively turned away.

"Dear lord, she's pretty. She's about the most beautiful girl I've ever seen outside of TV."

"Go talk to her."

"She's too much. I'd need another few drinks."

"Let me talk to her for you."

"No."

I got up from my stool. "Consider this a birthday present."

"Harlan—wait!"

I approached the solitary blond on the barstool.

"Hello. I'm Harlan."

"Hi. Cindy."

"Forgive me for being forward, but my friend over there thinks you're the most beautiful woman he's ever seen, and he'd like to talk to you."

"You mean the guy that looks like Edward Scissorhands?" She looked in Vincent's direction. I laughed.

"Yeah."

"Why won't he talk to me himself?"

"He's shy."

"I normally don't work well with shy guys."

"Oh. Do you ever watch the show *Grocery Store?*"

"Yeah."

"He created it. He's written every episode."

"Really? I love that show. Does he know the guy that plays Neil?"

"No, but he was best friends with the real Neil."

"Is the real Neil that hot?"

"No. Why don't you go talk to him? His name's Vincent."

"Wait. Tell me more about him first."

"Well, do you like Dunce Confederacy or Mary Cecil?"

"Yeah."

"He's written most of their songs."

She laughed.

"Whatever. Now you're pushing it."

"I'm serious. He's extremely prolific. He's even got a movie coming out."

"Okay, fine. It's two grand for the night."

Her favorite musician was Chad, her favorite TV show was *Situation Comedy*, and her favorite movie was *Shrek*.

"Oh. Huh. Well—"

"Come on. That's pocket change for a guy who's done all that, right?"

"Yeah, but I guess I'd be the one paying."

"Whatever."

"Could you not tell him I paid you?"

"Sure, for an extra two hundred."

"Make it one hundred."

"Deal. I'll be his 'girlfriend' for the night." Cindy executed air quotes with her fingers as she said "girlfriend."

"I don't know about this," I said. I looked over at Vincent, who was nervously looking at the girl. He turned away when he saw we were both watching him.

I studied him as he took a gulp of his whiskey and water. I studied the tinge of sadness in his mannerisms, his pathetic posture, his almost longish black hair with its foreshadowing of gray, his gloomy but earnest expression, his frosty paleness, his trace of acne, his sunken, melancholy eyes and the dark lines encircling them, his blushing cheeks, his reddish lips, his scrawny neck, his wiry arms, his scarred wrists, and his shaky phalanges wrapped around his glass. For the first time, I saw him as a work of art.

"Well, it *is* his birthday," I said. I turned my back to Vincent and wrote her a check. "Show him a good time. And please, be nice to him."

95.

Kuntzweiller had immediately begun working on *The New Wizard of Oz* after our meeting. He faced a major obstacle when none of our desired stars were interested. But Colin Farrell owed Drew Prormps a favor, and he complied with Prormps's wish for him to be in the movie. With Farrell attached, the other actors were more willing, except for Julia Roberts, who was busy doing a voice for the animated movie version of Kafka's *Metamorphosis*. The Wicked Witch ended up being played by Meg Ryan.

Since Vincent and I had a clear concept of how we wanted to market the movie, I requested that I be allowed to personally oversee the advertising campaign. Luckily, I had a valuable colleague in Drew Prormps, whom I still hadn't met. Prormps still had allies in marketing at IUI/Globe-Terner, and with his assistance, I was able to portray the movie as I desired.

Thus, the movie trailers began with the following voice-over: "In a world where all movie trailers begin with the phrase 'in a world,' it is possible for even the most sacred and beloved of our cultural institutions to be rediscovered and made into ONE KICK-ASS MOVIE, BITCH!!!" Then the trailer shows a car exploding, followed by the Oz cast dancing in a pornographic manner on the Yellow Brick Road. Every few seconds, one of Dorothy's passionate love scenes is shown. Close-ups of her cleavage appear subliminally. Periodically, the music stops, and after a brief pause, a one-liner is said, such as when the Scarecrow is embracing Dorothy, and she says, "Is that a garden tool in your pocket, or are you just happy to see me?" (Music suddenly stops...Brief pause...) "Neither. I have an erection." (Music resumes.) The trailer ends with this voice-over: "Just when you thought Hollywood couldn't get any lower..." And then the Tin Man is shown sitting on a toilet, shooting a rifle at some scantily clad Munchkins.

The film itself overflows with blatant movie clichés. There is running in slow motion, fake-sounding punches, and cameos by professional athletes. There is a black guy yelling, "That's what I'm talkin 'bout!," idiotic shoot-out scenes, and a twelve-minute-long car chase in the Emerald City. There is even an opportunity for the Cowardly Lion to dramatically scream "Noooooo!" when the Scarecrow is violently disemboweled by computer-generated monkey men.

In another scene, Dorothy is held at gunpoint by the Wicked Witch, forcing the Scarecrow to negotiate. He says, "I'll give you all the money if you let the girl go." The Witch agrees, only to predictably double-cross him by taking the money and then shooting Dorothy. Thankfully, Dorothy kept a "lucky scrap of iron ore" in her bra, which deflects the bullet.

And there had to be a scene in which Dorothy falls off a cliff, but a tree branch snags the strap of the purse she's carrying, saving her life. A close-up shows the purse is in danger of tearing, but just as the last fiber breaks, the Tin Man grabs her hand. To add to the tension, while all of this is happening, a car falls off the cliff in slow-motion and then explodes.

A critic would later call *The New Wizard of Oz* the worst movie of all time, but the most important movie of the millennium so far, because "if viewed properly, it is a blaringly loud wake-up call for the entertainment industry and audiences alike to, simply put, stop being so dumb."

When it was released a year and a half later, the film was a mega-blockbuster and was accompanied by a merchandising frenzy that sickened me. People were buying everything from *Wizard of Oz* 'do rags to ruby red flip-flops. But our movie served its purpose, because the industry understood its message, and the film's producer, director, and actors received gobs of bad press for destroying an American classic. Thus, the public was spared a bawdy, high-concept version of *Gone with the Wind* for another two years.

96.

"My life is one long disease," said Vincent the second I opened my apartment door.

"What's wrong?" I asked. He came in and collapsed on my new couch.

"I think that Cindy girl gave me something."

In retrospect, paying this lady was a mistake. After her services were rendered, Vincent got no relief from his depression, only desperate guilt. He had been unhappy since it had happened, especially since she had given him a fake phone number, making it impossible to establish a meaningful relationship. I prefer not to dwell on what their fleeting relations provided for, except that it was the same gift spread to the Western world by Columbus's men returning from their first conquest.

"To be so nasty, it's such a beautiful word. I've read that somewhere," said Vincent upon returning to my apartment after our visit to the doctor. "Syphilis. Requited syphilis. I'm tubercular and syphilitic."

Vincent made a melody to fit the words "tubercular and syphilitic." He sang it over and over again until the phone rang.

I answered. It was Steve.

"Mr. Lipowitz is ready to see you and Vincent," said Steve.

"Right now?"

"Yeah. He isn't going to make it much longer."

"Have you visited him?"

"No. He doesn't like having visitors. I think he wants to meet and thank you jack-rears before he dies."

Steve gave me directions to the nursing home, and Vincent and I left immediately.

"You won't tell him about my problem, will you?" asked Vincent in the car.

"No, but he probably already knows," I joked. Actually, Lipowitz stopped requiring me to send him Vincent's medical charts a few years earlier.

97.

We arrived at Goldencrest Nursing Home that evening. Goldencrest was a nursing home for the rich, resting on twenty-five acres of well-kept lawn and botanical landscaping. It also had a golf course. On the inside, aside from the gourmet chef, it was like any other nursing home with paneled ceilings, bright lights, white floors, beige walls, and the smell of feces and disinfectant. Vincent and I signed in, and a nurse gave us Mr. Lipowitz's room number.

In no hurry, we walked deeper into the nursing home. Vincent waved to an old woman holding a doll and received no response.

"God, I hate nursing homes," I said. I had spent a good fragment of my teenage years at nursing homes when several of my relatives, including my dad, were dying.

As we walked down the corridor leading to Lipowitz, I couldn't stop myself from looking into each room. I noticed Vincent did the same. Each room was depressing in its own way. The figures resting in the rooms were haunting shapes. Some moaned and cried for help. Bodies contorted into painful positions, mouths gaped open wildly, eyes reached out madly, and skeletal limbs tightly wrapped in veins dangled off the edges of beds. Bathrobes fit incorrectly, as if they didn't want to be involved in that person's wardrobe. A slipper, sometimes two, covered bluish feet. The occupants of these rooms barely looked human. I felt like a captive on a sterile alien spaceship docked on California soil.

At the end of the hall was Mr. Lipowitz's room. His door was ajar, and his lights were out.

"He must be asleep," I said. "Let's leave."

"No," said Vincent. "We should go in. He's expecting us, isn't he?"

Vincent pushed the door open, allowing the hallway light to spread across the room. In the middle of the room was a closed curtain. Vincent slid the curtain back to reveal a bed and several large blinking machines. On the bed, Mr. Lipowitz had been left lying naked, his withered genitals available for all to see.

98.

He was indeed asleep, curled into the fetal position on an adjustable bed he was unable to adjust because his body was broken down from bowels to fingertips. With his bald little head, he reminded me of a baby bird. His toothless beak looked stuck in a yawn, and I could hear him breathing.

Vincent turned on the light, but Lipowitz remained asleep. Vincent approached his bed and pulled a sheet over his emaciated body.

"Mr. Lipowitz?" he said quietly.

Lipowitz instantly awakened and looked up at Vincent. His eyes were wide and round and had a noticeable accumulation of crust in their corners.

"Oh. Hi. I'm Vincent Spinetti."

"Hello, Vincent," said Lipowitz. His voice was surprisingly strong and deep. He grunted as he turned over on his back. "And we have Harlan Eiffler over there."

I walked over to his bed and wondered if I should shake his hand.

"Hello, Mr. Lipowitz. It's so nice to finally meet you."

He offered a limp hand. I shook it lightly and let go immediately.

"Call me Foster."

He craned his head toward us and closed his eyes.

"Both of your hearts are beating *so* fast," he said.

Vincent and I exchanged a puzzled look.

"It's these hearing aids," said Foster. "Most expensive on the market. If it's quiet and if they're standing close enough, I can hear people's hearts. Especially if they're beating loud enough."

Vincent and I scooted back from the bed. Foster laughed and coughed at the same time.

"If I turn 'em up all the way, and if I concentrate hard enough, I could hear your thoughts."

I laughed nervously. Foster's face suddenly contorted with disapproval. I feared he was mad at me for laughing.

"I think those goddamn nurses left me here naked after they changed my bed."

"Can we do anything for you?" asked Vincent.

"You could raise my bed up for me."

He pointed a clawlike finger at a control lying at the foot of his bed. Vincent pressed the button, and the top half of the bed slowly folded upward with a mechanical hum. The bed sheet draped down on his lap, allowing me to clearly see eight electrodes hooked up to his bony chest. He also had a feeding tube protruding from his shallow stomach, an IV coming from his arm, and tubes running from his nose. All of these tubes and wires tangled around each other and ran to the machines and computers on both sides of his bed. I imagined the entire building being powered by his body.

Foster was now situated. He smiled at Vincent.

"Vincent, how are you doing these days?"

"I'm doing better, thanks."

"That's good to hear. I wanted to thank you for all you've done for us before I died. You've already left a legacy for us all." He looked at me. "He was the right one for this, wasn't he? Been through so much, and he's come out blameless and upright. Hasn't he, Harlan?"

"Yes, sir. He's the best."

"Thanks," said Vincent. "And I want to thank you for the opportunities you've given me. I had a fine education, and thanks for all you've done for me through the years."

"Don't thank me. Harlan's the one who's done all the dirty work. Harlan, I want you to know that your work hasn't gone unnoticed, either. I'm grateful for you, too. I know you were beginning to wonder when I would recognize you."

"Uh, to be honest, I had begun to wonder if you even existed," I said with a laugh. "I've been wanting to contact you for ages, but Sylvain and Prormps wouldn't let me. The only evidence I had of your being alive was that letter you sent me."

"What letter?"

"Well, I guess it was about fifteen years ago. It was a letter telling me all about New Renaissance and why I should take the job."

"Drew Prormps wrote that."

"Oh."

"He always handled most of the actual work. I'm more of a figurehead. I came up with the idea. I funded it all. I made the big decisions, and I got things the way I wanted them. But Prormps handled most of the paperwork and business side of it all. I trust he'll make a good successor."

We talked about all of Vincent's creations that had reached the public. As Steve had claimed, Foster was a fan of Vincent's. He complimented Vincent repeatedly, which Vincent relished until he saw that talking so much was making Foster weak. His voice was getting quieter, and he was coughing more. Vincent offered to recline the hospital bed, and

Foster allowed him to.

"Before I fall asleep, Vincent, I hope you realize how important you've been to the company. I hope you realize that you've helped," said Foster. "That's what I wanted to tell you while I still had the chance. Your suffering hasn't been in vain. You and the other New Renaissance kids have done a lot of good. But you've by far done the most. You've awakened a lot of people."

"Thank you."

"We better leave you alone so you can rest," I said.

"Rest in peace. I can do that now. It looks like things are better. That's what I wanted. Drew will say different. But I did it because I remembered something I had forgotten. I had forgotten about how I was in World War II. I was in a war but I didn't get killed, and I didn't kill anyone, and I didn't even get shot at a single time. You know why I didn't get shot at? Because I was playing music instead. I was good on the sax, so they let me be in the army band. I should have been killed like all those other poor bastards, but instead I got to play for dignitaries and soldiers alike, and everybody who just wanted to forget there was a war going on, even if they could forget about it for the few minutes at a time when we were playing. But I came back over here and forgot all about it somewhere along the way because I could afford to. Thank God I could also afford to make things better. I'm a lucky man. I bought renewal."

We told Foster good-bye, and he shifted back on his side and shriveled back into the fetal position. He died the next morning. I was informed of his death the same way all New Renaissance employees were informed: by fax. On the letterhead was the first place I ever saw the New Renaissance logo.

PART THREE

IX. KRISTINA

99·

Lipowitz's funeral was highly attended, though I heard no one present fell within the categories of family or loved ones. The attendees were predominantly business associates, and they were enough to fill the Temple Israel of Hollywood.

After the funeral ended, we well-dressed, nice-smelling entertainment types filed out of the temple in orderly fashion, following the plain pine box. When Vincent and I stepped outside, Steve whistled at us with fingers in mouth, causing most of the congregation outside to look in his direction. He hadn't seen Vincent for a while and gave him a forceful hug that nearly knocked him over.

"Hey, V-Diddy," said Sylvain.

"Hey, Stevedore," replied Vincent.

"Tell him, Vincent," I said with a smile.

"Okay. Steve, I wrote a screenplay for you."

"Get out of town, jack-rear."

"He did," I said. "He wrote the lead with you in mind."

"You rear-ball," said Steve as he pulled Vincent's slim frame in for another hug. "What's it about?"

"It's about a one-legged fallen celebrity who can't find love," answered Vincent. It's called *Impossible Woman*."

"I like it," said Steve, crinkling his brow.

We stood on the front lawn alongside several other huddles of men, waiting for the temple to empty so we could proceed to the next segment of funereal activities. On the sidewalk were a dozen camera-toting onlookers.

Toward the end of the line leaving the temple was a sharp-dressed man holding a digital camera. He had a handsome face and the suave demeanor of a leading man from a black-and-white movie. Behind sunglasses, he scanned the funeral crowd and smiled as if he were leaving a movie premiere.

"Did you see that freak in the sunglasses taking pictures of Lipowitz's coffin?" I asked Steve.

"Yeah," he replied. "That freak is our new CEO."

100.

While still on the front steps, Drew Prormps spotted Steve and waved. When he reached the bottom of the steps, he strode toward us, shaking a few hands on the way. Following him was an attractive young blond showing a hint of cleavage in her sexy black dress.

"Steve!" said Prormps as he approached us. "Is this they?"

"Sure is," said Steve.

Prormps was tall, slender, and distinguished looking. He wore a red pocket square that matched his tie, and I immediately noticed he had great hair. It was sandy brown and poofed up on top and appeared to have been recently cut.

Prormps turned to Vincent and greeted him, handshaking with both hands.

"You must be Vincent."

"Yes."

"Alas, I meet the marvelous boy. I'm Drew Prormps, the new CEO of New Renaissance."

"Hi."

"I just love your work. I'm thrilled to finally make your acquaintance."

"Thanks," Vincent replied.

Prormps turned to me and offered another double handshake.

"And you are Harlan Eiffler, I presume?"

"Yes, sir."

I instantly regretted calling him sir. He was not much older than I, maybe in his mid-forties, but he was the most urbane man I had ever met, and "sir" is what came out.

"Nice to finally meet you as well," said Prormps. "I believe we spoke on the phone once."

"That's right," I said. I noticed that a genuinely happy-looking smile seemed to be his default facial expression. His smiles were usually close-lipped and charming within the context of the rest of his well-tanned face and sunglasses. Prormps turned to Steve and offered yet another double handshake.

"How are you, Steve?"

"Getting better all the time."

"Oh, and this is Bridget," said Prormps, motioning an open palm to the blond. She bowed her chest at us.

"I'd love to get a picture of the three of you," said Prormps. "Three of New Renaissance's pioneers, together. And looking good, I might add."

Prormps turned on his little silver camera and stepped back.

"Vincent, I believe you're the shortest," he said. "Could you get in the middle, please, so I can have symmetry?"

With Vincent in the middle, the three of us smiled in our black suits. I'm sure all of our eyes were squinting because of the sun. I wish I had that picture.

After Prormps took the photo, we heard a commotion coming from down the sidewalk. A cluster of photographers and cameramen were walking backward, frantically taking pictures and yelling questions as their subject moved forward. The way this celebrity moved forward and the paparazzi moved backward in unison made them look like one big, flashing organism crawling down the sidewalk, like a loud, fierce mytho-logical monster spouting out rapid questions such as "How do you feel about Kristina Gomez marrying her backup dancer?"

"It's Chad!" exclaimed Prormps. "I told him he should make an appearance, and here he is! I'd love for him to meet you, Vincent."

Prormps left us to greet New Renaissance's biggest success.

101.

Prormps brought Chad over, and the paparazzi followed. As the camera flashes lit Chad's face, I thought about how photography isn't allowed in art museums since the flashes contribute to the pictures' fading.

Chad wore a black pinstripe suit and a chartreuse shirt, and as always, his pants pockets were turned inside out. These pockets must have been specially made for Chad; they showed cryptic symbols that matched his tattoos. His hair was now black with blond highlights, short and spiky. He shook Steve's hand and hugged him simultaneously, being photographed all the while.

"What's up, Sylvain?" said Chad.

"What do you say, Chad?" replied Steve.

"I guess we missed the funeral, man." Three young men and four young women stood around him, his entourage. "Tommy Lee had us over last night, and we're just now waking up."

"Chad, you've met Harlan Eiffler, haven't you?" asked Prormps, pointing to me.

"Oh, yeah, yeah. You were the one telling me not to party and shit. This guy's a trip. What's up, man?" He did something similar to shaking my hand, something cool that I didn't know how to do correctly.

"What up, Chad?" I replied, smiling.

"And this is Vincent Spinetti," said Prormps, pointing to the pale young man with the large, soulful eyes that were currently shifting their attention from the ground to Chad and to the ground again.

"What's up?" said Chad, coolly nodding.

"Hello," said Vincent.

"You're the one that wrote those songs, aren't you?" asked Chad.

"Yes."

"Those songs were cool as hell."

"Thank you."

"We should smoke some ganja sometime, maybe jam or something."

"Okay," said Vincent.

The funeral crowd had begun to disperse except for the gang surrounding Chad.

"We better get going," said Prormps. "My limo's in the procession. Why don't we all ride together."

Chad told all but two members of his entourage to wait for him at his house. As we walked to the back parking lot to Prormps's limo, a skinny middle-aged woman ran to Chad and hugged him. She had ridiculously large breasts and wore a tube top and miniskirt.

"Oh my God!" she shrieked. "I love you! I love you, Chad! I love you!"

"I love you back," said Chad.

"Oh my God. Hold on. Hold on." In a panic, she searched through her huge purse. "Dammit. I want your autograph, but I can't find a pen."

One of Chad's cohorts pulled out several markers from his satchel and handed the woman one.

"Ooh. Sign me, Chad." She pulled down her tube top, revealing a bit more of her chest. Chad quickly scratched out the four letters of his name above a breast.

"Hey, lady," said Steve with a grin. "This fellow here wrote a bunch of Chad's songs. Wouldn't you like his autograph?"

"Oh, yes! Sign me. Everybody just sign me."

Vincent smiled, and Chad expressionlessly passed him the marker. Vincent legibly signed his name above the woman's other breast.

"I recognize you, too," she said to Steve. "Sign me. Just everybody here sign me!" Chad's helper distributed markers to Steve, Prormps, Prormps's date, and me. We all dove in and signed the bumptious woman's chest. I couldn't resist drawing a penis on her.

102.

Vincent, Steve, Prormps's date, and I sat on one side of the limo while Prormps, Chad, and Chad's two male friends sat on the other. Chad didn't introduce these men. I gathered that the one with the markers was his personal assistant since Chad occasionally asked him questions regarding his own schedule. He ignored the other man, who sat silently holding a gold cell phone.

"What have you been up to, Sylvain?" asked Chad. "Haven't partied with you for a while."

"I've been staying at home, mostly. I think you party enough for the both of us. I'm sick of reading about your fanny every time you go out dancing."

"You getting jealous of the new generation of badboy, old-timer?"

"Oh, please, you jack-rear. You're an amateur."

"Shit. I'm gettin more ass than a firefighter after September eleventh."

I noticed Chad and Prormps's date exchanging glances. I also thought

I saw Prormps glancing at me, though it was hard to tell with him wearing sunglasses.

"Speaking of gettin some, when you gonna have another one of your parties, Drew?" asked Chad.

"I suppose when we have something to celebrate," said Prormps. "The last one was when your CD went platinum, was it not?"

"I think so. Your parties are off the hook, man. Do you still have The Hole?"

"Of course."

Chad laughed.

"You gotta have another party, man."

"You release another record that goes platinum, and I will. Have you started working on your follow-up?"

"Nah. Don't have the songs yet."

It had been four years since Chad's first record became a hit. He hadn't made another one since, as he was busy acting and setting up record deals for his friends.

"Vincent," said Prormps. "Have you written any songs for Chad's new CD?"

"No. Nothing has inspired me lately. But I can be working on them."

"Actually, I was thinking about writing the next record myself," announced Chad.

"Oh, really?" asked Prormps.

"Yeah. I can do it. A lot of people want to act like songwriting is brain surgery. But it's as easy as that." He snapped his fingers.

"It's only that easy when the songs are no good," I said.

With one hand, Chad rubbed his facial hair, a soul patch. He stared at me, visibly in deep thought.

"Hold up. Are you saying I couldn't write good songs?" he asked.

"No. But have you written a song before?"

"I'm confident I could if I just took the time to sit down and write one. I just never had the time to sit down and do it. I'm sure I could."

"Whatever you say," I said.

"Fine. Let's ask the songwriter," said Chad, looking at Vincent. "Do you think writing songs is easy or hard?"

"I don't know," said Vincent.

"What do you mean you don't know?" said Chad. "I mean, is it easy or is it hard?"

"It depends. Sometimes before you sit down and write, as you say, you have to go through things that—"

"Speak up, dude. You talk so quiet, I can't hear a word you're saying."

"Don't tell him what to do," I said.

"Was I talking to you?" said Chad.

"You wouldn't have a career without him."

"Man, you've always been all about the disrespect, haven't you? You oughtta—hold up."

A cell phone was ringing the tune of one of Chad's songs. The silent man holding the phone answered it. This was the first time I saw him move since we got in the limo.

"Hello?…Yes. One moment, please." He handed the phone to Chad, who said "What's up?" and began a spirited conversation with what sounded to be his girlfriend.

"Why doesn't he answer his own phone?" I asked as Chad was busy chatting.

"That's *his* job," said Chad's assistant, pointing to the silent man next to him.

"Oh, Jesus," I said.

"Harlan, let's not argue with Chad," said Prormps. "Not today."

"Yeah, all right," I muttered. Chad said, "Bye, baby," and returned the phone to its human console.

"Now, what was I talkin 'bout?"

"The disrespect," said Steve.

"Right," said Chad. "What's with the disrespect?"

I didn't answer.

"Look at how you dress, man," said Chad. "You look like you're from the thirties."

"You look like you're from this year."

"Duh."

"Gentlemen, please, let's tone things down a notch," said Prormps. "This day is about Foster."

"That's right," said Chad. "I'll show respect. I'll show you how to show the love. But the bottom line is I'm writing those songs."

"That's fine by me," I said.

We all stopped talking and stared out the windows. I remembered the last time I had been in a funeral procession. It was when my dad died, and though I regretted the circumstances, it made me feel important to ride in a limousine and have all the cars stop for us. I didn't feel like that this morning.

103.

Other than Chad's cell phone ringing, the burial of Foster Lipowitz occurred in a typically somber manner. Afterward, Prormps pulled Vincent aside and walked with him down a row of the cemetery. Chad and his employees had already departed; the assistant had called for Chad's driver to pick them up, likely since Chad didn't want to ride with me anymore. Strangely, Prormps allowed his date to leave with Chad, a matter that gnawed at my mind more than the fact that Vincent and Prormps were having a private conversation.

"I'm assuming Prormps brought that girl along as a front, right?" I asked Steve in the limo. "He didn't want to look gay in front of all these executives."

"No," said Steve. "They're actually dating. Drew's a bisexual. He's pretty open about it."

"Then why'd he let her leave with another man?"

Steve laughed.

"Drew's got a hundred girls like that. What does he care? It's good business to let Chad have one."

A smiling Prormps and a blushing Vincent returned from their walk. During the drive back to the funeral home, we discussed the future of Vincent's career. Steve and I agreed to concentrate on selling Vincent's older screenplays, which shouldn't be difficult with *The New Wizard of Oz* on its way. Prormps added that he had some exciting ideas for New Renaissance that he'd eventually be unveiling, big ideas that could affect Vincent's career and even change his life.

"But for now," he said. "Let's continue with business as usual."

When we arrived at the funeral home, Prormps asked to have a word with me. He and I stayed behind in the limo while Steve and Vincent loitered in the parking lot.

"Harlan, I just wanted to make sure that you and I are on the same page."

"Okay."

He scooted closer to me, causing the leather seat to squeak.

"You do know that just because Mr. Lipowitz has passed away doesn't mean that our special project will stop, right?"

"I had already stopped anyway," I replied.

"That's what I was afraid of. I was asking Vincent what he had been writing lately, and he said you had been telling him to relax and take a break. So why the new approach?"

"Well, Vincent tried to kill himself a while back."

"Right. Steve told me about that."

"So that's why. We went too far. We put him through enough, and we have plenty to show for it."

"We really do, don't we? I have newfound faith in mainstream audiences."

"Yeah. So anyway, I don't want to hurt Vincent anymore."

"See, here's the thing, Harlan. I totally see where you're coming from, but I'm thinking, we've gone this far, why not go ahead and take it to the next level?"

"What do you mean by that?"

"I'm not quite certain, but I'm thinking Vincent is a legend in the making. He has potential to be a demigod someday. An icon. The ultimate tortured artist. Now that I've met him, I can see he even has the perfect look for the role. The poor thing looks unhealthy."

"But we're not supposed to let the artists get famous. That's one of the cornerstones of New Renaissance philosophy."

"Right. But what if he were dead? It wouldn't matter then, would it? After all, the ultimate characteristic of a tortured artist, the key feature that solidifies their legend, is for them to die young, correct?"

I shuddered.

"Do you plan to kill him?" I asked.

Prormps laughed heartily.

"No. But he *will* die someday. I'm thinking long-term. That's what New Renaissance is all about, right? Longevity and posterity, not just box office charts and Nielsen ratings. Look, what I'm getting at is that for right now he just needs to give us more. More for New Renaissance and more for his legacy. He's obviously great. Everything he's done so far has been hot, but it's just that we need more. He gets better with each thing he writes, don't you think?"

"Sure."

"So I think he's just now reaching the apex of his artistic heights. I talked to him back at the cemetery to see where he's at right now, and I definitely detected *Kunstlerschuld*, or as I'm sure you know, artist-guilt, and that's bad for us, because he's come to the point to where he's considering the option of choosing life over art."

I was angry that he used a word I had never heard before.

"Well, if it makes you feel any better, I inadvertently arranged for Vincent to catch a case of syphilis," I said.

"Hey, that's something," said Prormps with a laugh. "Maybe he'll end up losing a limb to syphilis like Rimbaud!"

"Rimbaud isn't comparable to Vincent," I said. "Rimbaud was not a tortured artist so much as he was a little slut."

"Indeed. There is a fine line between the tormented and the dissolute."

"Yeah, I found that out in my research."

"I'm sure you did. You've been a fine employee. Tell you what, Harlan. Just one more round of inspiration for our artist. Just one more good barrage of espionage, and then you're done. How about it?"

Prormps smiled, as he had been doing for most of the conversation. I looked out the limousine window and watched Vincent wave away Steve's cigarette smoke.

"Can't do it," I said.

"You're a man of conviction. There aren't many like you in our business. I guess that's why you've worked out so well for New Renaissance." He patted me on the back.

"Listen, Mr. Prormps, I'll tell Vincent to try to write more. But he'll just have to get his pain the old-fashioned way."

"That sounds good. We'll play it by ear. So enough business talk, what are you doing tonight?"

"Nothing."

"Oh, yeah? Would you want to come over?" He placed his hand on my thigh and my entire muscular system tensed up. "Do you like hot tubs?"

"Mr. Prormps, I think I'd better get out of the limo."

"Oh, certainly. And call me Drew."

104.

The remainder of Vincent's twenty-first year was peaceful and enjoyable for both of us. Business consisted of meetings with movie executives, perfunctory meetings that were tedious but preferable to the conscience-vexing sabotage I had signed up for fifteen years before. At these meetings, Steve and I sold three of Vincent's screenplays, and three more were optioned.

One of the three we sold was *Impossible Woman*, which Steve was set to star in. Another was the aforementioned *The Best of Days Are the First to Flee*. And the third was *Heartbreak Academy*, which consisted entirely of one eighty-minute class period. The movie took place in real time, and despite being about a typical day in a high school English class, it managed to have a plot and subplot.

My personal life revolved around Monica. We saw each other every night and usually stayed home and watched pre-1990s movies. I also liked introducing her to my favorite bands. She was willing to sit and listen to my old CDs and even liked some. I often had her favorite food, barbecue, ordered and waiting for her when she came over after work. We were the highlight of each other's days. In January, we finally set our wedding date for the Friday after Thanksgiving.

I didn't see as much of Vincent as I did in Indiana. I often extended invitations, but he said he didn't want to interfere with Monica and me. Just as I had told Prormps I would, I encouraged Vincent to write, though I was not as emphatic as I once had been. I never asked to read his latest works, and eventually we scarcely talked about writing at all.

Vincent's new life in L. A. was made more pleasurable by the fact that he had become rich. With the ever-increasing royalties and screenplay sales, I shared the distinction of affluence with my prolific client. Vincent continued to send his brothers and sister the majority of his earnings, but he still had plenty left over. Even with his below-average cut of the profits, too many sales had been made to keep his income down.

With money to spend, Vincent gradually began leaving his condo more. He went to clubs to see his favorite bands, he went shopping for books and records, and he even began frequenting bars, sometimes with Steve, sometimes by himself, promising me he'd imbibe in moderation.

His extra money also afforded him a new computer. He had ruined his old one a while back in a drunken rampage. On this new computer, he fell into the lonesome habit of meeting local women on the Internet. With his many accomplishments, he so impressed them that they offered to rendezvous with him at bars. He had fun with these women, saying in case he had TB, he better make the most of his time by living as much as possible.

It was around the time he was dating his third and final Internet debutante that Vincent called to tell me he had been badly beaten and didn't know why.

105.

According to Vincent, at approximately seven-thirty that night, someone knocked at his door. He arose from the couch where he had been watching My Mother's Men, a sitcom he had written that became a hit, partially thanks to the beautiful lead actress. He looked through his door's peephole and saw a balding, mustached white man he had never met before. He opened the door hesitantly, and the stranger punched him in the eye.

"I fell to the floor and yelled, 'Ow! What was that for?' But he didn't answer. He closed the door and waited for me to get up. Then he punched me in the mouth, the ear, and the other eye, and I fell down again. As I lay on the floor, I noticed he was wearing flip-flops with dirty white socks.

"I asked what he wanted, but he just kicked me in the face. He couldn't kick well because his flip-flop nearly slid off with each kick. When I dodged one of his kicks, his flip-flop flew across the room.

"As he walked across the room to get his flip-flop, I stood up and got a good look at him. He was kind of big and stocky, balding on top, but straight brown hair flowed halfway down his back. He was about forty and had a baby face. His mustache was encrusted with what looked like dried mucus. He wore basketball shorts and a Co-Ed Naked Volleyball T-shirt, and he was sweaty.

"So I asked him what I had done to deserve this, and the skank passed gas. I laughed, and he blushed and lunged toward me. He punched me in the back of the head, and I fell down yet again. Then he turned me over on my back, sat on my stomach, and punched me repeatedly for about a minute. All the while I cussed at him and attempted to fight back. But I finally decided to fake unconsciousness, and he got up and left, and he calmly closed the door behind him."

After he called and told me all of this, I immediately drove to Vincent's condo. Both of his eyes were swollen, his jaw and both cheeks were bruised dark purple, his nose was bleeding from one nostril, and his forehead was marked by an unsightly knot. I insisted on calling the police. As we waited for them to arrive, Vincent called to cancel the date he had scheduled for later that night.

"Hi, Denise. This is Vincent...Well, actually I've been beaten up pretty badly...I don't know. This man just came in and beat me up. Anyway, I don't think I'll feel up to going out tonight...Okay then. Sorry about this...Bye."

The police couldn't do much for Vincent. After they ascertained that taking him to the hospital was not necessary, they asked for a description of his assailant. Then they asked him questions but didn't get any of the answers they wanted.

"Do you have anything of extreme value in this condo?" asked one of the policemen.

"No," replied Vincent.

"Do you have any enemies?"

"No."

"Do you owe anyone money?"

"No."

After this last question, a possible explanation for the assault dawned on me.

106.

"I swear, Harlan, I didn't know anything about this," said Steve on the phone.

"Do you have Drew's home phone number?" I asked.

"Yeah, but slow down. Why do you think Drew has anything to do with it?"

"Because he'd want it this way. Have you talked to him recently?"

"Yeah. I talked to him yesterday. I talk to him every week. You know that."

"Did you talk to him about Vincent yesterday?"

"Well, yeah. He usually asks what Vincent's been up to."

"What did you tell him?"

"I don't know. The same stuff you told me about him. How he's kind of becoming a ladies' man. You know, I guess I *could* see Prormps doing something like this. I've heard stories about him before, but I never really believed them."

"What kind of stories?"

"That he's put hits out on people. Lipowitz did it, too, supposedly."

"You told me those were nothing but tabloid stories."

"I didn't want to scare you off."

"Jesus. Are they gangsters?"

"Kind of, only there's more money involved. Hollywood has always had a kind of *Godfather* feel to it, you know? The most powerful men in the industry, oftentimes, are feared men. They've built this aura of intimidation around themselves, and sometimes you hear about *Godfather*-type stuff they've done to scare people. I thought you knew from the beginning that this was serious stuff you were getting involved in. Heck, even you have already done some pretty wicked stuff in this business."

"Yeah, well, I'm already regretting it and probably will for the rest of my life."

"I know what you mean."

Steve then relented Prormps's home phone number, which I immediately put to use.

"First of all, I realize you're excited right now, but let's tone things down a notch," said Prormps. "Secondly, yes, I hired a man to assault Vincent. Is Vincent okay?"

"Of course not," my voice was thick with contempt. "He's over there black and blue, trying to figure out what he's done wrong. He even had to cancel a date."

"I'm very sorry to hear that, but you can expect regular assaults until he starts behaving like an artist again."

"Oh, come on."

"I know it's awful. I put it off as long as I could. I kept waiting for Vincent to write some more masterpieces, but a year has passed without any. So I finally hired that man. I didn't know how else to keep Vincent beaten down, except by beating him down." He laughed.

"Well, just so you know, I'll be quitting my job because of this."

"I wish you weren't so perturbed. I'm merely adhering to our original plan. Vincent and you weren't doing your jobs. And most important, his lack of creativity perfectly coincides with his choosing girls and shopping over loneliness and alienation."

"So? Look at you."

"Yes, but my job isn't to suffer for the sake of art. My job is being the CEO of a company that I firmly intend to make the most important cultural institution of the millennium. I cannot make this happen if my top artist has forgotten how to make art."

"How is having him beaten going to remind him how to make art?"

"He canceled his date, did he not?"

I let out a frustrated growl.

"You're going about this the wrong way," I said.

"How so?"

"You're not being subtle. You can do it without being completely brutal and inhumane. You're going for physical pain. Mental pain is what you want. It's far more effective."

"I would imagine so. But this is such a bizarre job. Who could do it the proper way?"

"Steve and I have become too close to Vincent. What about Lipowitz's lawyer? He's been in on it from the beginning. Why don't you make him do it?"

"You didn't hear?" Prormps asked.

"Hear what?"

"Richard Resnick is dead. He shot himself. It was in the last company e-mail I sent out."

"I stopped checking those e-mails."

"Anyhow, Richard is obviously not the answer. Regrettably, I suppose I'll have to continue hiring random men to assault Vincent. I hope they won't harm him beyond repair. I'd plead with you for help, but you've already quit, right?"

I could almost hear him smiling.

107.

In the past six years, I had been involved in the negotiations of around thirty deals. This one was by far the most difficult: According to its terms, I would offer my unique motivational services to New Renaissance until November 28, the day of my wedding. From that date forward, I would serve New Renaissance only in the capacity of a traditional manager, and our tortured artist project would be officially terminated. I asked for a written contract with these terms, and Prormps complied. I signed with cold, clammy hands, knowing I would be lying to Monica about not hurting Vincent anymore.

It was obvious to me that at the root of Vincent's creative slackening were the freedoms allowed by his surplus of money. With this in mind, I visited Orphan Aid, a local charity. I explained to the elderly man in charge that I knew a rich friend who had more money than he knew what to do with, and I was certain he would make a generous donation, if only he were prompted. The man said he would send my friend a brochure.

"I figure he'd be likely to give more if you called him," I said.

"We could do that," said the man.

"And I'd appreciate it if whoever calls wouldn't mention me coming here like this. In fact, I'll make a contribution myself if you'll pretend I was never here."

The man laughed.

"Sir, it sounds like you're paying us to collect money from your friend."

"Well, you always hear about people paying other people to kill somebody for them. I figured paying someone to do something altruistic would be a welcome change for this world. Isn't it?"

My justification for this plot was my personal experience of poverty when my band and I lived in L.A. I knew what it was like to not have a bed and subsist on leftovers and Captain's Wafers. Plus, Vincent would be losing his money for a good cause.

Vincent donated the entirety of his riches to Orphan Aid, the Los

Angeles Humane Society, Ronald McDonald Children's Charity, March of Dimes Birth Defects Foundation, the American Cancer Society, Promises Rehab, and the Los Angeles Public Library. As I had predicted, being the generous, guilt-ridden fellow that he is, Vincent made a large contribution to Orphan Aid, which led me to pay similar visits to these other charities. Vincent became accustomed to needy phone calls and kept his credit card handy until he could no longer afford to give.

108.

One Tuesday night in early June, I invited myself to Vincent's condo to see if he had been writing. His place was empty except for a TV set, stereo, and couch. Just two months before, his home had been cluttered with CDs, cassettes, vinyl records, magazines, books, DVDs, and video-tapes. But more than anything else, the twenty-two-year-old's condo had been littered with toys: vintage Teenage Mutant Ninja Turtles, figures from the latest *Spider-Man* movie, reissues of old *Star Wars* toys. They were all gone now.

"What happened to all your stuff?" I asked.

"I had to sell it all."

"Why?"

"I got myself into serious debt to a couple of credit card companies. I seem to have given some charities more than I should've. Somebody's been giving my name out to all these charities, but I don't care. I didn't need all that money, and I didn't need all that stuff. I lost all my stuff once before, and I know it doesn't matter."

"Do you need to borrow some money?" I asked.

"Not anymore."

We sat on the couch after I declined his offer of water.

"Your face has almost healed," I commented. There were a couple of gray remnants of the assault, shading caused by fading bruises.

"I'm still as ugly as ever," he replied with a smile. His phone rang.

"Hello?...This is he...Oh, hi...I see. I think I have Thursday open. Let me check my calendar."

Vincent pulled out a planner from underneath the middle couch cushion.

"Yes, I'm available Thursday…Thursday at 2:30…Okay…Oh, um, I'm sorry, but could you send a cab for me? I don't have a car, and I'm afraid I don't have enough money for cab fare at the moment…Sure. A limousine would be fine."

He gave the caller his address and hung up.

"Sorry about that," he said.

"That's okay. Who was it, if you don't mind me asking?"

"It was some guy from Fox. He said they love my work and want me to help develop a new sitcom they're doing."

"So are you going to?"

"I doubt it. I've been meaning to tell you, I've been getting a lot of offers lately."

"I'm not surprised," I said. "Your name is really getting out there."

"I'm sorry I haven't told you sooner. I was afraid you'd be mad at me since I've actually met with a few people."

I took off my hat and pretended to examine it.

"I'm not mad. You're free to do whatever you want. Just remember, if I'm not involved, you're not working with New Renaissance. No telling whose pockets you'd be lining."

"I know. That's why I haven't agreed to anything yet. But they keep calling me and tempting me. They call with these huge offers, and I just get a little curious. Are you mad at me?"

"No. Don't worry about it."

"Thanks. I had been worrying about it a lot. I want you to know—"

His phone rang again. He took the call in his bedroom.

109.

"I'm sorry again," said Vincent. "That was this woman that's been calling me. She loves my writing. It's weird."

He blushed and tried to conceal a grin with his hand. He hadn't been seeing anyone since his assault because his bruised face made him feel self-conscious. Part of me was glad to hear he had at least been talking to a woman.

"Do you like her?"

"We've never met, but yes, I do. She has a great voice, and I could use a new muse."

"What's her name?"

"I'd rather not say."

"Who is it?"

"You're going to make fun of me."

"*Vincent,*" I said, bowing my head, staring into his big brown eyes.

"It's Kristina Gomez."

"Gross! Are you serious?!"

"Yes."

I was dumbstruck. I couldn't have manipulated a better turn of events myself. It was a fluke in the social order and couldn't end well.

"I thought she was married to one of her backup dancers," I said.

"They got a divorce."

"Are you going to ask her out?"

"I already did. She's going with me to *The Wizard of Oz* premiere this Friday. Are you going?"

"I wasn't invited. I can't believe you'd be interested in her."

"I know. But a bunch of girls have been calling me lately. She actually seems to be the sweetest of them all. And she's not after my money or anything since she's rich herself."

"How'd she get your number?"

"Her agent got it from Drew Prormps. She said *The New Wizard of Oz* was her favorite movie that she had ever been in, and she loves *Grocery Store* and some of Spoon 85's songs, and when she found out the same guy had written them all, she had the urge to call me. So she did."

"Did she mention you writing her some new material?"

"No. She didn't even know I wrote 'All Out for You.'"

"Yeah, right."

"Please don't be like that. I realize she might be after something, but can't you see the appeal in this for me? I've felt unwanted all my life, and now the prettiest, most famous woman in the world is interested in me. I know it's dumb. But can't you see—"

"Vincent, I'll be straight with you," I said, twirling my derby hat on one finger. "If you want to date stupid celebrities, that's fine by me. And if you want to take any of these job offers you're getting, that's also fine. But the reason I'm here today is that Prormps is really getting on my case wanting you to write more. Have you written anything lately?"

"Nothing good. Steve's screenplay was the last good thing I wrote."

"Why do you think you're having so much trouble writing?"

"There hasn't been much to write about since I moved. I'll be the first to admit, I haven't been worth a damn since my life has improved out here. That's pretty sad when all your life is good for is material."

"That's not true. You seemed to be enjoying life a couple months ago before you got the beat-up. Didn't you have two girlfriends at once?"

"I only did that to make creative tension for myself. I purposely put myself between those two Internet women. It didn't work, though. It was better when I was on the losing corner of a love triangle."

"You told me you were living it up like that because of your TB."

"I was. That was the truth. But the TB makes me want to get more written, and to get more written, I thought I needed more women problems."

I needed to collect my thoughts, so I told Vincent to turn on the TV. He turned it to Art TV, where Ernst Ludwig Kirchner's *Self-Portrait as Soldier* was on display. I concluded an ideal opportunity for giving Vincent an effective experience would arise on Friday, in time for his first movie premiere.

"You know, it doesn't have to be like this," I said. "You wouldn't have to worry about the TB so much if you got back on medication."

110.

I went about my final mission with the vigor of a man who knows he's good at his job. I assuaged my guilt with the knowledge that I would likely never have to commit another of these duplicitous acts again, though I couldn't shake my pangs of self-hatred every time I lied to Monica about what I was up to.

My final objective was to prevent Vincent from becoming a Hollywood "It Boy" and to ruin any chances of him becoming a socialite. I commenced my scheme as soon as I left Vincent's condo that night.

I called Sylvain, who hesitantly agreed to cooperate with my plan. He made use of his old drug connections to find me a pharmacist not known for ethics. I visited this shady pharmacist late that night after his drug-store closed. I paid him handsomely for a bottle of placebo pills and a bottle of codeine, and no questions were asked.

The next afternoon, I visited Vincent's condo again to bring him his new TB medication (the placebos), which I supposedly had attained by having his old doctor call in a prescription. I assured him this medication was different from the troublesome pills he had tried before, and I even had the pharmacist print up a fake label for proof.

"Thanks for the medicine," said Vincent.

"You're welcome. You promise you'll take it?"

"I promise."

"Good. Now, put on your suspenders."

"Why?"

"I'm taking you to a stylist. Don't you want to look good for the premiere?"

I paid the stylist in advance to give Vincent the most ungodly perm that money could buy. It was curly, effeminate, and disgustingly flamboyant. It puffed upward and outward and made Vincent resemble a poodle.

"I hold you responsible for this," said Vincent as he looked in my car's mirror.

"The stylist did it," I replied.

"*Let him do what he wants, Vincent. He's a professional,*" mocked Vincent.

"Sorry."

Friday afternoon, when Vincent opened his condo door, I was surprised to see he was completely bald. His skull was bulbous and covered in scabs from his long-time habit of picking his scalp.

"What happened to your hair?" I asked.

"I couldn't stand it looking like that. I shaved it."

Vincent closed the door behind me.

"You look sickly without hair," I said as I handed him his suit. I had come over under the pretense of bringing him a brand-new suit.

"I meant to just give myself a buzz, but I messed it up."

"I can see that. Go try on your suit. Make sure it fits."

While Vincent was dressing in his bedroom, I looked for his coffee mug with the Hollywood sign on it, a souvenir I had given him after my first trip to Los Angeles. Ever since he had been keeping his alcohol consumption to a minimum, he drank coffee constantly. He was always in the process of finishing another cup, so I was counting on this favorite mug of his to be somewhere in the condominium. I found it sitting on the floor by his couch, half-empty. I pulled out an envelope full of powdered codeine and poured it in the coffee. I stirred it with a straw I had brought, and with that, my torturous career was over.

111.

That evening, I phoned Vincent to wish him luck on his date. I was actually calling to make sure he was okay. He angrily informed me he had "broken out all over." I offered to come to his condo in case he needed to be taken to the hospital. Vincent told me not to bother and hung up as I was in midsentence. I went anyway.

He was half-dressed in blue slacks and an unbuttoned white shirt. Large, pink welts covered his face and neck. He rolled up his sleeves and lifted up his shirt to reveal even more splotches that were highly visible on his fair skin.

As I had noted years earlier, Vincent's mother had told me her son was highly allergic to codeine. Admittedly, in causing this skin irritation and the bad haircut that rendered Vincent so blatantly unattractive, I was breaking my own rule. I personally had never had a severe allergic reaction to anything, nor had I received a perm that inspired me to cut off all my hair. But I had always felt ugly, and I compromised my rule only because I was confident this would be my last act of torture.

"I told you not to come," said Vincent.

"I was worried about you. Does it hurt?" I asked.

"No, but I'm feeling itchy and hot all over." He clawed at his back with both hands.

"You must be having a reaction to your new medication."

"No. I know that's not it."

"How can you be so sure?"

"I haven't taken any of my new medication."

I was angered; this was to be my explanation for Vincent's sudden affliction.

"Vincent, you promised you would take it."

"I *will* take it. But I wanted to wait until after my date with Kristina.

I wanted everything to be perfect for our first date, so I didn't want to start a new medicine until afterwards."

"Well, if it's not a reaction to the medication, then what is it?"

"I don't know." He scratched his legs.

"It's got to be an allergic reaction to something. Tell me everything you've done today."

"The same things I do every day. I got up at about 12:30, I attempted to write, I drank some coffee, took a shower, ate some leftover pizza, attempted to write, drank some more coffee, then you showed up. Then I attempted to write again, drank more coffee, watched TV, and then I started itching."

"Maybe it's from stress. Are you nervous about this date?"

"Very much so. It's Kristina Gomez."

"Come on. You're way more talented than Kristina Gomez. In a perfect world, you'd be more famous, and she'd be the one breaking out in hives over you."

We heard a knock on the door.

"It's Kristina," said Vincent fearfully. "She's early. What do I do?"

"Go finish dressing. I'll get the door."

112.

The first thing that struck me about Kristina Gomez was this: She didn't know me. I don't think a day had passed in recent history without me seeing her in a magazine or on TV. Albeit in a minor way, she had been a part of my life for the past eight years. I knew her well, almost intimately. I had even seen her naked. Yet she didn't know me in the least.

"Vincent?" she asked.

"Uh, no, I'm his manager. Harlan Eiffler."

She didn't introduce herself. I suppose she stopped having to introduce herself a long time ago. She would not have to say who she was for the rest of her life.

"Is Vincent here?" she asked.

"Yes. He's getting dressed. Please, come in."

Kristina entered the barren condominium. A large, bald black man in a suit followed her. Kristina wore a low-cut brown dress that slinked over her voluptuous frame and made no secret of her perfect tan skin, especially her belly. A hole had conveniently been cut out of the dress's midsection. Her hair was long and snaky. She looked all around the room.

"Is he *poor?*" she asked.

"He is indeed," I answered. "Please, have a seat."

Kristina sat on the couch and crossed her shapely legs. Her bodyguard remained standing.

"Can I get either of you something to drink? I think all Vincent has is coffee and water."

"No, thanks," said Kristina. The bodyguard shook his head.

Silence ensued. I didn't know what to talk about, and Kristina obviously wasn't interested in confabulating. She seemed preoccupied with her nails.

"You about ready, Vincent?!" I yelled toward his bedroom.

"Yes!" he yelled back. "Hey, Kristina!"

"Hey!" she hollered.

"I'll be out in a minute!"

"Okay!"

I sat on the other end of the couch.

"So, Vincent tells me you're a fan of his work."

"Yeah. I love what he did with *Wizard of Oz*. I can't wait to see it."

"We were really pleased with your version of his song," I said. "I guess he told you that was the first thing of his we sold."

"No. He didn't tell me, but I knew it."

More silence followed.

"Harlan, could you come here, please?!" shouted Vincent from his bedroom.

"Excuse me," I said, rising from the condo's lone piece of furniture.

I entered Vincent's bedroom. With his bruises, hives, and baldness, he looked out of place in a new suit.

"What should I do?" he asked, itching the top of his bald head.

"Go on out there."

"But look at me."

"You don't look that bad. Besides, she's already here. You can't tell her to just leave. This is a big night for you. Go on out there."

"But I don't want to frighten her. Will you please go tell her what's happened to me?"

"Just go on out there," I said.

"Please," Vincent pleaded.

I sighed and returned to the living room.

"Miss Gomez, Vincent wanted me to warn you before you saw him. His skin is a bit unhealthy at the moment. He's mysteriously broken out in hives, probably an allergic reaction to something."

"Oh," she said. "Is he contagious?"

"No. It's not that bad. Also, his stylist messed up his hair, and now he's kind of bald. He just wanted me to let you know that he normally looks better."

Kristina looked confused and scared.

"Exactly how bad does he look?" she asked.

"You can see for yourself. Vincent!" I yelled. "You can come out now!"

113.

"Hi," Vincent said as he sheepishly entered. I could feel the nervous tension he brought with him into the living room. He fidgeted in his shiny blue suit. He kept his hands in his pockets and didn't scratch himself. Kristina arose from the couch and studied her date.

"Hey," she replied.

"You look so beautiful."

"Are you sure you feel like going?" she asked.

"Yes. I feel fine. I'm sorry about this. You probably don't want to be seen with me."

Kristina looked at the floor.

"No, it's just—well, maybe you shouldn't go."

"I'm sure the hives will go away soon. For now, I can wear one of Harlan's hats and a pair of sunglasses if that will help. I've really been looking forward to this."

"I think I should probably leave you alone," said Kristina, still looking at the floor.

"Kristina, please. Would you at least want to hang out here a little while with me?" asked Vincent, also looking downward. "There's still plenty of time before the premiere."

"Thanks, but I think I'll go on and leave."

"But I was your date."

"I don't think I'll have any problems getting in without you."

"Oh."

Her favorite band was Spoon 85, her favorite TV show was *Grocery Store*, and her favorite movie was *The New Wizard of Oz*.

"Nice meeting you. Sorry about this." She turned and walked to the door, which her bodyguard already had opened. Just before her exit, she turned to Vincent across the room. "I'd love to do some more of your songs or have a part in another one of your movies. Have your agent call my agent when you have something for me."

Her posterior swayed rhythmically out the door. As soon as she left, Vincent threw his blazer on the floor and scratched himself violently.

"Sorry," I said.

He looked at me and said nothing, shaking his head. He loosened his tie and lay on the floor, occasionally scratching himself. He silently stared at the ceiling for five minutes and continued to do so even after his phone rang.

"Do you want me to get that?" I asked after three rings.

"No. I want you to throw my telephone away."

He jumped up from the floor and stood tall.

"And I want to be left alone," he said, looking me in the eye. "Tonight I begin my opus."

X. SHERILYN

114.

In keeping with our agreement to have the smallest wedding possible, Monica and I invited only our closest relatives and friends. I invited my mother, brother, aunt, uncle, and a few cousins from St. Louis. Monica invited more family than I, as well as a few of her girlfriends from Kentucky. I flew everyone to California. The only L.A. residents invited were Steve and Vincent.

On that sunny November day, I nervously paced in the backstage area of St. Victor Catholic Church. Vincent entered in a plain black suit, black shirt, and red tie that matched my outfit. He held a rectangular box wrapped in the comics section of the newspaper.

Five months after the incidents surrounding his first movie premiere, his hair had grown back, though now the gray hairs were numerous enough to threaten a Pyrrhic victory over the black. He looked tired and true to the fact that he had recently recovered from his second breakdown.

"Hey," he said with a weak smile. "How are you feeling?"

"I'm not sure. I can't stand this collar being so tight."

"Why don't you unbutton the top button and loosen your tie like you always do?" suggested Vincent.

"I shouldn't. It's my wedding. It might look bad."

"Here," said Vincent, unbuttoning his shirt. "I'll do it, too, so you won't look funny."

"Thanks," I said as I unbuttoned my shirt.

"Here's my wedding gift. Go ahead and open it."

He handed me the box.

"Oh, thank you."

I ripped off the funny papers and opened the box. I pushed aside the tissue paper to see a bound script with a mint-green cover.

"Whoa. Is this it?" I asked.

"That's it. I even typed it out for you."

I opened the cover to see the title page which read:

HARLAN AND ME

an original screenplay by

Vincent Spinetti

At the bottom of the page was an inscription that read: "Harlan, All I own, I owe you."

"Thanks. Course, you really don't own that much," I said with a chortle. Vincent was slowly rebuilding his bank account. I had stopped having the charity collectors call, and with *The New Wizard of Oz* becoming a box office hit, he would soon be on his way to economic recovery.

"You know what I mean," said Vincent.

"It's your writing that pays my bills. All I own, I owe *you*." I cleared my throat. "But enough pillow talk. Congratulations on finally finishing this. What's with my name in the title?"

"It was originally supposed to be my life story, but halfway through it, I realized I was telling your story just as much as mine. So I made you the lead character."

"I doubt I'd make a good lead. All I do is go to meetings and fill out paperwork."

"You're more interesting in the screenplay."

"Can't wait to read it."

"And I ended it with your wedding day. I took some artistic liberties and ended it exactly the way I wanted. I think that screenplay is the only thing I've ever written that I like."

115.

"There is only two letters' difference between 'worrier' and 'warrior.'" I remembered this quote, as it is my favorite line from *Harlan and Me*. The character based on me says the line to the character based on Vincent after the character based on Kristina Gomez haughtily exits.

In accordance with the events that inspired it, the screenplay tells of its scorned writer accepting the mysterious boils on his body and using his art to persevere through loneliness, poverty, and pain. The estranged young man feverishly works, writing defiantly, shirtsleeves rolled up and arms akimbo when they're not being used to strike lyrics upon page. His loyal manager/mentor constantly encourages him, and the artist pushes himself to the point of exhaustion.

Vincent viewed *Harlan and Me* as a last-ditch attempt to make sense of his life, his ultimate artistic purge, a one-hundred-thirty-page catharsis that, once it was perfect in its creator's eyes, might allow him to move on and live a normal life. "If I get this one the way I want it, I'm going to feel at home," he said.

As he worked day and night, he nearly lost sight of reality. He flirted with his breaking point for months. I noticed the margins of his notebook were becoming wider and wider, while the writing itself was becoming an increasingly narrower column of dark, jumbled prose. I remembered his writing taking on the same appearance before his suicide attempt.

His overwork was at the expense of eating and sleeping. By late October, he stopped talking, save for the phrases "Yes, sir" and "No, sir." I insisted on his hospitalization, and he was given strong medication that resuscitated his mind.

In the end, the warrior was not broken, and the carcass of his kill was neatly bound in a gift box, ready for my perusal. He stood by my side, his trust in his art stronger than ever. My best man.

As for my bride, she had beauty to spare, so abundant inside that it seeped through her skin. I looked forward to staring at her in the morning before she awoke from now through elderliness. Never had I seen a woman with such an equal balance of spunk and grace. My heart screamed "I do," and the girl was mine. I was the luckiest forty-three-year-old in this galaxy or any other.

We would live in my apartment until we found a house. I was giddy at the prospect of finally owning the place I could call home, a place with a front yard and a garden, and an extra-big backyard where curious little feet would have room to explore.

When I was a kid, my favorite place was my backyard. I liked playing, digging holes, and building a clubhouse for myself by draping blankets over my jungle gym. I had no ambitions because the backyard was enough.

Soon, I'd have a backyard again, complete with a wife and a home, and maybe even a little dog. It would all fit nicely with my normal job, which from this day forward stood the chance of being something I could be proud of. I would be Vincent Spinetti's manager, and there would be nothing uncivilized about it.

116.

"Congrats, lucky-butt," said Steve, shaking my hand at the reception at the Renaissance Hollywood Hotel.

"Thanks, Steve. Hey, I made sure the bar had some of that fancy Scotch you introduced me to. You want some?"

"No thanks, bra," he replied. He was now completely bald on top, and what hair remained was graying faster than Vincent's.

"You sure?" I asked. "It's an open bar."

"I've quit drinking. I'm trying to take better care of myself."

"That's great. Lipowitz would be proud of you."

"Yeah, well, I'm really amped up about this new movie, and I want to be in good shape for all the promoting and whatnot."

Vincent joined us, holding a tall glass of beer.

"Hello there, my little honky," said Steve.

"Hey, Stevedore," said Vincent.

"I was just telling Harlan, I'm really getting amped up about *Impossible Woman* coming out. It's something I can actually be proud of, you know? I mean, I didn't even have to take my shirt off in this one. And I have you to thank."

"I'll have to write you another one," said Vincent.

"Shift yeah! That'd be awesome." Steve noticed that I was staring at him disapprovingly. "You know, then again, why don't you take a break from writing? I know you about busted your rear on that opus of yours. Besides, judging by what Prormps told me, you aren't going to have much time for writing anyway."

"What are you talking about?" I asked.

"Ah, you don't want to talk business now, do you?"

"No, but I'll worry if you don't tell me."

"Tell us, Steve," said Vincent.

"But it might upset both of you."

"Now you have to tell us," I said.

"Fine. Prormps has this idea. Actually, it's more than an idea because he's got it all planned out and assures me it's going to happen. The whole deal is that he's tired of New Renaissance being this, he said *subversive* company, and he thinks we could accomplish more if we, like, you know, put ourselves *out there* more."

"What does that mean?" I asked.

"It means he wants to present to the media an actual event called The New Renaissance. He wants to put all his top artists on display and call attention to what they've done over the years for the entertainment world. He wants New Renaissance alumni to go on a promotional tour, he wants T-shirts with the New Renaissance logo on 'em, he wants books written on it, he even wants the New Renaissance TV special. He wants it to be this phenomenon, like some sort of happening like the original Renaissance."

"Unbelievable," said Vincent.

"I believe it," I said. "Seems about right."

"And that's not the worst part," said Sylvain. "He wants Vincent to be the New Renaissance poster boy."

Vincent and I laughed.

"I'm serious. He sees you as the marquee figure for the whole thing. He wants you to be world-famous and to promote you as, like, the modern-day Renaissance man."

"Well, I think that's my cue to turn in my resignation," I said.

"I hear that," said Steve.

"You with us, Vincent?" I asked. He picked at his scalp and didn't answer. "*Vincent?*"

As Steve and I stared at Vincent, Monica ran up and embraced me.

"Hey, babe," I said.

"Hey. Is something wrong?"

"Nah."

"Harlan, I could tell from across the room that something's bothering you. What is it?"

I paraphrased Prormps's plan for my wife.

"Damn," said Monica. "What is with that Prormps guy?"

"He smells money," I said.

"But it's more than that," said Steve. "I've known him a while now. I think he honestly thinks he's doing good and furthering our cause."

"It reminds me of when they brought Woodstock back," said Monica. "The tickets were one-hundred-fifty dollars, and Pepsi sponsored it. And then a bunch of girls were raped at it. There's no place for something like a Woodstock or something like a Renaissance anymore."

"Yeah. I'm not touching it," I said. "But Vincent's scaring me."

"Why?" asked Vincent.

"You haven't said whether or not you'll cooperate with Prormps. Surely you're not tempted, are you?"

"If he wants to do it, maybe he should do it," said Monica, patting Vincent on the shoulder. "It's not like he hasn't paid his dues. He should do what makes him happy."

"No," said Vincent. "Harlan's right. I don't want to be a tool. I'm with you guys."

"Are you sure?" I asked. "You can do whatever you want."

"I'm sure. I only hesitated because I was thinking that getting famous might increase my chances of finding the right girl. But then again, I'd probably just find more bitch goddesses like Kristina Gomez."

"Trust me, Vince," said Steve. "Fame's not what it's cracked up to be. Just like you said, I haven't had an honest moment with another person in decades. Which reminds me—Monica, I was meaning to ask you about that maid of honor of yours."

"That's my sister," said Monica.

"Really? She's not a fan of mine, is she?"

"Sorry. I don't think so."

"Then could you introduce us?"

117.

I remember the week of my honeymoon as being the best week of my life. The entire time I wore a boyish smirk that refused to go away, its perpetuation assisted by Monica's similarly inexorable smile. I made it a point to recognize and fully appreciate the sanctity of each moment because it was one of the few times since childhood that I was unmistakably *happy*.

We had decided to honeymoon in Las Vegas. We figured the glitzy city would have a campy yet classy feel that would appeal to us. I drove us in my six-year-old Volvo. I felt as if the road had been built just for our benefit, intended as a pathway from my apartment to our honeymoon suite at the Las Vegas Palms Hotel.

I rolled down the window and turned on the radio. I normally hated radio, but it now seemed tolerable. I heard the beauty in Black Sabbath. I could hear the laughter in sadness. The wind felt so good slapping my oily face.

Monica and I spent a substantial portion of the week in our hotel room, inseparably clinging to one another high above the Vegas Strip. When I had the chance, I read *Harlan and Me*, which I soon realized was Vincent's best work. I considered the screenplay perfect except for its unlikely ending in which the character based on me marries the character based on Veronica. In the margin next to this ending, Vincent inscribed, "I'm sorry to Monica about this. Just wanted Mom and me to have a happy ending, too. Is this selfish of me?"

118.

When we returned to Los Angeles, I heard Steve's voice on my answering machine telling me he had news. I returned his call.

"I went ahead and quit New Renaissance," he said.

"You did?"

"Yeah.

"What'd you tell Prormps?"

"I told him the truth. I told him I didn't like the direction he was taking the company, and that it's just as well because I want to start acting more."

"How'd he take it?"

"He tried talking me out of it, giving me a bunch of his rhetoric, but I stood my ground. He made me swear I'd never tell anyone about what we did to Vincent, and he wished me luck. He was nice about it."

"I guess Vincent and I should wait awhile to resign. We probably shouldn't all abandon him at once."

"Do whatever you want. I won't hold it against you if you stay. It's still a pretty cool gig, you know?"

"I don't like the sound of where it's going, though. I'll hear Drew out, but I'm through. Vincent and I will just have to go independent."

"Anyhow, I want you to know it was a pleasure working with you, Harlan. I know I sound like a girl, but I mean it. And I guess I can tell you this now. You were hired for this job because we thought you were a sociopath."

"I'm not a sociopath."

"I know, but you had the right profile at the time. We figured we needed someone dangerously antisocial but not completely psychotic. Anyhow, you ended up being the right person for the job. You kick my rear."

"Thanks. Thanks for everything. And keep in touch."

"Hey, just because I'm not Vincent's agent anymore doesn't mean I'll stop being friends with you and him. Make sure you tell Vincent that, okay?"

"I will."

"Oh, hey. Remember that maid of honor I liked?"

"Yeah. She's my sister-in-law."

"I took her out before she had to go back home, and I love her. I mean I really *love* her. We've been talking every day."

"That's great. That family has some good genes."

"I know. I never thought I was capable of—"

"Steve, I got a beep. Could you hold on, please?"

"Ah, that's all right. I'll let you go."

"You sure?"

"Yeah. I'll see you soon."

"All right, then. Bye."

"Laters."

119.

Drew Prormps beeped in to personally invite me to his party since he knew I seldom checked my e-mail. He would be throwing the party at his house that Saturday, and the occasion was to celebrate Chad's new record going platinum. Chad wrote all the songs on the CD, titled *Venis and*

Pagina.

Prormps said Vincent and I had to attend his party since we were so important in the making of Chad's first CD, which was still considered one of New Renaissance's biggest triumphs. After unsuccessfully rummaging my mind for an excuse, I accepted his invitation. He told me to bring my new wife and Vincent.

"I don't want to celebrate that record going platinum," said Vincent when I called him. "Have you heard it? It's an atrocity."

"I know it is. But Drew says we have to be there, and I already told him we're going. Besides, if we're quitting the company, I guess we owe it to him."

"We owe him nothing. I hate parties."

"I do, too, but we'll go suffer together. Maybe we'll find you a girl while we're there."

He agreed to go.

120.

Five days later, on Saturday, December thirteenth, at 8 p.m., Vincent and I passed through the copper gates of the Prormps estate. Monica couldn't go because she was stuck on the phone comforting her sister, who was distraught since Steve hadn't returned her calls in two days. "That's just Steve," I told Monica. "Sometimes he's just not there for you."

I drove up a mile-long driveway that led to an expansive three-story mansion of contemporary design. It was composed of plain white concrete, triangular columns needlessly jutted out of its facade, and the roof was flat. All the windows were brightly lit.

We got out of the car and heard the dumb thump of a techno drumbeat and the shrieking of girls. I gave the valet my keys and walked to the front door. I rang the doorbell and a tall woman with chicly slicked-back hair opened the door, unleashing a mixed burst of laughs, shouts, screams, and robotic music.

"Name, please," said the woman. She held a flat piece of black plastic. She pressed a button, and the top of the object flipped up to reveal a screen.

"Harlan Eiffler and Vincent Spinetti."

She pressed some more buttons and looked at us.

"Welcome." She flipped the screen back and let us in the circular white foyer. We walked down a hall toward the noise. I recognized the song as we moved closer to its source. It was a remixed dance version of one of Chad's new songs, titled "Middle Finger." "Why should I say the words when I can just lift the finger," sang Chad. "Guess I should wear mittens."

At the end of the hall was a large rectangular doorway. Once we were at the doorway, a startling scene spread before us. It was a phantasmagoria of shocking, ever-shifting images, almost too much for one pair of eyes to process all at once, even though the overall sight was unmistakable. We were at an orgy.

121.

"Let's get out of here," I yelled above the music.

"Okay," yelled Vincent, still transfixed by the twisted images.

Just as we turned away, I heard a friendly shout.

"Harlan! Vincent! Welcome!" Priggish as ever, Prormps bowed and shook my hand with both of his. He did the same to Vincent. Again, he was wearing sunglasses despite being indoors, as well as another fine suit with a pocket square, and his hair looked freshly cut. But that night, his face was badly sunburned. Tiny flakes of skin were peeling off his forehead and cheeks at the expense of his elegance.

"You both look so good," he said. We were wearing our usual outfits, me in my brownish gray suit and Vincent in his gray pants, suspenders, and white dress shirt. "Can I get either of you anything?"

"We're leaving," I yelled. His handsome red face sank with disappointment.

"You can't leave!" he shouted. "I have something very important that I need to tell you."

For once, he wasn't smiling. His lips stayed straight and serious. Concerned, I considered staying, but then my peripheral vision observed gyrating nude flesh, and I thought about Monica's brown eyes.

"Sorry, Drew," I said. "We're leaving."

"Steven's dead," he yelled. "His body was found earlier tonight."

I didn't believe him. I gaped at him, as did Vincent, who was no longer engrossed by the Dionysian scenery in the background.

"Please, come with me to my office," said Prormps. "We must talk."

Vincent and I followed the CEO across the room, which required us to walk among the copulating partygoers. Most of the women were nude except for surreal masks, reminiscent of the Tom Cruise–Stanley Kubrick film *Eyes Wide Shut*. These faceless women were being penetrated in various manners by fully clothed, unmasked men with their pants around their ankles. Many of these men were celebrities whom I'd love to mention.

As we were walking past Kristina Gomez rapturously engaged in a threesome (I mention her only because of her pertinence to my story), Prormps turned to us and asked if we'd like a drink. Shaken by the bad news, we accepted his offer. He led us to the bar where we both asked the topless bartender for whiskeys and Coke.

"You do mean Coke the drink, right?" she asked.

"Yeah," I answered.

"I always ask to make sure."

As she fixed our drinks, I watched the people dance and have sex and thought about Steve being dead. I saw Chad in a white tracksuit dancing with two nude women to a song he wrote titled "Night Bodies (The Sexy Body Song)."

122.

Prormps led us down a hall in which a few more couples were adjoined. We walked into his office, and he shut the door, muffling the music. His office was spacious and empty, brightly lit and overwhelmingly white. It was sparsely decorated by three nude sculptures. About ten feet behind his giant desk was a wall entirely composed of a window.

"Please, have a seat," said Prormps. He sat behind the desk, and we sat in front. Our chairs and his were the only pieces of furniture in the office besides the desk. "I'm sorry I had to tell you about Steven the way I did."

"I just can't believe it," I said.

"I can't either. He was supposed to be here two hours ago to bring me something before the party started. He didn't come, so I tried calling his home phone and then his cell phone. He didn't answer, so I sent an assistant to go pick up what I needed from Steven's house. My assistant said the door was unlocked, and he walked in and found Steven lying in a pool of dried blood. He was shot in the head, and a gun was in his hand."

Vincent finished off his drink as if he were angry at the glass.

"Would you like another?" asked Prormps.

"Oh, no thanks," said Vincent.

Prormps walked to the office's bar area. He put ice and whiskey in a glass and brought it to Vincent, along with the whiskey bottle.

"It's okay, Vincent," said Prormps. "If there were ever a time to drink, it's now."

Vincent grabbed the drink and finished it in a few furious swallows. Prormps poured him another.

"So you're saying that Steve committed suicide," I said.

"It appears that way. Yes."

"No way," I said. "I talked to Steve on Monday. He was happier than I've ever seen him."

"I won't deny the possibility of murder," said Prormps. "Steven had been involved in some sordid drug deals with some shady characters."

"But he quit drugs," I argued.

"I'm not so sure about that. I didn't want to mention this, but the aforementioned *thing* that Steven was supposed to bring me was cocaine for my guests. Nevertheless, we will leave it to the authorities to sort this out. In the meantime, New Renaissance is left with a void. Steven was one of our finest agents."

"But he had already quit," I said.

"Oh, yes. He told you?"

"Yeah." I finished off my drink.

"May I get you another?"

"No. I'm driving. I think we'll leave soon."

"Please, stay awhile. I want to go over some ideas with you while I have both of you here. Like I said, Steve has left a void, especially for you, Vincent. After all, you are now without agent."

Vincent seemed to be hardly listening. He stared at his lap and occasionally took a drink. By now his ice had dissolved.

"However," continued Prormps. "I'm thinking we can find you a new one, this time an acting agent rather than a writing agent. In fact, I've already taken the liberty of contacting John Shapiro for you. He represents Keanu and Reese and the Rock. Now, you're probably wondering why I'd want you to have a high-profile acting agent."

"We know why," I interrupted. "You want Vincent to be a celebrity and promote The New Renaissance." I said the last phrase with exaggerated grandeur.

"I presume Steven told you," said Prormps, his smile straightening. I nodded. "What do you think of my plans?"

"Do we have to talk business right now?" I asked. "You just told us our friend was killed."

"Yes. Of course. Forgive me. I'm so passionate about my plans for this company that I sometimes lose sight. Let me just ask this. Vincent, Mr. Shapiro is interested in you. Should I set up a meeting for you two?"

Vincent shook his head. "No, thank you," he said.

Prormps suddenly screamed and pounded his fist on his desk. The impact was so powerful that Vincent jumped in his seat.

"Why the fuck not?!"

123.

Stunned, Vincent stared at Prormps across the plateau of the desk.

"Oh, Vincent. Forgive me," said Prormps as he got up and walked around his desk. "Please forgive me. I'm so upset about Steven, I don't know what I'm doing. I've got it in my head that this new version of New Renaissance is the answer to all my problems. I'm a mess. Forgive me."

He poured Vincent another drink.

"It's okay," said Vincent.

"Thank you," said Prormps. He returned to his seat. "I'll let both of you go, but first, please just tell me why you don't want an agent. This is quite an opportunity."

Vincent took a drink. "I—Harlan, you're my manager. Talk to him, would you, please?"

"We don't think New Renaissance should be turned into something it wasn't supposed to be," I said. "We don't think Lipowitz would've liked the way it's heading, and simply put, we don't want to be a part of it."

"I see," said Prormps. "You think it's going to become too commercial, don't you?"

"Well, Steve said you wanted T-shirts and TV specials, right?"

"This is true, but allow me to explain. As you know, in the sixteen years since New Renaissance was established, the combined efforts of our writers, managers, agents, and lawyers have resulted in a noticeable improvement of mainstream entertainment. Remarkably, we've done so largely undetected by the public eye. Our work has almost been subliminal. Unfortunately, our studies have shown that our numbers have peaked, and to reach the kind of widespread masses we originally hoped for, New Renaissance needs more exposure, which would necessitate the help of media and commerce. And with the help of media and commerce, we will turn our writers into celebrities."

"Oh, yeah. That's definitely what this world needs," I said. "More celebrities."

"Writers are what make entertainment possible," retorted Prormps. "They should be just as famous as the actors and singers. Furthermore, once our writers become famous, we can use *their* name recognition in addition to the movie stars and rock stars to draw even bigger audiences."

"I understand that, but I think we've made our mark well enough," I said. "Vincent and the other students were taught well, and we've got their work out there, and it will be there to influence future generations. We don't need to get any bigger than we are. The less we're in the public eye, the greater our longevity."

"Yes, but in keeping with the spirit of the original Renaissance, we want to focus on the here and now, not the hereafter. And in the twenty-first century, we have tools that the original Renaissance didn't, such as globalization and cybernetics. The New Renaissance could change the world. A much-needed intellectual revival for dumbed-down humanity."

"New Renaissance is just a catchy name," I argued. "Don't treat it like it's the second coming of the Renaissance, because that's not going to happen in this world. The best you'll be able to do is get the New Renaissance kids on MTV, make them seem cool, and sell some more movie tickets. It'll be a fad at best. It'll be old news in four months, and we don't want any part of it. Do whatever you want, but we're quitting the company."

"Vincent, is he speaking for you as well?"

Vincent stared at his lap and nodded.

"Vincent," said Prormps. "Look me in the eye and tell me you want to quit New Renaissance."

"I can't," said Vincent with a giggle, visibly under the influence. "You're wearing sunglasses."

124.

"I would only do this for my biggest star," said Prormps as he took off his sunglasses. His face was pale where the glasses had been, not sunburned. The white of his right eye was not at all white but dark yellow, and its tiny pupil lazily crossed toward his nose. "I'm blind in this one," he said, pointing to his right eye. "When I was four, my dad was drunk, and he got me in a headlock, and with his other hand, he pried my eyelids open and made me stare at the sun. He said he wanted to see what would happen." He put his glasses back on.

"I'm sorry," said Vincent.

"I am too," said Prormps. "I shouldn't have confronted you with all this, what with Steven dying. Please, before you quit on me, just think about the things I've said."

Vincent nodded. Prormps picked up the phone.

"Yes. Beth, could you please send one of the girls to my office...One of my finest, please." He hung up the phone. "The gods would despise me. I've not been a hospitable host. Luckily, I've assembled Los Angeles's most beautiful models and harlots for tonight's festivities. To redeem myself, I'll have one of my best girls take care of you, Vincent, while Harlan and I discuss a few more things."

"I think that's enough for tonight," I said.

"No. I insist. You're quitting your job when I need you the most. The least you can do is talk to me five more minutes."

"Fine," I said with a sigh.

Prormps got up, walked around the desk, and poured Vincent another drink.

"And Vincent, Steven would want you to have fun tonight."

An extremely well-built nude woman with long red hair opened the door without knocking. I thought about my wife and quickly turned back around.

"Excellent," said Prormps. "Isn't she heavenly? Or would something that beautiful come from hell?"

"Hell," Vincent answered. He managed to turn back around.

"What's your name?" Prormps asked the woman.

"You can call me Sherilyn," she shouted from behind her mask. There was no need for her to shout; the music wasn't that audible in Prormps' office. When people talked loudly, I imagined the TV volume in their household was always turned up high.

"You've been to lots of these, haven't you, Sherilyn?" asked Prormps.

"Yeah. Been coming for, like, five years."

"This is one of my finest," said Prormps to Vincent. "Let her be good to you."

"I don't want to," said Vincent.

"You don't have to touch her," said Prormps with a laugh. "Just talk to her, let her show you around. Let her show you my paintings. I've got a Pollock, a Gorky, and some Rothkos. Show him around. You can do that, can't you, dear?"

"Yeah," she yelled. "I'm trippin pretty hard and don't feel like doin it anyhow."

"Wonderful!" said Prormps. "Go ahead, Vincent."

Vincent looked at me.

"Would it be okay?" he asked.

"I guess. I'll come get you in a minute," I said. "We'll leave soon."

With his drink, Vincent walked to the woman. She took him by the hand, and they exited.

125.

"Harlan, I understand where you're coming from," said Prormps, taking his seat. "But despite all you've learned about business through the years, I can see you're still not a businessman. Because if you were a businessman, I think you'd see that commercializing New Renaissance is a logical extension of what we've done all along. Sure we're patrons of the arts. But we're corporate patrons, and we have always exploited our artists for money. Vincent more so than anyone."

"Even if we did exploit our artists, it was for the greater good, not maximum profit, remember? You wrote that in the letter you sent me before I was hired."

Prormps laughed.

"Not for maximum profit, huh? New Renaissance gets a quarter of all profits just because our writers got scholarships to a school that trained them to think money is bad. Foster Lipowitz came up with a system that allows us on the business end to take 92 percent of song royalties and 60 percent of TV and movie sales, and our artists find that acceptable because we taught them to seek deprivation over reward. Vincent was our guinea pig for the most extreme case of deprivation, an experiment which, by the way, was my brainchild, not Lipowitz's. So take it from me, as much good as we've done, don't fool yourself. A lot of people have made a lot of money from Vincent and the other artists, and you're one of them."

His favorite band was Radiohead, his favorite TV show was *Inside the Actors Studio*, and his favorite movie was *Kinky Positions*.

I got up from my chair. "I'm not at all surprised the experiment was your idea, because I think you're sick," I said to my adversary. "And I was well aware that no one had more to gain from New Renaissance than the businessmen involved. But I reconciled that a long time ago. All of us that profited will be able to die rich, but we'll still be dead. Vincent and all those other gifted kids didn't make as much money as they should've, but they've created things that will outlast their bodies. And our bodies."

Prormps stood up and walked around his desk.

"Indeed," said Prormps. "As Andre Malraux suggested, art is man's only way to revolt against death. But then again, it's not really the only way. Hemingway said, 'Killing is the feeling of rebellion against death which comes from its administering.'"

The way he said it made my nerves feel prickly.

"Jesus Christ," I said. "What are you saying?"

"I'm just saying that artists and murderers have more in common than one might think."

"I think you are completely wrong about that."

There was a knock on the door. Chad entered. He now had his head shaved and a bleached blond goatee.

"What's up, Drew?!" said Chad. "You gotta let me give it to The Hole, man. I've been waiting all night!" The pants pockets of his white tracksuit were tucked in. So many people had taken to the inside-out trend that it was no longer hip.

"One moment, Chadwick. Let me finish up with Harlan here."

"That's all right," I said. "I think we're done."

"Yes, I suppose we are." Prormps shook my hand with both of his. "Harlan, I do admire your conviction, and I thank you for all of your work. New Renaissance will miss you."

"Thank you."

"And I trust you'll always honor the terms set forth by the contract concerning our treatment of the artist?"

"Of course."

As I passed Chad to leave, he recognized me.

"Whoa. Hold up. You're that one guy. Listen to that." Another of his horrid songs was playing down the hall. "Told you I could write songs."

"Yeah. I stand corrected."

"That's straight. No hard feelings. Hey, have you tried The Hole?"

"No."

"Come check it out."

"I don't think he'd be interested," said Prormps.

"Just let him see it. This is *craaazy*."

Prormps pulled a remote control from a desk drawer and pushed several buttons, causing a square of carpet to slide away, revealing an orifice neatly carved into a patch of dirt. It was lined with a flesh-colored material.

"That's the ground, man," said Chad. "That part of the floor is right on the ground. He had it built like that. It's made of this special material and feels just like the real thing. In the daytime you can look out the big window when you're doing it. It's cool. It's spiritual. You have no idea how many important dudes have done it. And to show that I ain't mad at ya, I'll let you go first."

"No thanks. Good-bye." I walked to the door.

"Ah, man. He's gotta be a hater," said Chad to Prormps. "He don't love the world like we do."

"We'll see you at Steven's funeral," said Prormps with a smile.

I nodded and closed the door as Chad pulled down his pants.

126.

I walked down the hall to the main party room but didn't see Vincent, though I did see Jerry Van Dyke curiously watching the couples mate. I walked down another hall, and a couple of doors down, I saw Vincent and the nude redhead sitting on the floor at the foot of a bed.

The woman was sliding Vincent's suspenders off his shoulders. Then she erotically tilted her head back. She touched her palms to the carpet and arched her back, pointing her breasts at Vincent, who stared at her while blindly reaching behind himself for his glass.

"Vincent, let's get out of here," I said.

Vincent jumped up and pulled his suspenders over his shoulders.

"What gives, man?" asked the loud-talking masked woman as she looked up at me. The look turned into a stare.

"Wait a minute," she said. "I know you. I know you. Is your name Harlan or something like that?"

"Maybe," I said, exchanging a surprised look with Vincent. I looked back at the woman.

My heart began pumping dangerously fast. My body became hot with anxiety.

"Let's go. Let's get out of here right now," I said to Vincent.

"But she knows you," said Vincent. "His name *is* Harlan."

"Oh, my God," she said, looking up at Vincent. She stood and held a hand over her genitalia. "What's your name?"

My face filled with blood. My armpits poured sweat.

"Vincent," he said.

"Let's leave, goddammit!" I yelled, taking Vincent by the wrist.

"My name is Vincent!" he screamed as I dragged him across the room to the doorway.

Before I got us out of the room, the woman took off her mask and used it to partially cover her ample bosom.

"You remember me, Vincent?"

I still had Vincent by his skinny wrist, but he pulled away from me with more might than I knew his delicate body could produce. I let go.

He stared at the woman across the room.

"Yes," he said. "I remember."

"What's up?" the woman asked, smiling gorgeously.

"Hey, Mom."

XI. MONICA

127.

Veronica was as beautiful as ever. Her face hadn't aged, though the flesh looked unnaturally tightened. Also, her breasts had grown. She walked across the bedroom to her son and attempted to hug him. Before she could touch him, he stepped back.

"Put some clothes on," he said.

"Oh, yeah," she said, turning around and covering her behind. She opened the closet door and looked inside. "This is so messed up. I knew something seemed familiar about you, but you're all grown up, and I'm out of it, and—I can't find no clothes."

"Here," I said. I took off my sportscoat and tossed it at her. She put it on, covering herself sufficiently.

"What are you doing in L.A.?" she asked.

"I'm writing," said Vincent. "I'm a successful writer. Didn't you know?"

"No. What have you written? Anything I've heard of?"

"I hate you," said Vincent.

"Vinny! Don't say that! I haven't seen you in ten years."

"Twelve years," he corrected. "Why'd you leave us?"

"I was gonna come back."

"Why'd you leave us?!"

"Stop it! Don't be all mad at me. You oughtta be mad at him. If I'd have stayed, I'd have been doing just like him." She pointed to me. "Do you still fuck with him?" she asked me. I knew she would do this. I knew no good could come from her appearing. She would ruin everything without thinking a thing of it.

"He's been a better parent to me than you ever were," interjected Vincent.

"You don't know nothin, Vinny. You don't know nothin! You don't know nothin! You don't know nothin! You don't know nothin!"

128.

"She's losing it," I said. "Let's get out of here."

"Oh, no. I'm not gonna be the bad guy no more," said Veronica. She spoke like an irate guest on *Jerry Springer*. "I'm comin clean. It's time he knows anyway."

"Veronica, be quiet," I said.

"What's it worth to you?" she asked. "Huh? I'll shut up, but what's it worth to you?"

I shook my head incredulously.

"What's she talking about?" asked Vincent.

"I don't know," I said. "She's on drugs."

"I'll tell you what I'm talking 'bout. When you was little, this man come to our home and told me he wanted to screw with your life. He said it'd help your writing. He had contracts and everything for it. He was gonna keep it a secret from you forever."

Vincent looked at me.

"She's out of her mind," I said.

"Remember when your dog died? He did that. He poisoned your dog. He thought it'd inspirate you to write."

Vincent looked at me again, this time smiling nervously.

"He's probably been screwing you all along. Have you ever had a girl-friend? He said he wouldn't ever let you have a girlfriend."

"I had one."

"But she upped and left you I bet, didn't she?"

"Kind of."

"He's done it." She frantically pointed an accusing finger at me. "He's done it. I swear on all Bibles. It's a conspiracy. He wanted me in on it, but I'm not in on it no more. I love you."

"What's she talking about?" Vincent asked again.

I shrugged my shoulders. I was so tired.

129.

Veronica walked up to Vincent and grabbed him by the shoulders. He had grown taller than his mom.

"Hey. Hey, Vin," she said. "What's the worst thing that's happened to you in this life?"

"My mother leaving me."

"Besides that."

"What do you care?"

"Just tell me. What's the worst thing that's happened to you since I left?"

"I don't know. Lots of stuff. I'm dying of tuberculosis. Supposedly."

"What's that?" asked Veronica.

"It's this disease that not many people die from anymore," he said. "A bunch of great writers had it." He shook his shoulders free of his mother's hands and turned his back to us.

"I bet you anything he gave it to you," said Veronica, pointing at me. Vincent turned around and looked at me.

His face was red. Mine was too.

"She's telling the truth, isn't she?" he quietly asked.

"Yes."

Vincent stared at me sadly, knowing the whatness of his life for the first time.

130.

"I'm so sorry," I said. "Words can't give enough credit to how sorry I am."

"What all did you do to me?" asked Vincent, his voice trembling.

"Most of it," I answered.

"See!" shouted Veronica. "I told you so."

"You kept the girls from me?" Vincent asked.

"Yeah. I paid some of 'em off. They were no good."

"I didn't want no part of it, Vinny," said Veronica. "That's why I left. I didn't want him putting me up to anything that'd hurt you. That's why I left."

I rolled my eyes.

"I tried to stop," I said. "I *did* stop for a while. But then Prormps sent that man to beat you up—I had nothing to do with that—and I was forced to do it some more. I'm so sorry."

Vincent looked at both of us and suddenly walked out of the room.

"Vin!" yelled his mom. He ran down the hall and into the main room. Veronica and I chased him, but the mindless sexuality cluttering the room made it impossible for us to catch up. He was soon on his way out of the mansion. By the time I reached the front door, he had already vanished into the warm California winter.

131.

As Veronica and I stood in front of the mansion surveying the area, Prormps came outside.

"What is going on?" he asked. "I saw Vincent running off."

"He just found out about our project," I said.

"He didn't!" cried Prormps.

"This whore you sent him off with is his mother."

"Shut up! Don't be calling me no whore!"

"Why not? You obviously are one. Do you honestly think you're not a whore?"

Veronica lunged at me. She tried to claw my face, but I caught her wrists in time. Prormps took her by the torso and pulled her away from me.

"Tone things down a notch!" he screamed, standing between us. "Harlan, how did he find out?"

"His mom just blurted it out."

"Miss Spinetti—"

"It ain't Spinetti. I changed it to Thunderheart."

"I don't care what your name is," continued Prormps. "That was not a wise thing to do. You are under a lifetime contract to never tell anyone about that project. You are in serious trouble."

"I know I done wrong," she said. "But Vinny needed to know."

I found myself agreeing with her.

"Have you told anyone else of our secrets?" asked Prormps.

"Nah," said Veronica. "I told the kids that I've had since movin out here, but they're retarded and live in a home, so I didn't think it'd matter."

"I'll deal with you later," said Prormps. "For now, we must find Vincent."

I immediately had the valet retrieve my car. Prormps called his security and told them to drive around the neighborhood and search for a young man.

"Can I go home now?" whined Veronica to Prormps.

"Yes. Go put on your clothes. I'll have my driver take you home."

"That's okay. I got my own car."

"I insist," said Prormps. "You're in no condition to drive."

"Whatever." Veronica scurried back into the mansion.

"At least we finally found her," said Prormps. "I hated the idea of having someone who knew our secrets roaming around freely out there."

The valet pulled up in my car.

"Call me if you find Vincent," said Prormps. "And make sure he doesn't take this to the media. We cannot let what we've done to him get out. I've worked too hard to have The New Renaissance ruined before it even begins. In fact, if he acts like he's going to the media with this, don't be afraid to threaten him."

"I'm not going to threaten him."

"Then threaten him on my behalf. Your career is on the line, too. He could ruin all of us. We'd be vilified for all of eternity."

I said nothing as I got in my car and sped away from the party, the last party I ever went to.

132.

I couldn't find Vincent. I drove all around Prormps's neighborhood, then to Vincent's condo, and then to his favorite bars. At around midnight, I went back to his condo and sat in front of his door. I waited two hours before leaving, and on his doorstep I left a message for him to call me.

Early the next morning, I futilely called Vincent's condo ten times. Monica suggested that he had gone to his mother's house. I found Sherilyn Thunderheart's address in the phone book.

Veronica lived in a small house in a run-down neighborhood. Her lawn was in desperate need of a mowing. After opening the flimsy screen door, I saw the front door was ajar.

I knocked. No one answered. I pushed open the door and said "hello" before I looked down and saw Vincent sitting on the floor in front of a shabby Christmas tree, holding his bloody mother's limp hand.

It was a heartbreaking image. What one writer called the most unpoetic of all God's creatures, the poet, was holding the hand of what another writer called the most poetic subject, a beautiful woman prematurely dead.

133.

"Jesus Christ," I muttered. I noticed bits of meat on the couch and blood splattered on the tabloid-covered wallpaper. Veronica was lying fully clothed, still wearing my sportscoat. She had been shot through the temple.

Vincent looked up at me. His expression slowly changed from sorrow to rage. He dropped his mother's hand and in one instantaneous motion jumped to his feet and leapt toward me, his fist leading the way.

He hit my left eye before I could block my face. With my face covered, he pounded viciously at my skull. I crouched on the floor with my head wrapped in my arms.

"Stop it!" I yelled from within the cocoon I had rolled myself into. "Stop it!"

"You did it, didn't ya?!" roared Vincent as he hit my arms.

"No! I didn't! I swear I didn't! Please stop hitting me."

He stopped hitting me and rolled over on his back. He lay panting on the ashy carpet, staring at the ceiling. Blood stains streaked his white dress shirt.

"I swear I didn't do this," I said, sitting next to him. "I'm not that bad."

"*Somebody* did it," said Vincent.

I was dumfounded. Two people I had known were found murdered within twenty-four hours.

"Oh, God," I said. "I gotta call Monica."

"Why?" asked Vincent. I pulled out my cell phone from my pants pocket and began dialing.

"I gotta tell her to get out of our apartment."

"Why?"

"'Cause they'll probably try to get you and me next."

134.

"Hello?" said Monica.

"Get out of the apartment, right now," I said. "I'll explain later. Just get out of there."

She was crying.

"A man came over," she said. "He just left. He had a gun and a ski mask and he ran all through the apartment looking around and then he left. I called the police and I was trying to call you but I kept dialing wrong 'cause I'm so nervous and—"

"Monica, pack a suitcase for both of us as fast as you can. Vincent and I are in serious danger, and we're gonna have to leave town, okay?"

"Okay."

"Vincent and I will pick you up as soon as we can. Try to get out of the apartment before the cops get there. I love you."

"I love you."

"Come on," I said to Vincent as I opened the screen door.

"I'm not leaving Mom here."

"Vincent, you gotta listen to me. A guy came to my apartment just then. He had a gun. He was going to kill me. He's going to kill you, too, if he finds you. We gotta get out of town. Come on. You gotta listen to me."

"First you ruin my life, and now you're wanting to save it."

"Yeah. Come on."

"Hold on," said Vincent. He turned around and knelt in front of his mother's corpse. He bowed his head, then got up and followed me to my car.

135.

"It's Prormps doing this, isn't it?" asked Vincent. We were in the car, speeding across Los Angeles to Monica.

"There are too many coincidences for it not to be," I replied.

"Did he have Steven killed?"

"Probably."

"Why would he kill his own employees?"

"It's an easy way to solve his problems, and he's too powerful to be caught."

"I know that," said Vincent. "But why?"

"The secret things we were doing to you—that officially ended on my wedding day. I negotiated that. Now that it's over, it looks like Prormps wants to erase any evidence that it happened, because if it got out, his career would be over. And he told me if it got out, The New Renaissance could be ruined. And so there were only six people that were in on what we did to you. Prormps was one of them. Lipowitz died. Richard Resnick allegedly killed himself. Steve allegedly killed himself. Then there was your mom. That leaves me. And now you."

"Steve was in on it?"

"Afraid so."

Vincent looked out the passenger-side window and didn't turn around for the remainder of our drive.

"Where'd you go last night?" I asked the back of Vincent's head. "I was worried sick about you."

"I hitched a ride into town. Then I just walked around and thought about things."

"Then what?"

"I finally decided I wanted to talk to my mom, but by the time I found her place, it was too late."

"I heard Prormps kind of threaten her last night, but I didn't think anything of it. He wanted me to threaten you, too."

"Shouldn't we call the police about all this?"

"No. How would we explain? Where would we begin? Anyway, I've heard Prormps has the police in his pocket."

"So are we just going to run from him the rest of our lives?"

"Well, at least for a while."

"Maybe I don't want to run away with you."

"I don't care," I said. "If I don't take you with me they'll kill you or you'll kill yourself."

Vincent silently stared out the window. I turned on the radio, and one of his songs was playing. We both reached to change the station.

136.

Monica was waiting for us in the parking lot when I pulled up to my apartment building. I got out of the car and grabbed the suitcases.

"What happened to your eye?" she asked. "Did you get in a fight?"

"I'll explain everything. Just get in the car." Vincent got out of the car so Monica could have the front seat. As I was putting our suitcases in the trunk, he approached me.

"Hey. Do you still have any of that absinthe left?" asked Vincent.

"Yeah."

"Could we bring it with us?"

"We need to get out of here. I'll buy you some whiskey later."

"I'm a nervous wreck after all that's happened. I need something strong. Can't you go get it really quickly?"

I hurried up to my apartment and got the absinthe. After all that had happened, Vincent knew he could have asked me to do anything.

I jumped in my light blue Volvo, tossed the bottle and a clean white dress shirt to the backseat, and rushed to the bank. I closed my account and collected all of my cash and insisted that Vincent do the same. Pockets and glove compartment stuffed with our pay, we left Los Angeles.

137.

I drove east, not knowing where I was going, constantly checking my rearview mirror. Vincent wouldn't talk. His stubborn silence in the backseat made me acutely feel his presence.

He hadn't been so silent with Monica while I fetched the absinthe. She later told me he had asked her about the man who came into our apartment. She described the man's tacky apparel and the hair creeping from underneath his mask, leading Vincent to conclude that Prormps's mercenary was the same man who had assaulted him earlier that year.

Then Vincent had told Monica how sad he was about losing his mother, and that he had always considered his mom the idée fixe of his entire body of writing. A lover of classical music, Monica explained to me that an idée fixe was a recurring melody that links different movements together.

As soon as I got in the car, Vincent ended his conversation with Monica. He changed shirts, took a sip of the absinthe, and became silent.

I explained to Monica what we were escaping from and why someone would possibly want to kill Vincent and me. Like me, she was as concerned about Vincent's mental health as she was the increasingly distant threat of murder. The world inside Vincent's head had undergone apocalyptic changes in a matter of hours.

"It's enough to kill somebody," said Monica.

"I know, but he's tough," I said. "He'll make it. Before I met him, he'd cry over a bowl of ice cream. I've been conditioning him his whole life to be able to endure a day like this."

138.

I drove until the late afternoon when Monica and I could no longer ignore our hunger. Somewhere in Arizona, we ate inside a Burger King, the restaurant of Vincent's choosing. Coincidentally, Burger King had run a *New Wizard of Oz* promotion five months before.

Vincent wouldn't look up as he ate his plain hamburger and heavily salted French fries. Monica looked at me and mouthed "talk to him."

"Vincent?" I asked. "How are you feeling?"

He shrugged his shoulders and continued staring at his food.

"Vincent, can we do anything at all for you, honey?" asked Monica. He finally looked up.

"No, thank you," he said. "I'm sorry if I've seemed rude. My head's kind of a mess right now."

"Honey, don't you apologize for a thing. You've been through so much. You act however you want, and if you ever want to talk about anything, Harlan and I will listen."

"Thank you."

He resumed eating. Monica glared at me and then Vincent, her eyes saying I should try talking to him again. I waved a fly away and cleared my throat.

"Vincent, I feel like I should talk to you about everything, but it's too much. I realize we can't resolve the last fifteen years with a heart-to-heart talk. But for right now, I just want you to know I am incredibly sorry, and

I swear I'll be honest with you from now on. And Monica's right. If there's anything you want to talk about, we're here. If there's anything at all you'd like to ask me, I'm an open book. I know you must have a lot of questions. Is there anything you want to ask me?"

He morosely looked up from his empty tray.

"Could I have another hamburger?" he asked. I laughed.

"Of course. Least I can do."

<h2 style="text-align:center">13₉.</h2>

At a 7-Eleven, I bought toothbrushes, toothpaste, aspirin, razors, *Rolling Stone*, *People*, and *Star* since their covers featured some musicians and actors that Vincent had written for. The cashier commented on my black eye, presenting me with the opportunity for a joke I had always longed to tell. "You should see the other guy," I said.

I filled my gas tank to its capacity and drove until I was in need of sleep, which was at around 1 a.m. Somewhere in New Mexico I checked us into a Days Inn under the name "Dickinson." I asked for one room; I wanted all of us to sleep in the same room to guard Vincent.

As Vincent was brushing his teeth, Monica told me what he had said to her at Burger King while I was buying another hamburger. He told her he felt like he had lost a mother *and* a father since he had discovered I had been lying to him all these years. She told me I should talk to him some more, but when he came out of the bathroom, I could only ask if he was ready for bed. He nodded and crawled under the covers. Monica and I situated ourselves in the other bed, and I turned out the lights.

"Good night, Vincent," said Monica.

"Good night, Monica."

"Good night, Harlan."

"Good night, Monica. Good night, Vincent," I said.

"Good night."

With the extra-thick drapes, the hotel room was pitch dark except for the blinking red light on the ceiling. It was silent except for the occasional bass-heavy door slam down the hall. I thought about how when I was a kid on family vacations, my brother and I loved to goof off after the lights were out in our hotel room. We would simulate flatulence, imitate

Sylvester Stallone, and talk like we hadn't seen each other all day. Eventually our dad would say, "All right now. That's enough," but this would only make us laugh more.

"Look on the bright side. At least you don't have TB anymore," I found myself saying in the dark. "And you can stop taking that medication. They were placebos." I giggled.

There was no response from across the chasm of our beds.

"And check this out," I continued. "I was thinking, if we were trying to make you a tortured artist, then our relationship is actually perfect."

He still wouldn't respond.

"What do you mean?" asked Monica.

"Most tortured artists had bad relationships with their fathers. I found that out when I was researching for the job."

No one commented, but I wasn't ready to sleep yet.

"One of my favorite things I learned from my research was about Dalí. I read about how he had a castle built for him and his wife, Gala, but then he would only allow himself to go there by her invitation. She was his muse, and he deprived himself of her so he'd be more inspired."

"I read that Dalí once collaborated with Walt Disney on something," said Monica.

"That figures. But Vincent, artists like Dalí would probably pay for an abusive manager like me. There are tons of rich kids in art school that could use me, too. The 'woe is me' types."

I gave up after Vincent remained silent.

"All right, then," I said. "Good night."

140.

"I didn't know my father," Vincent suddenly said in the dark.

"I know," I replied.

"So you can't say I had a bad relationship with my father if he's non-existent."

"I just meant that you hate me right now, and I've kind of been your guardian."

"Some guardian," said Vincent.

"Hey, now. Believe it or not, I was always looking out for you. Even when I was manipulating the things around you, I was protecting you at the same time. In my own way, I was trying to keep you in line like a father should."

"You killed my dog."

"I was teaching you about the pain of death. You were taking it lightly."

"You made me break out in hives."

"You were getting in with the wrong crowd with people like Kristina Gomez. Everything I did was for good reasons. As ridiculous as this may sound, I don't think you could find a more caring, concerned manager than I."

"He's telling the truth," said Monica. "He always cared about you so much, Vincent. It used to make me jealous when we were first dating because he'd put you before me. He loves you. He thought he was doing good. I believe that, or I couldn't have married him."

"Sorry I made you jealous," said Vincent.

"Oh, you hush," said Monica. "I'm over it."

"Vincent, do you believe me when I say I did the things I did for good reasons?" I waited for an answer to come out of the dark.

"I believe you, but it doesn't matter. You've ruined my worldview."

"That sounds awful. How'd I do that?"

"I always thought of myself as a filter for other people's hatred. If someone did something hateful to me, I'd use it as inspiration, and it would come out of me in the form of writing, which is something positive and beautiful. That was my worldview and my justification for the bad things in my life, and I was okay with it. But now I've found out that someone else saw me the exact same way. You used me as your filter, and you even got paid to do it."

"Yeah, but I didn't like it. It was torture for me, too. Sorry." I didn't know what else to say, but I was able to go into that night's slumber with the satisfaction of having had a conversation with Vincent. I hoped that someday we could talk to each other with the lights on.

141.

None of us slept well. We had breakfast at the hotel and departed at around eight. I paid cash at the hotel and everywhere else.

Vincent and Monica wanted to know what our plan was. I told them I didn't have one. We would simply continue driving east, hiding ourselves, and faking our names. I told them if they had any ideas, I was open to suggestions. Monica wondered if we could stay with her family in Kentucky or my family in Missouri. I told her that, for now, it was too dangerous to retreat to the obvious places.

So I drove, sleepily progressing across the northern block of Texas, cruise control set at sixty-five mph so as not to risk a ticket. Perhaps I was being paranoid, but assuming Prormps still had the worldwide networking of IUI/Globe-Terner at his disposal, I would not have been surprised if police forces across the United States were anticipating us.

I didn't feel like listening to music, and we seldom talked. Somewhere in Texas, Monica finally initiated a conversation.

"You doing okay, Vincent?"

"Yes. Why do you ask?"

"You just look troubled."

"You're so quiet back there," I added. "I almost forgot you were here."

"I hate it when people say things like that," said Vincent. "You're being just as quiet."

"That's true. I'm sorry."

"He's got a lot to think about," said Monica. "I don't blame him for being quiet."

"I wish I could stop thinking," said Vincent. "From the moment I woke up, I started replaying my life in my mind, trying to make sense of everything."

"I'm sure it's a lot to sort out," said Monica. "But at least you have Harlan here to help if you need anything clarified."

"Yeah. Do you need anything clarified?" I asked.

"I don't know. I was wondering, did you pay off the kids at school so I'd always be alienated?"

"No. That happened on its own."

"Maybe if you would tell me in detail everything you've done to me, I'd be pleasantly surprised. Maybe you didn't lie as much as I think."

"Yeah. Okay. I don't know where to begin," I said. "Well, I guess it was in high school that I began developing misanthropic qualities..."

142.

As we passed by the infinite rows of power lines, I told Vincent his life story, the one he had erroneously documented in *Harlan and Me*. I recounted every detail from the original choice I gave him when he was seven to the final conversation I had with Prormps. I told him how, yes, I did manipulate his love life, and no, I had nothing to do with his acne; yes, I gave him amphetamines to help him work more, and no, I never gave him downers that made him depressed; yes, I gave him a fake case of TB, and no, I didn't mean to provide that genuine case of VD. And I absolutely never planned for a suicide.

"Can I ask *you* something now?" I said after relieving myself of every lie.

"I guess."

"Did you ever suspect me of anything?"

"You knew I never totally bought the TB thing. And I always felt like you were rooting against me having a girlfriend."

"Sorry."

"I thought there was definitely something strange about you being in the 7-Eleven that night with Jane. Actually, just then when you told me about her, I had a flashback. I'm pretty sure she told me about what you were up to, but I was so drunk that I forgot. You lucked out."

"She wasn't supposed to tell you. I wouldn't have been sending her checks if I had known she had already told you."

"It's not nice to be lied to, is it?" asked Vincent.

"Oh, Vincent, come on. I know I deserve anything you say to me, but listen. Most tortured artists were complete failures when they were living, and their work only reached the public after they were buried. As bad as I've been, I've kept you alive, and I've kept you successful."

"You've kept me sad."

"Yeah, I know. I'm horrible. I'm no good. That's why I'm whisking you across the country to save your life."

"How are you so sure they're going to kill me?"

"Prormps implied it to me a couple times before, and now he has more reason to than ever before, because he knows you'll never cooperate with The New Renaissance. The only way he could market you would be if you were dead, which is what he always wanted anyway. That's the ultimate, he said. Dead artists are more marketable. A violent death would be even more marketable. You'd be an instant legend."

"I don't think he could find us."

"He's a former executive for the world's largest media company. He has connections everywhere that there's electricity. You want me to drop you off to die?"

"No. I wouldn't want to be marketable."

143.

After crossing the border into Oklahoma, we stopped for lunch at McDonald's. As we were waiting in line, I noticed the boy behind us was wearing an Apology Accepted T-shirt under his hooded sweatshirt. He was an average teenager with zits and Nikes.

"Hey, believe it or not, this guy has written songs for that band." I pointed to Vincent.

"No way," said the kid.

"I swear. His name is Vincent Spinetti. You'll see his name on their CD's liner notes."

"Are you serious!?" exclaimed the boy, looking at Vincent.

Vincent nodded.

"What'd you write?"

"'A Dog Named Pathos' and 'God's Forehead on My Windowpane.' And a few others."

"Those are some of my favorites."

"Thank you," said Vincent.

"Just out of curiosity, what do you like about that band?" I asked.

"I don't know," he said. "They rock."

It was our turn to order. After waiting for our food, we sat on hard plastic seats in the nonsmoking section. As I commenced eating my fish fillet, I noticed Monica hadn't spoken for some time.

"Are you all right, babe?"

"Yeah," she replied without looking at me.

"Monica, what's wrong?" I could not stand to see her adorable face frowning.

"You lied to me."

"I did?"

"You went behind my back and tortured Vincent some more after you said you wouldn't."

"Oh." I hadn't realized that I revealed this in the car. "Didn't I explain that Prormps had my back against the wall?"

"Yes, but I wish you had told me about it."

"I'm so sorry. I always felt awful about it, but it was my chance to get Vincent and me out of everything. Please forgive me." I held her hand and squeezed it.

"I forgive you," she said sadly.

"Baby, I'm so sorry," I said. I slid across the plastic booth and embraced her. We kissed and then continued eating. Vincent smiled at both of us.

144.

After McDonald's, I filled my tank up at a Citgo and returned to the interstate, continuing east across Oklahoma.

"Hey, Vincent," said Monica. "Tell Harlan what you were telling me when he was getting gas."

"I doubt he'd want to hear it."

"Sure I would," I said.

"I was just saying that New Renaissance and that top-secret project were both inherently flawed."

"Uh huh. Why do you think so?" I asked.

"First of all, New Renaissance operates under the notion that entertainment and art are the same thing, but they're not."

"Right, but our goal was to bring them closer together."

"You should have been patrons for authors and painters, not screenwriters and pop songwriters."

"Our audience was the mainstream. Authors and painters don't have the influence on the mainstream they once did. They've been replaced by actors and athletes and rappers. We thought the best way to improve culture would be to improve the work of the celebrities."

"Tell him about how contrived it was," said Monica.

"The way you groomed me to be an artist was so contrived," said

Vincent. "My mom found you through an ad in a magazine, and then you found me through telephone interviews. That's not how artists should be discovered."

"It wasn't my idea," I said.

"And then your secret project or experiment or whatever it was. It was absurd. Experiments are scientific. There's no art in science. You researched and tried to condition me to be an artist as if I were a school project. Art should grow organically. It shouldn't be processed."

"I agree, but so why did our experiment succeed?" I asked.

"I guess because entertainment is big business, and business *can* be processed. So can celebrities. But I wouldn't call the experiment a success."

"Why?"

"I'm never going to write again. I don't think that's what you were hoping for."

145.

At around eight, I could no longer tolerate the open road. Shortly after crossing into Arkansas, I took an exit and checked us into a Best Western under the name "Plath." As Monica and Vincent got settled in our room, I filled our ice bucket and bought three overpriced Cokes from a vending machine. Then we watched TV the rest of the night, Vincent lying on one bed, Monica and I on the other, all of our shoes on the floor.

I insisted that Vincent be in charge of the remote control. The hotel had cable, so Art TV was available. But it was Monday night, and Vincent opted to watch the faux violence of WWE wrestling. He made a fine selection, as we were finally ready to laugh again. The wrestlers were good entertainers.

During a commercial break, Vincent flipped through the channels and found a show he had written. It was a dark sitcom titled *Nobody Home* and was set in a mental institution. Vincent had already written the second and third seasons, set respectively in a halfway house and the suburbs. The setting would continue to change every season, following the tribulations of an unstable alcoholic who failed a suicide attempt. The show was both intelligent and hilarious, as well as a ratings success, partially thanks to heartthrob Josh Hartnett as the lead. I wondered who would write future episodes now that the series' creator had disappeared.

After we watched *Nobody Home*, Vincent flipped through some more channels and stopped when he saw Steve on an entertainment news program. They were showing clips of a body bag being wheeled out of Steve's house. A cop at a press conference called it a suicide.

The voice-over spoke of the buzz surrounding Steve's superb performance in his last role. They showed snippets of him in *Impossible Woman*, which was to debut in theaters Wednesday. We planned to see it in whatever town we ended up in that night.

Then David Letterman made us laugh, and we said good night.

146.

After an early breakfast at Denny's, we continued east. I drove for about six hours before we were ready for lunch. We decided to eat in Tennessee at a mom-and-pop barbecue establishment, the name of which escapes me.

Over lunch, Monica and I talked about how we had always wanted to go to Graceland. Vincent revealed the same desire, so we agreed to go since we were nearing Memphis. After lunch, I drove to Memphis and struggled to locate the famed estate, only to find no tours were offered on Tuesdays. This was just as well. We were growing sick of traveling, and at this point, our fear of being hunted down by a trashy assassin had subsided. It was time for a vacation, so we decided to stay in Memphis for a while.

I couldn't resist selecting Elvis Presley's Heartbreak Hotel for our shelter. When Vincent found that the hotel had special themed rooms, he excitedly insisted on staying in the "Burning Love" suite, even offering to pay for it himself. I told him to keep his money, and I checked us into the Burning Love suite under the name "Woolf."

The three of us marveled at the kitschy splendor of our hotel room, which looked as if a drunken cherub had regurgitated blood all over in mid-flight. Everything was red, making it excessively romantic and decadent enough to be Satan's childhood bedroom.

By evening we were tired of watching TV, despite the free HBO. I suggested we go out, and Monica and Vincent complied. We took the

Elvis Express shuttle to Beale Street, famed for its blues music (among other forms of entertainment), and occasionally cited as the birthplace of rock 'n' roll. We ate at the Hard Rock Cafe.

After dinner, we explored the rest of the Beale Street entertainment district. We patronized several clubs and ordered familiar beers. As Vincent was christening the latrine in one of the blues clubs, Monica and I had an important conversation that lasted all of three minutes, abruptly ended by Vincent's return.

"Everything come out okay?" I asked Vincent.

"Yeah." He laughed.

"How you doin?" asked Monica.

"I don't know. I like it here, but I just can't get into the blues. The blues make me sad."

Monica and I laughed.

"Listen, Vincent," I said. "Monica and I were talking, and we have a proposal for you."

"Okay."

"I know you still might be mad at me for everything, and that's understandable."

"I forgive you."

"Wow. *Really?*"

"Yes."

I assumed it was the Coors Light making him so merciful, but I accepted it.

"What's the proposal?" asked Vincent.

"Once Monica and I settle down—and I don't know when or where that'll be—but once we do it, we'd like for you to live with us."

Vincent smiled.

"I'll have to think about it. It *would* be nice, though."

We toasted to the future.

147.

The next afternoon we went to Super Wal-Mart so Vincent could buy some new shirts, pants, underwear, and a denim jacket. He had been wearing the same clothes for five days now. Then we went to Graceland.

In the front lawn we saw both a Nativity scene and a giant Santa with a sign that said, "Merry Christmas to All, Elvis." On the hour-long mansion tour, we saw the Jungle Room, the basement, and the trophy house. Poinsettias were everywhere. At Elvis's grave, Vincent got the giggles, which caused Monica and me to laugh. When the tour guide looked at us, I said, "That's enough, now, Vincent."

I remember everything feeling normal that day. We were able to laugh and behave as if no one we knew had been shot in the head, as if none of us had been secretly tormented for years. We refrained from talking about any of those serious issues, just like any family.

Back at our Burning Love suite, we lounged around and watched the hotel's special channel on which Elvis movies played twenty-four hours a day. After dining on room service that evening, I drove us to the movie theater. The seven-twenty showing of *Impossible Woman* was crowded with a receptive audience. Vincent wanted to sit in the back. I think he wanted to observe the audience's reactions.

There was truth to the buzz; Steve was mesmerizing in a role he seemed born to play. I could hear sniffs and muffled weeping all around me at the end of the movie when Steve's character didn't get the girl.

Monica sobbed. As we stood up to leave the theater, she hugged Vincent.

"Honey, that was just beautiful," she said. "You are brilliant."

"Thank you."

I shook his hand and congratulated him.

"I loved it," I said.

"Thanks for selling it," said Vincent.

"Thanks for writing it," I replied.

148.

Back at our crimson hotel suite, Vincent seemed worried about something, and I noticed him staring at both Monica and me. If either of us looked back, he quickly turned away.

"Are you all right, Vincent?" I asked.

"Why do you ask?"

"You just look like something's bothering you."

"Uh, I was just wondering...would you guys want to celebrate my movie by having some drinks?" he asked. He was blushing.

"Okay," I said.

"Sure," agreed Monica.

I called room service and ordered a bottle of whiskey. It was promptly delivered. I bought an overpriced Coke from the vending machine since Monica liked to mix her whiskey with it. I mixed mine with water, and Vincent drank his straight with ice.

Over our whiskeys, we talked about how great the movie was, even with a murderous rap star and a *Playboy* Playmate in its supporting roles. Monica seemed in awe of Vincent, praising him lavishly. He enjoyed the attention.

As the night progressed and the bottle emptied, I noticed Vincent kept closing one of his eyes.

"Why do you keep winking at me?" I asked.

"Oh, I've had these contacts in too long. They're killing me. I really need to take them out, but they're the only pair I have, and I don't have any solution to put them in."

"Do you need me to go buy you some solution?"

"No. Let me drive your car. I'll get it myself."

He knew there was no way I'd let him go.

"You can't drive with one eye, and you've been drinking more than I have," I said. "I'll drive."

"Would you?"

"Yeah."

"Then can I just stay here? I'm feeling nauseated."

"Sure." I didn't mind. I needed some solution for my own contact lenses, come to think of it. "Monica, take care of Vincent while I'm gone, okay?"

She replied with a drunken belch.

"Better yet, Vincent, take care of Monica."

It took me a while to find a store open that sold solution. I returned to the hotel about an hour later, at eleven. As I approached our suite's door and got out my key, I could hear Elvis singing through the wall.

I entered. No one was in the living room where we had been drinking. The TV had been left on. An Elvis movie was playing at an absurd-

ly loud volume. I saw the old bottle of absinthe on the coffee table, nearly empty. I instantly became nervous.

I walked over to the bedroom doorway, where I saw pale flesh undu-
lating amid red sheets. The image has never left me.

I watched for about three seconds and then walked back to the living
room. I set Vincent's contact solution down. I then emptied my wallet
and pockets of cash and left all of it for them on the coffee table. I had
plenty of money left over in my car's glove compartment.

I didn't pack anything. I walked out the door and left the building. I
got in my car and drove off, speeding down a road, then a highway, flee-
ing across a state, free and miserable, as I have remained sixteen years
later.

XII. NORMA JEAN

149.

My name is Harlan Joseph Eifflerdorf the fourth. I am fifty-nine years old. My father was a banker. My mother was a grade-school English teacher. I grew up in St. Louis, Missouri. I was reasonably happy until my father died when I was sixteen. Then I learned to play guitar and started a band. I hoped to become a star because I thought that meant having the best life possible. I drank too much and was expelled from college. I took my band to California and failed to get anywhere with my music. I got a writing job. Then I was hired by New Renaissance, a progressive entertainment company whose goal was to improve American culture. My job was to manipulate the life of the most talented prodigy we could find, so that he might always be inspired to create things we could sell. Fifteen years into this job, the prodigy found out what I had been doing, and he seduced my wife.

Following that, I drove around a while before going back to St. Louis. For a year, I lived with my mother in the big house I had bought her. My brother and his family lived there, too. I got to know my nephews better. They liked several of Vincent's TV shows and probably wondered why their eccentric uncle left the room every time one of these shows appeared.

I was completely willing to risk an assassin coming for me in my hometown, though, admittedly, I was still scared. Hearing car doors slam late at night frightened me. I often looked through the window blinds to make sure no menacing figures lurked outside. I regularly had nightmares in which people killed me in gruesome, unspeakable ways.

But no killers ever came for me, and I eventually became less paranoid. I decided to use my real name again and attained a passport. I took a vacation to Europe, something I had always wanted to do. Since I could afford to, I decided to stay there. In various hotel rooms, I lived in Germany, Italy, Spain, and France. Ten years ago, I settled in London, which is where I currently reside. Home is the Hilton Trafalgar.

My mother, brother, and his family visit me annually, and in turn, I stay in St. Louis periodically. I decided a while back that despite my family living so far away, London would be my permanent home. I planned on someday dying in this hotel room. It could be sadder; Eugene O'Neill both died and was born in a hotel room.

For years I was able to subsist on those hastily withdrawn savings I had stashed in my car. After all, I rarely went anywhere, and I liked being hungry. In more recent years, I have found sufficient income from the publication of a book I wrote under the pseudonym Franz Sandler. The book is a collection of profiles of modern and contemporary painters, writers, and other creators. My publisher insisted that the title of this book should be *Lives of the Artists 2: The New Generation*. It was pretentiously marketed as a sequel to Giorgio Vasari's monumental Renaissance work. I hated the idea, though it apparently worked; I sell enough books each year to continue living in this suite.

I labored on the biographies of these artists for years, spending most of my long, uneventful days in drafty old libraries. Each profile focuses on the artist's childhood, school experiences, love life, obstacles, tragedies, neuroses, addictions, and diseases. In an effort to make the profiles as entertaining as possible, I went into explicit detail about the artists' personal torments, such as Chaim Soutine suffering in such squalor that a nest of bed bugs lived inside his ear.

I wrote the book to pass the time and to give myself a purpose. I chose this particular subject because of my admiration for artists. I maintain that artists are far superior to any CEO, president, or king, though still inferior to most women.

I have been working on this, tentatively titled *Torture the Artist*, for a year and three months now. I don't know if it will see publication, but the goal for me is to complete the book once and for all. If this is actually being read, then this story has been published, unless it is being read by a literary agent or editor or one of their assistants who will either accept or reject my manuscript. I would be surprised if it is published, because the manuscript will likely be difficult to sell. Because of its synthesis of humor and pathos, comedy and drama, highbrow and lowbrow, it might be labeled a "tweener," too risky to publish. And unlike Vincent's brilliant in-betweeners, I have no well-connected businessmen representing my work. I fired the agent who sold *Lives of the Artists 2*. For a while he was my only friend, but I grew to hate him.

I should now remind my audience that the six of us who knew about Vincent's unorthodox inspiration had signed contracts long ago saying we would not make public any accounts of the project while any of its participants remained living. Every character in this book, myself and Vincent included, is presently deceased. Otherwise, my audience could not be reading of their triumphs and foibles in this printed form, as this book could not be legally released. So even if my manuscript should be published, which is doubtful, I will be dead and buried before it appears in bookstores.

But for now, I am here.

In the last sixteen years, I have become an ascetic. I look the part. I have stoic posture. I gave up contact lenses in favor of wire-rimmed glasses. I no longer slick back my hair, which is now gray and combed neatly to the side. I still wear suits, even on days that I don't leave my room. These days I occasionally wear three-piece suits, as I have grown to appreciate vests.

If I'm not in this hotel room writing, I'm in this hotel room reading. I read musty old books by the dead masters. I often find myself revisiting Spengler's and Mann's works, and if I'm feeling indulgent, I'll read some poems by Edwin Arlington Robinson. I do not watch movies or television, and I do not own a stereo.

I don't smile. I can't smile. I cannot even frown. My mouth is just there. It yawns a lot. At the designated time, I like to sleep. It is the only true pleasure I have these days. I always wake up.

I no longer say "hello." I only say "good-bye," usually at inappropriate times. I don't bother getting to know anybody. I no longer honor "what's up," "what's going on," or the like with a response. I will not tolerate being asked how I'm doing.

I no longer become aroused. Everything is a turnoff. My heart won't congeal. It won't function. I couldn't even love my wife.

I eat to live. For a while, when I first settled in London, I drank to live. On one drinking binge which coincided with a personal nadir, I mischievously searched the classifieds and found an ad for an artist looking for work. I called and told him I wanted a mural painted in a bar I owned. I gave him the address of an actual bar and told him to meet me there the next day. I didn't mention the fact that it was a wild, run-down gay bar. The boy was so excited about getting a job that I felt awful for deceiving him. I pictured him walking into the bar with his portfolio, then startled by the leather-clad men dancing, then his face reddening when he finds that no one there had called. Sometime after that, I stopped drinking and started writing.

I accepted my loneliness. I have become accustomed to being horribly, horribly sad. I own a gun but am afraid to use it. My life is my work, and my work is almost done.

150.

In the movies, usually comedies, an easy way to provide the plot its denouement is to show each character with a one- to three-sentence caption summarizing his or her fate while an upbeat song plays. *Animal House* and *Fast Times at Ridgemont High* are earlier examples of films that have ended this way. I will admit to appreciating this convenient device.

Veronica Djapushkonbutm's murderer was not found. She was given a pauper's burial, and nobody came.

Vincent's older brother, Dylan, was sent to prison for rape. His younger brother, Ben, was murdered during a drug deal. Grateful for his years of financial support, his sister Sarah named one of her five children "Vincent."

Steven Sylvain is remembered today for his last performance in *Impossible Woman*, as well as for the *Blood Lust* movies. His murderer was not found. At the Oscars, he received the most applause during the dead celebrity montage.

Daphne Sullivan married and divorced twice, has two kids, and works as a nurse.

Kari DuBrow dropped out of the New Renaissance Academy to marry Neil Elgart. They divorced two years later when Neil left Kari for another woman. Kari became a high school teacher, and Neil works at a plastic factory.

Jane Pearson's novel did not sell well, and Globe Books dropped her. After this, she was unable to sell another manuscript. She became a librarian and is currently single.

Kristina Gomez is forty-seven and not as pretty as she used to be. Her popularity has waned for years, especially since she started concealing her midriff.

Chad Carter enjoyed another decade of success without Vincent's songwriting. Terner Bros. gave him a movie deal, and he nearly had the opportunity to fly into outer space. But like Kristina Gomez, his recent sales have dwindled, and he is currently in rehab.

Any other singers or bands whose recording careers were initiated by Vincent's songwriting found their careers declining within two to three years. Their subsequent releases were mediocre at best, rendering their success fleeting but lucrative, typical of any pop music act of their time.

Some of Vincent's TV shows diminished in popularity after less talented writers took over. Others continued to pull in ratings. Imitations of his successes cheapened the originals, such as a working-class drama titled *Gas Station*, and a channel called Hotty TV, which only shows pictures of celebrities in sexy outfits.

The New Wizard of Oz remains popular and is shown in some art schools as an example of Dadaism. *Impossible Woman*, *The Best of Days Are the First to Flee*, and four more of Vincent's films achieved both commercial and artistic success, paving the way for plenty of sequels.

IUI/Globe-Terner is as powerful as ever. Through the years, there have been reports of the company's financial woes, but it's still everywhere, still growing.

One year after Vincent and I fled from California, The New Renaissance was presented to the media. It was a complete failure. Despite intense marketing hype, the public was not interested. That same year, the New Renaissance Academy was shut down halfway through the semester.

In a mass e-mail to all of his employees, Drew Prormps declared the end of the New Renaissance company. He returned to his old marketing job at IUI/Globe-Terner. He died of AIDS three years ago, and I presume he is no longer a threat to my well-being.

Except for the occasional genius who lucked into his or her work being sold, entertainment has become increasingly hideous with each passing year. Art has become increasingly irrelevant.

Some remember a year or two there when the things they saw and heard seemed to be getting better.

151.

I won't reduce Monica's life to a three-sentence summary.

The day after I left Memphis, she called my mother asking if she had heard from me. She continued calling my mom every day for weeks. When I came home, Mom made me call my wife, who was living with her own mother in Kentucky.

"Hey."

"Oh, God. Harlan. Where have you been? What have you been doing?"

"Driving around."

"Why did you leave?" Her voice trembled. She was crying.

"I saw you and Vincent in bed together."

"I was drunk. I was really, really drunk. He was drunk, too. He came on really strong. He did everything he could to seduce me, and I couldn't take it anymore. But we didn't have sex. I swear we didn't."

"Bullshit. I saw you."

"He tried, but he couldn't. He was impotent."

"You still intended to sleep with him. You still kissed and groped him. I saw it."

"I'm sorry, Harlan. I'm so sorry. I could kill myself. I hate myself. I know it's no excuse, but I was out of my mind. That wasn't me."

"Oh, I saw you looking at him before you even did that, and fawning over his movie. You probably wanted him all along. No wonder you wanted him to live with us."

"No. Don't say that. You're the love of my life. The last few weeks have been hell without you."

"Well, they've been hell for me, too."

"Can I come see you?"

"Where's Vincent?"

"I don't know. I passed out, and when I woke up the next morning, he was gone. Both of you were gone. I was so scared."

"Was there money on the coffee table?"

"Tons of money. You left it?"

"Yes. Did he leave that contact solution he sent me out for?"

"Yeah."

"I thought so."

"Can I come see you?"

"No. I'm not ready to see you yet."

"Then when?"

"I don't know. I think I'd like a divorce."

She sobbed explosively, shrieking, "God, no, why?"

"That was the worst thing you could have possibly done to me. You knew how hard it was for me to let my guard down and trust you, but I did, because I thought you were different from all the rest. But you aren't. The love of my life tried to fuck a kid I considered to be a son. I'm sorry, baby, but I can't let that go. That's an image I just can't shake."

She cried and cried, "God, no, why."

"It's not completely your fault," I said. "I think I was meant to be alone."

The divorce papers were sent through the mail. I never saw her again.

152.

There is one more of us ghosts I have left floating around.

Vincent Spinetti is thirty-eight years old. His father was unknown. His mother was a whore. He grew up in Kramden, Illinois, and Kokomo, Indiana. When he was seven, his mother sold him to a progressive entertainment company whose goal was to make money. For fifteen years, his life was manipulated just because a very ambitious man came up with a ridiculous marketing scheme that other ambitious men were fooled into thinking was a good idea. In those fifteen years, Vincent created works of art that were exhibited nationwide on radios, televisions, and movie screens. These works were intended to improve the mind of America, and I choose to believe they did, in an insignificant, fleeting way. Fortunately, his works are still there for anyone to see, and they will be there forever, available for purchase.

From the moment I saw the intolerable act in Memphis, I cut Vincent out of my life. He reciprocated. Nevertheless, I thought of him often and wondered if he was alive, where he was, what he was doing, how he was doing, whether or not he was writing, and whether or not he hated me. I didn't hate him. Part of me wanted to talk to him, but the closest I came to reestablishing contact was typing "Vincent Spinetti" on an Internet search engine at the library. I also typed in Monica's name from time to time. The searches never led to their whereabouts, and I assumed I'd never cross paths with Monica or Vincent again.

About a year and three months ago, I received a letter in the mail, a rarity for me. It had no inside address.

My Dearest Harlan,

I know you might disagree, but I don't think we're put on this Earth to suffer. I also think you and I have suffered long enough.

I gave up on you a while back. I tried looking for someone else, but as I expected, there is no one else for me. I hate everyone else. They all seem so lame compared to you, my dear.

Let's get back together before we start getting too sick to enjoy one another. I figure you might come home for Thanksgiving. Meet me in St. Louis at the airport's Concourse A baggage claim on our wedding anniversary at 1 p.m.

Please, let's be happy again.

Immortal Beloved

And oh, my sweet Lord, I wanted to go. But I could not. I thought of one hundred reasons not to go, though two stood out. My one true love had been untrue to me. And I deserved it. I spent Thanksgiving in my hotel room.

153.

The week after Thanksgiving, I saw Vincent through the peephole of my hotel room door. He had knocked on this door as if a generation hadn't passed since we had last seen each other.

I opened the door, and Vincent smiled. His eyes opened wide, and his eyebrows slanted worriedly. His open-mouthed smile made me smile back. It's all I knew to do.

He didn't look much different from the twenty-two-year-old version of himself. The only sign of aging was his receding hairline, visible because he now wore his hair short. He still had plenty of black hairs to even out the grays.

Beyond his hair, the only other change was his clothes. He wore black loafers, raggedy blue jeans, and a black T-shirt, but he still had his long black wool coat. Standing behind him and clutching his leg was a little girl with long black hair.

"Hey, Harlan." His voice was the same, still tired and warm.

"Hey, Vincent." My heart pounded. I hadn't felt so excited in ages.

"Is it okay that I'm here?"

"Yes. I'm just—please, come in."

They entered, and I closed the door behind them.

"Who's this?" I asked, nodding at the girl.

"This is Norma Jean Spinetti. My daughter. Norma Jean, this is my old manager and friend, Harlan."

"Hello, Norma Jean," I said. "I like your name."

"Thank you." Her smile revealed a missing tooth. Her eyes were big and brown. She continued to hide behind her dad.

"Her mom wanted to name her after Marilyn Monroe, but I insisted on Marilyn's real name."

"How old are you?" I asked the timid little thing.

She held up five fingers.

"That's a good age," I said. "Please, have a seat. Can I get either of you anything to drink?"

"No, thanks," said Vincent. They sat on the couch in the living room area of my suite. "I hope you don't mind us popping in like this. I didn't think a phone call would give the gravity of our reunion the justice it deserves."

I laughed.

"How'd you find me?"

"Through your publisher. I loved your book."

"Thank you. How'd you know it was mine?"

"Norma Jean and I go to the bookstore and buy a book once a week, one for her and one for me, and the other week I saw your book, and it looked good, and then when I got home and opened it, I was shocked to see the dedication was for me. I knew it had to be you."

The dedication of my first book read: "For Vincent Djapushkonbutm Spinetti, I'll always be sorry."

"Have *you* been writing?" I asked.

"No. Between working and Norma Jean, I really don't have time to. It's been years since I've written a thing. There for a while I would write something and then stuff it into a beer bottle and throw it into the Gulf. But I've stopped drinking, so I don't have any more beer bottles."

"The Gulf?"

"Yeah. That's where I've been living all this time, on the Gulf of Mexico in a little town in Florida called Hackle. I started living there a year or so after I took off. It was the first place I got to I really liked, so I stayed there. How'd you end up in London?"

"Same as you, I suppose. Just liked it here. I like feeling that I'm away from everything."

"I know you were never that fond of your home country," remarked Vincent.

"I don't know. It's not that. Nowadays, everywhere is the same really. Even since I've been over here, I've seen it getting to be the same as any place."

Norma Jean sat perfectly still and watched whoever was talking. I felt bad for not paying more attention to her.

"So Norma Jean, what do you do for a living?" She tilted her head sideways and gave me a funny look. Vincent laughed and playfully tousled his daughter's hair.

"I don't do anything," she said.

"Hey, neither do I. Isn't it great? What do you do, Vincent?"

"I'm working at this credit union place, mostly answering phones and dealing with angry customers. I had a couple factory jobs before that."

"I take it you haven't been collecting the royalties you have coming to you either, huh?"

"No. I lived off what I saved for years, but I didn't want to risk anyone finding me, so I didn't seek out any more checks."

"Me neither. I wonder if we could still get them," I said.

"I don't really care about that money. I think of it as being dirty money."

I nodded. "Did you hear about Prormps?"

"No."

"He died."

"Did he?"

"Yes."

Vincent grinned.

"What?" I asked.

"He asked me not to tell you about this, but I guess it doesn't matter now. He made a pass at me after Lipowitz's burial."

I laughed.

"Right there at the cemetery, in front of the tombstones," he continued. "He caressed the back of my neck and asked if I liked hot tubs."

"Don't feel too special. He made a pass at me in the limo that same day."

We laughed.

"What a whore," said Vincent. "Baby doll, do you wanna watch some TV? Or some telly? That's what they call it in England."

Norma Jean looked up at her dad and nodded.

"Do you mind if she watches your TV?"

"Not at all." I walked to the bedroom and turned on the set. Vincent led Norma Jean in, and she hopped up on the bed. I handed her the remote.

"We'll be in here catching up, okay?" said Vincent.

"Okay."

Vincent returned to the couch and lay across it. I sat in a chair.

"Harlan?"

"What?"

"Are you mad at me?"

"No. I had been for years, but then I forgave you, and when I saw you through the peephole, I just felt relieved. I was afraid you were dead."

"The main reason I came here was to tell you I'm sorry for what I did. So, I'm sorry."

"Well, I've had a long time to think about it, and the way I see it, you and I are even."

"I'm still sorry," said Vincent.

"I'm sorrier for all I did to you. I deserved what I got. But can I ask you why you did what you did?"

Vincent picked at his scalp and sighed.

"I still can't believe I did it. It was by far the cruelest thing I've ever done. Just remember the state of mind I was in. I was mad at the world, and I blamed you for everything. I hated you so much. So I figured I'd hurt you really good, and then I'd kill myself."

"Why didn't you?"

"I wanted to live a little more first. I got on a Greyhound bus and went to Panama City, and I went wild and partied and spent a lot of money, and then I found Hackle and decided to live there. Then I met Norma Jean's mom, and she made me not want to die anymore. I got married."

"Are you still with her?"

"No. We got a divorce." He looked at me suspiciously. "Hey—did you have anything to do with my marriage falling apart?"

I didn't know what to say.

"I'm kidding," he said with a laugh. I shook my head and smiled.

"Our marriage was an absolute wreck," he said. "We loved each other hard, but she was crazy. I mean literally crazy. Violently crazy. And it didn't help that she loved drugs. I think she loved drugs more than she loved Norma Jean and me. When I had my wisdom teeth pulled, she took almost all of my pain pills for herself and her friends. I couldn't stay with someone like that."

"So you got custody of Norma Jean?"

"Yeah. By that point, my wife was in a mental institution, so getting custody was no problem. So it's just Norma Jean and me. We have so much fun together. I love her more than life itself." He smiled another toothy smile.

"I'm so happy for you," I said. I meant it. "It's just too bad you stopped writing."

"I know. I can't have it both ways, though. The way I see it, I wrote enough when I was young to last a lifetime. You doing okay, kid?!" he hollered.

"Yes!" she yelled back.

"Anyhow," continued Vincent, "I also came here to let you know I've come to terms with all you did to me. If it means anything to you, I really do forgive you."

"Thank you. I wish I could forgive myself. I ruined everyone's life."

"Oh, Harlan, it wasn't so bad. What you and those other men did to me was cruel and unusual, but everybody goes through their hell on earth if they live long enough. You talk about tortured artists, but artists don't have a monopoly on torture. What about a worker dragging himself home every day with a broken back? Or a handicapped child being made fun of at school? Or an elderly person being widowed and alone? I never had parents that beat or molested me. I never had to beg for spare change. I never had to go off to some strange country and fight in a war. Everybody is tortured. I had it better than most, because I was fortunate enough to be able to do something with my torture. You made sure of that. Most people don't have that luxury."

154.

We talked about everything we had been doing in the last fifteen years. Vincent had much more to report than I. He had Norma Jean's entire life history to tell. I just wrote a book and occasionally went to church.

Toward the end of our conversation, he presented me with one more topic, one that has proven crucial to the remainder of my life.

"Harlan, there was one other reason why I wanted to visit you."

"Okay."

"I wanted to ask you why you didn't show up where you were supposed to the day after Thanksgiving."

"You sent that letter?"

"Yeah. One to you and one to Monica. Why didn't you go?"

"I don't deserve her," I muttered grumpily.

"Why not?"

"I was a heathen all those years. I knew it was wrong the entire time, but I kept doing it."

"I said I forgive you."

"It doesn't matter. I can't trust her anyway. She was my wife. She was the ultimate. If I can't trust her, who can I trust? I'm just as well staying over here."

We stopped talking and heard cartoon sound effects coming from the next room.

"Well?" asked Vincent.

"Well what?"

"Don't you want to know if she showed up or not?"

"No."

"Are you sure?"

"Yes. I appreciate what you tried to do, but this is the life I've chosen."

"No fulfillment, just frustration, huh?"

I nodded.

"At least you have your work, right?"

I nodded again.

"That's good, but I know from experience, you can't go to bed at night with your work. You can love it all you want, but it can't love you back."

"That's enough, Vincent."

"Sorry." He smiled and calmly stared at the ceiling. I noticed his complexion looked healthier, not quite as pale. "So what are you writing now?"

"Nothing."

"Why not?"

"Don't know what to write."

"And that makes you feel even more worthless, doesn't it?"

"Yes."

"Why don't you write about you and me?" asked Vincent. "You have fifteen years' worth of drama there."

"I can't. We all signed those contracts. I'd be breaking the gag order."

"What about writing it for yourself, then?"

"That would be pointless."

"I don't think so. But if you need an audience to validate your work, then get an agent to shop around your manuscript posthumously."

"Why don't you write it?" I asked.

"I already did, remember? But I got it completely wrong. Besides, I'm through with writing."

"I don't know. It's a pretty unbelievable story."

"Present it as fiction," suggested Vincent.

"I'll think about it."

155.

There was little left to talk about. Vincent lazily sat up on the couch.

"So are you sure you don't want to know about Monica?"

"I'm sure."

"All right. I sure am sorry I ruined everything for you two."

"You didn't. I never believed in love anyway."

"You depress me," said Vincent. "You make me feel like I did when I was young."

"Sorry."

"It's okay."

Vincent stood, and so did I. "Norma Jean! Let's go!" he yelled. She turned off the TV and ran to her father, who was crouching down to pick her up. He hoisted her up, and she put one arm around his scrawny neck.

"Thank you for letting us visit," said Vincent.

"Thanks for coming. Are you in town long?"

"No. We're leaving tonight. I have to get back to work."

Vincent reached out with his free arm and shook my hand. His grip was strong.

"I'm glad you don't hate me, Harlan."

"I'm glad you don't hate me," I replied. I shook Norma Jean's fragile hand. "Nice to meet you, Norma Jean."

"Nice to meet you," replied the girl. I thought that maybe I could be an uncle-like figure to her, always visiting her and sending her gifts, but I decided this role would end up hurting.

"Vincent, promise me you will spoil this child."

"I'd love to, but I don't make enough money."

"I don't care. Find a way to spoil her rotten."

"I'll try."

I opened the door. Vincent walked through it and then turned to me.

"Maybe we'll see each other again before another fifteen years pass," said Vincent, his arms tightly wrapped around his girl. "Maybe we could go fishing or something."

"Maybe," I said with a laugh. I didn't see it happening. I somehow felt that he didn't either. Our work was done here. Furthermore, the girl would be needing him more than ever in her next fifteen years.

"Bye, Harlan."

"Good-bye," I said before closing the door and locking it.

I haven't seen or heard from Vincent since, except for a note I found slipped under my door that night. It was a folded-over piece of hotel stationery. It read:

She was there. She waited for you for five hours. You made her cry. Stop being selfish.

Vincent

156.

That night, one year and three months ago, I got to thinking, and I made myself sad. I pictured another universe, another realm of existence where the love of my life and I remained inseparable. In that world, not a day goes by without seeing her smile, making her laugh, hugging her, kissing her, placing my hands on her hips, looking into her brown eyes, and saying "I love you." Hearing "I love you." Seeing her pink lips say the words. We have good days, we have bad days, but we have each other. We get depressed, but not alone. We don't go to parties. We lie on the couch together in our messy home, watching TV. We stay warm. We don't worry about getting old. We age holding hands.

I compared this to the universe I have known, here where it won't stop raining and I don't know a soul, here where I have drunk and drunk alone in my hotel room. Days have gone by without me uttering a single word. All I do is think, and my thoughts hurt. What's she doing? Who is she with? Did she have a good day? I sit in the corner by the lamp, and I read, and I write. My only comfort is my knowledge of how the world I've extracted myself from is a doomed one, because it's getting dumber every day, losing its values, gradually turning into one great orgy where the only kind words are orgasmic grunts.

And then I saw that other life again, where my bride and I have a child that seems to glow, and suddenly I can't wait for the holidays. Our child is perfect. She cries. We pick her up, and she smiles and forgets why she was crying. We make her feel safe, and she makes us feel at peace. But we do worry about her constantly. Nothing bad can happen to our baby, or we'd die. But she always ends up in her bed at night, and we tuck her in and say, "Good night. I love you." She doesn't know what a corporate oligarchy is, and I don't bother telling her.

Back in this life, I wear a nice suit that will never receive a compliment, and it is too late for a child. I think about how I was happy to see my old friend, the artist I once knew. I thought about how he and I tried to cultivate the deadlands, but we ultimately failed. It was a nice thought.

"In the room the men came and went, talking of Pamela Anderson. I found a boy who gave us hope. I tied his feet and hands with strands of blond and brunette rope. I tortured the artist. I tortured him good. And I sold his suffering to Hollywood." My pretty words. All I have, but I have used them.

Also that night, I thought about that other world where happiness is possible, where love can exist with a wife and a kid and summer vacations. Then I thought about this place I've chosen, where the closest thing to a child I'll ever have is that book I wrote, and that very night I decided I wanted to have another.

I made myself sad, and I got myself pregnant. It took more than nine months. It has taken fifteen months. But I've purged it out of me. It might end up being cleansed of its bloody infantile residue, wrapped in a jacket, and available for public viewing behind a window. Or it might be stillborn, known only by me, forgotten once my brain dies. I don't care, just so it's out of me, just so it's done, because once it's done, if the fates allow, I am going to find that woman, the one from that better universe. I am going to tell her that she was the muse that has saved a wretch like me, and that she has given me my grace, because I've known for a while now how I would end this letter to the world.

I will fall in love again. I will make my way through the whores of the world and find her. I will anxiously sit in the airplane and look out the window the entire flight. I will jump off the airplane stairs wounded, and I will land on the tarmac reborn. I will find her and love her with everything I've got. And because it is written, I can love as long as the deathwish sun keeps coming back for more.

ACKNOWLEDGMENTS

I want to thank:

My mother, Nancy, and my sister, CeCe, my most devoted supporters, who have done everything for me, and whom I wish I could do more for.

Kate Nitze, Pat Walsh, Tasha Kepler, David Poindexter, Dorothy Carico Smith, and everyone else at MacAdam/Cage. They each conduct business with far more humanity than any character in this book.

Bart (David Bartholomy), Michael Bruner, the Dillinghams, the Walkers, Susie Thurman, Jason Sheeley, and the United States Postal Service, for various reasons.

Anyone who read *The Anomalies*.

And Micah Beth Williams, who makes me want to give books happy endings.